THE FIRST MOUNTAIN MAN
PREACHER'S JOURNEY

WILLIAM W. JOHNSTONE

THE FIRST MOUNTAIN MAN
PREACHER'S JOURNEY

PINNACLE BOOKS
Kensington Publishing Corp.

http://www.kensingtonbooks.com

PINNACLE BOOKS are published by

Kensington Publishing Corp.
119 West 40th Street
New York, NY 10018

PUBLISHER'S NOTE
Following the death of William W. Johnstone, the Johnstone family is working with a carefully selected writer to organize and complete Mr. Johnstone's outlines and many unfinished manuscripts to create additional novels in all of his series like The Last Gunfighter, Mountain Man, and Eagles, among others. This novel was inspired by Mr. Johnstone's superb storytelling.

All Kensington titles, imprints, and distributed lines are available at special quantity discounts for bulk purchases for sales promotions, premiums, fund-raising, educational, or institutional use. Special book excerpts or customized printings can also be created to fit specific needs. For details, write or phone the office of the Kensington special sales manager: Kensington Publishing Corp., 119 West 40th Street, New York, NY 10018, attn: Special Sales Department; phone 1-800-221-2647.

PINNACLE BOOKS and the Pinnacle logo are Reg. U.S. Pat. & TM Off.
The WWJ steer head logo is a trademark of Kensington Publishing Corp.

ISBN-13: 978-0-7860-2848-1
ISBN-10: 0-7860-2848-3

First printing: January 2005

15 14 13 12 11 10 9 8 7

Printed in the United States of America

ONE

Sometimes days went by when he did not think of her, and when he realized that, it saddened him. Sometimes on an evening, when he sat by his lonely campfire—not staring into the flames, mind you, because that ruined a fella's night vision and was a damned good way to get him killed in a hurry in this wild country—but just sitting there, he tried to conjure up the image of her face, and he couldn't. No matter how hard he tried, he just couldn't remember *exactly* what she looked like. The caress of her voice, the music of her laugh were equally elusive.

Jennie.

He had been fond of her when he was a boy, he had loved her when he was a man, and now she was gone, foully murdered by a son of a bitch not worthy of kissing the hem of her dress or even licking the sole of her shoe. Her death had been avenged, but the pain of her loss was still there, lurking in the back of his mind more than two years later, ready to leap out like a hobgoblin when it was least expected.

For a time, the pain had been his only friend. Well, that and the big, wolflike dog known only as Dog. But eventually it began to recede, washed away by time and hard work and the glorious surroundings of the Rocky Mountains. He had welcomed the easing of the pain, until he realized that it meant the memories were beginning to fade too. That was bad, because he never wanted to lose any of his memories of Jennie.

One generation passeth away, and another generation cometh; but the earth abideth forever. The sun also ariseth. . . .

That's what it said in the Good Book, in the part called Ecclesiastes, and he knew it meant there was no way to turn back time. The sun would go down, and the sun would come up in the morning, until the end of the earth, forever and ever, amen.

Ecclesiastes . . . also known as the Preacher.

Just like the man who sat beside those lonely campfires and rode the high mountain trails.

Preacher reined in the big hammerheaded dun and sniffed the air. He thought he smelled snow. Beside him on the trail, Dog whined softly. Preacher grinned down at him.

"You smell it too, old fella? Winter's comin' on. Be here before you know it. But it's time, I reckon."

He was a tall man in buckskins and a coat made from the hide of a bear. Lean but not skinny, he packed plenty of hard muscle on his frame. When he shaved—which wasn't often—and when he was around womenfolk—an even rarer occurrence—the gals seemed to find him handsome. At the moment he sported a thick mustache and a beard that he kept cropped relatively close with a hunting knife. Under a brown felt hat with a broad, floppy brim, his hair was black as a raven's wing. His age was difficult to tell, because he had always looked a little older than his true years. He was thirty-one, and he had been making his own way in the world since he was twelve. Sometimes with help, friendship, at least companions, but often alone, except for a horse or a mule, and the dog. When he was little more than a boy, he had made a promise to a dying friend that he would come west and "see the creature" for himself, since they couldn't go together as planned. And he had done it, traveling to the Shining Mountains, as they were sometimes called in those days instead of the Rockies, and he had seen the creature, all right. He had seen it aplenty.

Now he saw something that shouldn't have been there—a tendril of smoke climbing into the pewter-blue sky above the valley spread out before him.

Preacher's pale gray eyes narrowed. There shouldn't have been anybody in that valley. With winter coming on, the prime fur-trapping season was over for a while. Some of the mountain men had gone back to St. Louis or elsewhere closer to civilization to spend the winter; others would pass the months of cold weather with friendly Indians. A few, like Preacher, would live alone, travel their own paths until Rendezvous in the spring. But he was acquainted with most of those men and knew that none of them planned to winter in this valley.

Besides, no mountain man worth his salt would build a fire big enough to give off that much smoke. It would announce his presence to any unfriendly Indians who were in the area, and besides, it was plumb wasteful.

Must be white men, he thought, *and pilgrims at that.*

He heeled the dun in the flanks and rode toward the smoke. He could have ignored it, could have ridden the other way, but he had a powerful curiosity and most of the time he went where it took him.

Curiosity could be a hazardous vice in the mountains, so he was well armed. Behind his broad leather belt he carried a pair of pistols, each of them double-shotted. He had two more pistols in saddle holsters, with the butts turned toward him, and two more in his saddlebags, loaded but not primed. A heavy-bladed hunting knife rode in a beaded sheath on his left hip. Strapped to his right calf was a smaller knife, more of a dagger, really. The butt of a Hawken rifle stuck up from a saddle boot under the right fender of the saddle, and he carried another Hawken balanced in front of him. Men who saw Preacher for the first time sometimes said he was armed for b'ar, but truth was he was armed for just about any kind of trouble that up and came at him.

That smoke meant trouble. Pilgrims always did.

Time was, these mountains had been the sole province of the Indians. Then the fur trappers had come, first Frenchmen down from Canada, and then, after Lewis and Clark's expedition to the Pacific, Americans who traipsed out from St. Louis, following the Missouri River. A fella named Manuel Lisa had bankrolled the first American fur trapping party. Others had followed. Colter, Bridger, Holt, and Clyde Barnes and Pierre Garneau, who had saved Preacher's life and become his friends . . . these and hundreds more like them had come to the mountains to harvest the beaver pelts. Some of them had gotten along with the Indians and some hadn't, but they hadn't disrupted life in the high country too much.

Movers were a different story.

Immigrants from back East had just gotten started heading west in the past year or so, and already there were too damned many of them to suit Preacher, traveling in those big wagons that came a-rollin' and a-creakin' across the plains and through the passes, leaving ruts that marred the ground and might not ever come out.

He couldn't blame people for wanting to improve their lives; hell, he had come west himself when he wasn't much more than a greenhorn, hadn't he? But too many of the pilgrims didn't really *care* about the country they were passing through. They weren't going to make their homes here. The mountains didn't mean anything to them except as obstacles to be crossed. And they sure as shootin' didn't care about the folks who actually did live here, both red and white.

Still, if there was trouble, Preacher couldn't turn his back on it. He just wasn't made that way.

He topped a rise, reined in again, and looked down on a tree-lined stream meandering along through some lush-grassed bottomland. Four wagons with mule teams hitched to them were parked alongside the stream. Canvas arched high over the rear of the wagons. Preacher leaned over in the saddle and spat. Movers, all right. Immigrants had to have wagons like that because they hauled so damned much stuff with them.

They were off the trail too. They wouldn't get anywhere going the direction they were headed except deeper into the mountains. Had to be lost.

The smoke came from a big fire near the creek. The pilgrims had gathered broken branches into a large pile and set them ablaze. Preacher's keen eyes made out a big iron pot set on stands at the edge of the fire. They were either cooking stew or heating water for something, and he didn't smell any stew. Neither did Dog, who sat next to the dun and growled, and not pleasant-like either.

"Yeah, my teeth are a mite on edge too," Preacher told the dog. "You reckon we ought to ride down there and turn those folks around, send 'em back where they come from? If we get to talkin' to them, they're liable to ask me to lead 'em on to the Promised Land, and I ain't in much of a mood to play Moses."

Dog just growled again.

"That's what I thought," Preacher said, but he was suddenly alert as a new sound came to his ears through the clear, crisp air.

Somebody in one of those wagons started screaming.

The screams came from a woman, Preacher judged,

although he supposed it might have been a man who was really hurting like blazes. The odd thing was that several people were moving around the wagons, tending to the mules and chores like that, and they didn't seem the least bit disturbed by the agonized screeches. They just went on about their business, unhooking the teams and evidently settling in for a long stay.

"Good Lord A'mighty!" Preacher exclaimed. "Don't they know somebody's torturin' that poor gal?"

Dog turned his head sharply toward the east, and his growling took on a new, deeper, more menacing tone. Preacher's instinct for trouble started to bubble up even harder than before too, and he looked in the same direction as Dog. What he saw made his hands tighten on the Hawken across the saddle in front of him.

A half-dozen or so figures were slipping along the creek toward the wagons, sneaking through the aspens and cottonwoods that grew along the banks. Preacher saw buckskins and feathers and a few bright splashes of color that told him the stealthy figures had painted their faces. Painted for war . . .

Indians were notional folks and hard to predict. And they differed greatly from tribe to tribe. But once warriors from any tribe had daubed on the war paint, they did not turn back. They were bound for trouble, and nothing would make them spit the bit.

"Aw, hell," Preacher said softly. It looked like his mind had just been made up for him.

He was about three hundred yards from the creek. A ball from the Hawken would carry that far without any trouble. He would make sure of one of the Indians first, then gallop down there and deal with the others. Backing the dun into the shelter of some trees, Preacher swung down from the saddle and then turned the horse so that he could rest the barrel of the rifle across its back.

Dog's neck fur was all bristled up. He wanted to

charge down there and bite somebody, but he wouldn't do it until Preacher gave him the word. "Don't get your fur in an uproar," Preacher said quietly as he cocked the Hawken and drew a bead on the warrior who was closest to the wagons. As Preacher watched, the Indian drew an arrow from his quiver and nocked it on his bowstring, pulling the string back and taking aim at one of the movers.

Well, that settled the question of whether or not they were hostile, not that Preacher had had any real doubts in his mind about it.

He pressed the trigger. The hammer snapped, setting off the priming charge, and an instant later the powder packed in the barrel ignited with a roar. The buttstock kicked hard against his shoulder. The unexpected sound must have thrown off the Indian's aim, because the arrow he loosed whipped harmlessly past the head of one of the settlers. A heartbeat later, the heavy lead ball smashed into the Indian's body, entering just under his left arm, driving down at an angle through his left lung, ripping the bottom off his heart, and lodging deep in his right lung. The Indian staggered, blood welling from his mouth, and then pitched forward on his face.

Up on the rise, Preacher vaulted into the saddle and kicked the dun into a gallop.

The fight was on.

TWO

Now that their surprise attack was ruined, the Indians burst from the trees and raced toward the wagons, whooping and shooting arrows. Preacher's shot had warned the immigrants, though, and they went diving for the cover of the wagons. As guns began to bang and puffs of smoke came from behind the bulky vehicles, Preacher gave the pilgrims a little reluctant credit for being prepared. At least they had some loaded weapons close at hand.

Preacher swapped rifles as he rode, pulling the loaded one from the saddle boot and ramming the empty back in its place. He guided the dun down the slope with his knees. When he had the Hawken primed and ready, he left the saddle and landed on his feet, running forward a few paces before he bellied down on the ground. Arrows cut the air above his head.

He fired without seeming to aim, but the ball flew true. It struck one of the warriors right where his arm joined his shoulder and busted the socket to smithereens, shredding so much flesh in the process that the arm wound up attached to the Indian's body only by a couple of strands of meat. The warrior flopped on the ground, his lifeblood pouring out onto the grass from the hideous wound.

Dog flashed by, a gray streak low to the ground, as

Preacher surged to his feet and drew the pistols from behind his belt. He had covered enough distance in his
initial charge that he was now within range for the short
guns. An arrow tugged at the fringe of his buckskin
jacket as he cocked and leveled the right-hand pistol. It
roared and bucked in his hand, launching its double-
shotted load of death.

The first ball caught an Indian in the belly while the
second smashed his kneecap and dropped him.
Preacher was already pivoting and drawing another bead
before that warrior hit the dirt. The left-hand pistol
thundered. Only one of those balls hit its target, but
since that one smashed through the throat of one of the
remaining Indians, it more than did its job. The Indian
spun around crazily, blood fountaining from severed ar-
teries.

Preacher saw that only one Indian was left, meaning
there had been five to start with. The lone survivor had
a bullet burn on his arm, a souvenir of the volley that
had come from the wagons, but the minor wound didn't
slow him down as he charged at Preacher, screaming out
his hate as he lifted his war 'hawk.

Preacher dropped the empty pistols and yanked the
hunting knife from its sheath. He got the heavy blade up
just in time to block the tomahawk stroke. Preacher
grunted under the impact. The Indian was strong and
fast, a worthy opponent. Preacher slashed at him with
the knife, making the warrior give ground for a second.

At times such as this, when Preacher was locked in a
struggle for his life, he didn't burden his brain overmuch with thinking. His eyes, his reflexes, his muscles all
knew what to do already. He acted. Later, if he lived, he
would think about what had happened, because despite
his rough exterior and his sparse education, Preacher
was a thoughtful man.

He grabbed the wrist of the hand in which the warrior

held the tomahawk. The Indian grabbed the wrist of Preacher's knife hand. Muscles straining, they stood there locked together, each knowing that the first one who slipped or eased up would probably die. Their faces were only a few inches apart. The warrior's features were contorted with hate behind their war paint. Preacher's jaw was tight with strain, but he didn't hate the Indian. Likely the fella believed he had a good reason for wanting Preacher dead. For his part, Preacher just wanted to stay alive, and he knew that meant killing the Indian.

The Indian suddenly tried to hook Preacher's leg with his foot and pull it out from under him. Preacher shifted his stance with blinding speed, and the warrior missed his try. That gave Preacher his chance. He got a heel behind the Indian's leg and jerked, and the Indian went over backward. Preacher went down with him, using the impetus of his fall to break free of the Indian's grip and plunge his knife into the man's chest. The muscles in Preacher's arm and shoulder bunched as he turned the knife and ripped to the side with it. The blade rasped against ribs and cleaved through flesh and organs until it reached the heart. The warrior spasmed for a second underneath Preacher before dying nerves relaxed. The Indian's fingers opened and let the war 'hawk fall on the ground beside him. Blood trickled from the corner of his mouth as he stared up into Preacher's eyes and died.

Preacher pushed himself up and tugged the knife free, then wiped the blade on the dead warrior's buckskins as he knelt beside the corpse. "Mighty good fight, fella," he muttered.

It had been pretty hectic while it lasted, which was no more than three minutes. In that time, five men had died. At least five, Preacher amended to himself, because he didn't know if any of the pilgrims from the little wagon train had gone under.

He turned toward the wagons, thinking to see if any of

the immigrants had been wounded or killed, when he got a surprise. One of the pilgrims came at him, rifle in hand, and pointed the gun at him in a threatening manner.

"Stand right there, mister! Don't move or I'll shoot!"

Most times, pointing a gun at Preacher was a mighty efficient way of getting dead, but today Preacher controlled his instincts and didn't throw the knife in his hand. He knew a flick of his wrist would have buried the blade hilt-deep in the damn fool's throat. Still could, if the tarnal idjit didn't lower that rifle.

"Better point that thing at the ground, friend," Preacher rumbled. "Case you didn't notice, I just risked my own scalp to keep these Injuns from takin' yours. We're on the same side."

"You're one of those wild mountain men!" the man with the rifle said. "I don't trust you! How do we know *you* won't try to kill us?"

The man was tall and fairly muscular for a pilgrim, with a shock of black hair and bushy black eyebrows. He was also scared half to death, which was a dangerous thing. He might pull the trigger without even meaning to.

"Peter!" someone shouted from the wagons. "Peter, wait!"

The man turned his head toward the shout, and that was all the opening Preacher needed. In a flash, Preacher was across the open space between him and the man. His left arm hit the barrel of the rifle and knocked it aside as flame geysered from the muzzle. An instant later, Preacher's right fist, which was still wrapped around the handle of the knife, crashed into the man's jaw and sent him flying backward. Preacher had pulled the punch a little; otherwise he would have broken the man's jaw or maybe even killed him with the blow.

The man landed on his back and lay there motionless, stunned. The rifle was empty and posed no danger now. Preacher didn't think the fella was likely to get up any time soon, let alone come after him using the rifle as a club.

"Back away from him! If you try to hurt him again we'll kill you!"

Preacher looked toward the wagons and saw that another young man and two older ones were advancing slowly toward him. The older men were armed with rifles while the younger one held a brace of pistols.

"Hurt him again?" Preacher repeated scornfully. "He was the one wavin' a rifle around. Like I told him, I'm on the same side as you folks, or I wouldn't have come ridin' down here to give you a hand."

"That makes sense, Roger," one of the older men said. "I think Peter just lost his head."

"This man saved our lives," the other old-timer put in.

Preacher was glad to see that somebody understood that. He said, "Why don't we all just take a deep breath here and calm down?"

The young man called Roger lowered his pistols. "Yes, you're right, of course. I'm sorry." He nodded toward the man still lying dazed on the ground. "My brother just lost his head."

"Might have lost it literally, as hard as that fella punched him," one of the old-timers said as he nudged the other one in the ribs with an elbow and grinned.

Roger came forward. "I'm Roger Galloway," he said, introducing himself. "That's my brother Peter, there on the ground, and these are our uncles, Geoffrey and Jonathan Galloway."

The mountain man nodded. "Call me Preacher."

One of the older men—Preacher didn't yet know which was which—stared at him and said, "Not *the* Preacher?"

"Why, you're famous!" the other one said.

Fame was not something Preacher had ever sought, but when mountain men gathered at Rendezvous or other places, they liked to swap yarns. Some of the best ones were about Preacher, who despite his relative youth had already lived a full and very adventurous life. They would talk about how he had skirmished with river pirates on the Mississippi when he was naught but a boy, fought the British at the Battle of New Orleans alongside Andy Jackson when he was only a little older, and killed a grizzly bear with nothing but a knife, nearly dying himself from the mauling he had received. And the best story of all, at least to the mountain men, was the one about how Preacher had gotten his name. Captured by Blackfeet, he would have been put to death if he hadn't gotten the idea to start preaching to them, inspired by a street preacher he had seen one time back in St. Louis.

Preacher was a spiritual man, but not a religious one. He worshipped in his own way, in places of his choosing, instead of in some gloomy church where a fella couldn't quite breathe right. But for a day and a night and part of another day, he had given forth with the Gospel of the Lord, and as the appointed time of his death had approached, the Indians had decided he was crazy and given him a reprieve. None of the Blackfeet wanted to risk harming one who might be under the protection of the Great Spirit. Before that incident, he had been only Arthur, his given name, or more commonly Art. After it, forever and always, he was Preacher, and his name was spoken in every fort and trading post and isolated settlement where frontiersmen gathered.

Now he shook his head and said, "Never mind about me. What are you folks doin' up here in the high country?"

Before any of the men could answer, another shriek came from the wagons. Sometime during the ruckus, the screaming had stopped without Preacher really noticing. He couldn't miss it now, though, as it started up again.

"Lord have mercy!" he exclaimed. "What's that?"

"Don't worry," Roger Galloway said. "That's just my wife—"

He didn't have a chance to explain why his wife was inside one of the wagons yelling her head off. A shout came from the trees back along the creek bank, followed by a burst of savage growling.

Preacher swung around and stepped over to his horse, which had come to a halt nearby. He jerked the pair of pistols from the saddle holsters and went toward the trees at a run. The Galloways stayed where they were, gathered around the fallen member of their clan.

When Preacher reached the trees, he followed the growling until he came to a spot where Dog stood over a buckskin-clad body that lay half in and half out of the water. Preacher had wondered where Dog had gotten off to during the fight, and now he knew. The big wolflike animal had sniffed out another of the hostiles. Preacher had been right in his original estimation: there had been six of the Indians.

This one was dead too, his throat torn out by Dog's savage fangs. Preacher rubbed Dog's ears and said, "Good boy. This fella must've seen things were goin' bad and tried to slip off. If you hadn't stopped him, he would've gone back to his village and likely brought the whole bunch of 'em down on us. Reckon you saved the day, you old varmint."

Preacher dragged the dead Indian out of the creek. He would gather up the corpses later and bury them.

In the meantime, he wanted to get back to the wagons and see what all that other screaming was about.

He had a feeling he wasn't going to like the answer.

THREE

Preacher had made a mistake. It was rare, but it happened every now and then. He was human, after all. Though he had eyes like an eagle, not even he could see everything.

There had not been six members of the war party that had attacked the wagons. There had been *seven*.

Now the seventh warrior, a young man called Nah Ka Wan, crouched shivering on the bank of the creek several hundred yards from the spot where the wagons of the hated white men were parked. He had made it into the water when the huge gray wolf attacked him and his companion while they were attempting to get away. Running from a fight went contrary to everything Nah Ka Wan believed in, but it was necessary that someone return to the main band and let Swift Arrow know what had happened. Swift Arrow and his warriors had been searching for these whites for some time, and the war chief would be displeased if they were allowed to escape from the righteous vengeance of the Sahnish people.

While his companion had struggled with the wolf, Nah Ka Wan had slipped into the deeper water and started swimming, staying under the surface as long as he possibly could. The water was cold, very cold. On some morning soon, a skim of ice would appear on it, and after that it would be only a matter of time until the entire surface was frozen over. For now, though, it was just brutally frigid, but Nah Ka Wan could stand it for only so long. Then he had to crawl out onto the bank.

Instantly, he felt even colder when the wind hit his soaked buckskins and his wet skin. Not even a single particle of heat equal to the faintest ember in a long-extinguished campfire was left inside him, he thought as his teeth chattered. They clicked together so hard and so loud that surely the whites must hear the noise, especially the tall, hair-faced one who had killed so many brave Sahnish warriors. Nah Ka Wan did not know who that man was, but surely he was the most dangerous white man in this part of the country.

A shaft of sunlight found the young warrior where he lay in the brush and warmed him slightly, but not enough to make him stop shivering or still his chattering teeth. He had to move, a small voice in the back of his head warned him. If he continued to lie here, he would freeze to death before much longer.

Death might be welcome. He would cross over to a warmer, friendlier land, where the sky was clear and the hunting was good and there would be a beautiful young woman to greet him and keep his lodge. It was said that for every man there was a woman and for every woman a man, and since Nah Ka Won had not yet met his woman, if he died then surely she would be waiting for him on the other side of that great barrier.

But if he lived, the voice in his head told him, he might still find the one who was fated to be with him here in this world.

Could there be *two* women, one in this world and one in the land beyond death? That was an interesting thought.

But the question could not be answered unless he lived.

He pushed himself onto hands and knees, then

climbed slowly and laboriously to his feet. Back to the west, along the creek, the white men talked among themselves. Nah Ka Wan could hear their voices, though their words made no more sense to him than the prattling of a squirrel.

He turned and began to walk, heading east toward the spot where he and the others had split off from Swift Arrow's group to search in this direction for the wagons. Though he felt dazed and found it difficult to think, he was confident that his instincts would lead him in the right path. He would backtrack until he found the others, and then he would tell his story to Swift Arrow. It would be a proud moment when he told the war chief where to find the hated whites.

Nah Ka Wan moved one foot, then the other, one foot, then the other, again and again, until it seemed that he had been walking forever. His brain was so numb with cold that it was several minutes after he had fallen before he realized that he was no longer moving forward. And then even that awareness slipped away from him. He lay there senseless. . . .

So senseless he was completely unaware of the snuffling and the crashing in the brush as the bear approached.

When Preacher got back to the wagons, he saw that Peter Galloway was on his feet again, although still looking a little dazed from the punch that had laid him out. Those bushy eyebrows drew down in an angry frown as he saw Preacher striding toward him.

Peter's brother Roger stood by him, with the two older men, Geoffrey and Jonathan, behind them. Roger was shorter and slighter than Peter, with sandy hair, and looked a little older. He seemed older too as he put a hand on Peter's arm and said, "Don't lose your temper again. This man is here to help us."

Peter nodded grudgingly. He said to Preacher, "Sorry I jumped you, mister. I guess I was just too worked up from those Indians attacking us."

Preacher didn't think the apology sounded completely sincere, but he nodded in acceptance of it anyway. "I don't hear no more hollerin'," he said as he jerked his head toward the wagons. "Mind tellin' me what's goin' on?"

"I was just about to," Roger reminded him. "That's my wife Dorothy you heard earlier. She's, ah, in the family way and is about to deliver."

Preacher's eyes widened. "You mean there's a baby bein' birthed in there?" Would wonders never cease?

"Yes. To put it a bit indelicately, there is indeed a baby being birthed in there," Roger agreed.

Preacher shook his head.

"Is there something wrong with that?" Roger asked.

How to tell a man on the verge of being a proud papa that he was a damned fool for subjecting first a pregnant woman and then a newborn babe to the wilds of the Rocky Mountains? And on the verge of winter, to boot!

Preacher just said, "Babies got a habit of comin' into this world whenever they take a notion to, and there ain't nothin' anybody can do about it. You got anybody in there helpin' the lady?"

"My wife is helping," Peter said.

"She knows about such things, does she?"

Roger said, "Both of our wives have had children before, Mr. Preacher. They're not without experience in the process."

"No mister, just Preacher." He noticed three kids peeking at him from the back of one of the wagons. The oldest one appeared to be a towheaded boy about ten. The other two were a brown-haired girl, five or six years old, and a black-haired boy a year or so younger. They wore expressions of mingled fear and curiosity, but as usual with young'uns, curiosity had the upper hand.

He told himself he could sort out who was who and which youngsters belonged with which set of parents later on, then decided he wouldn't be around long enough for that to be necessary. But a moment later, as more screams came from one of the wagons, he knew that he wasn't fooling anybody, least of all himself. No matter how much he wanted to, he couldn't ride off and leave these pilgrims to fend for themselves in the wilderness.

"Sounds like she's havin' a mighty hard time of it," he commented.

"It's been a difficult labor," Roger admitted. "A difficult time for Dorothy all around, I'm afraid."

And yet you dragged her out here anyway, Preacher thought.

Roger went on. "But I'm sure she'll be fine. Women always scream when they're giving birth."

"You'd know that if you'd ever been around any civilized women," Peter added.

Preacher's jaw tightened in irritation. "I been around civilized women," he snapped. Jennie had been a prostitute, but nobody could say she wasn't civilized. And he'd had a mother, of course, although truth to tell, Preacher barely remembered her. Most of the women he'd been around while they were giving birth were Indians, and the men of the tribe stayed far away while that was going on, leaving the process in the capable hands of the squaws. So Preacher supposed Peter Galloway had a point, whether he wanted to admit it or not.

He turned away from the others, saying, "I better do something about them bodies."

"We can help you," one of the older men said. He was stout, with white hair and a mustache. He stuck out a hand and introduced himself. "I'm Jonathan."

"And I'm Geoffrey," the other old-timer said as Preacher and Jonathan shook hands. He was shorter and slighter than his brother, clean-shaven, with wispy gray hair under a broad-brimmed hat. All of them wore functional homespun, leather, and whipcord garments, no doubt purchased back in St. Louis or wherever they had started from. At least they had the sense not to sport their fancy Eastern duds out here. They weren't totally unfamiliar with firearms either, although they had burned quite a bit of powder during the fracas with the Indians and hadn't done any significant damage. They might not be completely hopeless, Preacher told himself.

With Geoffrey and Jonathan trailing him, he walked back to where the bodies of the warriors lay scattered. For the first time, he had a chance to really study the way they wore their hair, the markings on their faces, and the decorations on their buckskins. What he saw made him grunt in surprise.

"What is it?" Jonathan asked. "They're all dead, aren't they?"

"They've gone under, all right," Preacher said. "I'm just a mite surprised to see that they're Arikara."

"That's the tribe they belong to, you mean?" Geoffrey said.

Preacher nodded. "See them bits of horn in their hair, stickin' up like they was real horns? That's a sure sign of them bein' 'Rees, which is what some folks call 'em. They call themselves the Sahnish."

"I thought all Indians were pretty much the same," Jonathan said. "They're all savages, aren't they?"

"Not hardly. Some tribes are right friendly to white folks, even though we came into their part of the country without an invite. And it goes deeper than that. Every tribe has its own way of doin' things, its own beliefs. I reckon a fella could spend a whole lifetime out here and not get to know everything there is to know about Injuns."

"You sound almost like you like them," Jonathan said in amazement.

"I do. Some of 'em anyway. Never had much use for Blackfeet or Pawnee, though."

Geoffrey gestured toward the sprawled bodies. "Surely these creatures are from one of the more warlike tribes."

Preacher scratched his bearded jaw and then shook his head. "That's what's got me a mite puzzled. The Arikaras can be fierce when they want to be, but most of the time, if they're let alone, they let folks alone in turn. A few years back, there was a spell when they were on the warpath because some idjits traded 'em bad whiskey for beaver plews. I was mixed up in that little dustup myself. But they got over it, except for one warrior who stayed so mad at the whites he went over to the Blackfeet and called himself a Blackfoot, just so's he could still make war."

Preacher didn't go into any more details about how the Arikara warrior Wak Tha Go had carried out a vengeance quest on one particular white man, namely Preacher himself. In the end Wak Tha Go had died and Preacher had lived, and that was all that needed to be said, or remembered.

"Since then, the Arikara have been pretty peaceful," Preacher continued. "Not only that, their usual stompin' grounds are at least a hundred miles east of here. Something must've really got 'em stirred up for them to be way over here in the mountains, attackin' wagon trains. You boys know anything about that?"

"Of course not," Jonathan replied immediately. "We've never even seen any Indians like these before, have we, Geoffrey?"

"No, I don't believe we have."

Preacher wasn't sure whether to believe the two old-timers or not. Some instinct made him doubt what they had just told him. Yet he had no evidence that they were lying. They might really have no idea why the Arikara had attacked the Galloway wagon train.

"Let's get these old boys buried," Preacher said. The rest of it could wait until after that grisly task was completed.

FOUR

Preacher didn't bother digging a grave for the six corpses. He found a nearby gully, dumped the bodies in it with the help of Geoffrey and Jonathan, and caved in the bank to cover them. He knew it was a mite disrespectful not to treat them according to the customs of their own people, but he wasn't a 'Ree, and besides, they'd tried to kill him. He might not hold that against them, but it didn't make him inclined to do them any special favors neither.

When he and the two old-timers got back to the wagons, Preacher saw the towheaded boy standing near the dun. "Does he bite, mister?" the youngster asked.

"He just might," Preacher said as he strolled over. "Might nip a finger right off. You got to worry more about gettin' behind him, though. He's liable to kick you if you do, and you don't want that to happen."

"No, sir," the boy agreed solemnly. "I'm Nathan. They call me Nate."

"Pleased to make your acquaintance, Nate. They call me Preacher, but you know what name I was borned with?"

"No, what?"

"Arthur."

Nate made a face. "That's not a very good name."

"Why, sure it is!" Preacher said with a grin. "Ain't you never heard of King Arthur and his knights?"

"Well . . . I reckon maybe. But you're not a king, are you?"

"No, but I'm somethin' better than a king."

"What's better than a king?"

"A mountain man. A fella who lives free, who goes where he wants and ain't tied down to no old throne. I wouldn't know for sure, but I suspect it's a whole heap o' hard work bein' a king. I wouldn't want the job, no, sir."

Nate laughed. "I don't think I would either."

Preacher inclined his head toward the wagons. "I saw a couple of other young'uns earlier."

"Those are my cousins, Mary and Brad. I don't have any brothers or sisters, but I will soon. That's my mama who was yelling a while ago. She's having a baby."

Preacher nodded. "So I heard. You want a brother or a sister?"

Nate made a face again. "I don't particularly want either one. But I guess whatever I get will be fine."

"You best be grateful you won't be an only child no more. I got a brother and sister, but I ain't seen 'em in twenty years. I miss 'em somethin' fierce sometimes."

"Then why don't you go and see them?"

"I'll do that," Preacher said. "One of these days. Run along now, and don't get too near this old horse. He's used to me, but he ain't very friendly with other folks. Same with the dog."

"What's your dog's name?"

"Dog," Preacher said. He left Nate with a puzzled frown on his face and walked toward the wagons, where Roger, Peter, Geoffrey, and Jonathan were standing and talking. As he approached, Preacher saw that another man had joined the group. He was older too, and there was a resemblance between him and Geoffrey and

Jonathan. Another Galloway brother from the older generation?

That proved to be exactly right. Roger said, "Preacher, this is my father, Simon Galloway."

Simon was stocky like Jonathan, but clean-shaven and mostly bald. He shook hands with Preacher and said, "Thank you for what you did to help us."

"Folks out here in the mountains got to stick together," Preacher said. "Even when they shouldn't ought to be here."

"What do you mean by that?" Peter asked sharply.

"I mean we got to have a talk about what you folks are doin' here and what you ought to do next."

"What we're doing is simple," Roger said. "We're going to Oregon to settle there."

Preacher shook his head. "There's ways to get to Oregon, but this ain't one of them. You ought to be south and west of here, heading for one of the passes through the mountains."

"No," Roger said stubbornly. "We're going to go around the mountains to the north."

For a moment all Preacher could do was stare, sort of like Roger had suddenly grown a second nose or a third eye in the middle of his forehead. Finally he repeated, "Around the mountains to the north."

"That's right. A guide we talked to a trading post a few weeks ago told us there was no good way through the mountains, so the smart travelers go around them to the north."

Preacher closed his eyes and scrubbed a hand over his face. There were so many things wrong with what Roger Galloway had just said that Preacher didn't know where to begin. He settled for asking, "This fella you talked to, what was his name?"

"Let me think . . . Drummond, I believe he said."

Preacher nodded. For all its vastness, the frontier

could be a small place at times, and though he didn't know a man named Drummond, there was a good likelihood he would run into the son of a bitch sooner or later. If he did, he intended to hand him a good beatin'. Anybody who would send a bunch of dumb pilgrims off to almost certain death deserved at least that much.

"Drummond told you wrong," Preacher said mildly. "There ain't no way to go around these mountains. They run from somewhere way up in Canada all the way down to Mexico. You could go north from now on and never get to the end of 'em."

All five of the men looked at him with worried frowns. Jonathan said, "That can't be right. Mr. Drummond seemed so sure."

"He was havin' some sport with you. Reckon he didn't care that what he told you might wind up gettin' you killed."

"It can't be that bad," Simon said shakily. He had the reddish nose and the veined eyes of a heavy drinker. Preacher wondered if earlier, during the Arikara attack, he had been hiding out in one of the wagons, sucking on a jug of whiskey.

"It's that bad," Preacher said, his voice flat with certainty. "Winter's comin', and probably comin' fast. There's been a snow or two already in these parts, and one day soon a sure-enough blizzard will come roarin' down out o' the north. When that happens, the temperature will drop down to thirty or forty below zero, the wind'll blow so hard you won't be able to stand up, and when it's all over there'll be three or four feet of snow on the ground, deeper in the drifts."

Peter turned pale, which made the bushy black eyebrows stand out even more against his face. "My God! How could anyone live through something like that?"

"You can't unless you've got some good shelter, which same you ain't likely to find around here."

"Then what should we *do*?" Geoffrey asked.

"Maybe we could go south to one of those passes you mentioned," Roger suggested to Preacher.

"If it was earlier in the year, maybe, but those passes are all blocked by snow already. They're only open for a few months during the summer and early fall. Hell, nobody goes west at this time of year."

"We were delayed leaving the settlements, and we had no choice but to press on."

"You had a choice. You could've waited until next spring."

Roger shook his head. "No. We couldn't."

"Well, you're in a mess now, pure and simple," Preacher said. "Way I see it, there's only one thing you can do: turn around and hit back east as fast as you can. There's a little settlement 'bout a hundred and twenty miles east of here called Garvey's Fort. You could winter there and start out again next spring, with a real guide this time. Folks don't need to start across the mountains without somebody who knows where he's goin'."

"A hundred and twenty miles will take us at least two weeks," Roger pointed out. "You said a blizzard could strike at any time."

"It can. But who knows, maybe you'll be lucky and the really bad weather will hold off for a spell. You'll make better time once you get out of the mountains and back on the plains. It'll be close, but it's the only chance you got."

Roger asked the question that Preacher had been dreading. "You'll take us there?"

"You must know the way, Preacher," Jonathan put in. "We'll get lost again if we don't have a guide. You as much as said so."

Roger frowned a little. Preacher had already figured out that Roger was the leader of this ill-advised expedition, despite being younger than his father and uncles.

Roger seemed to be the driving force for them being here in the first place. Preacher's harsh words had struck a blow at his pride.

But Roger was practical too, and knew the party needed help. Quietly, he said, "We won't have a chance if you don't show us the way."

Preacher sighed, knowing that it was true. "I reckon I ain't got nothin' better to do," he said. "It's too late in the day to pull out now, but first thing in the mornin' we'll get these wagons turned around and head east. If the birthin' is over and done with by then, I mean."

There hadn't been any screams from the wagons for quite some time, but there hadn't been the squall of a newborn baby either, as Preacher had halfway expected to hear. Now, Peter looked toward the wagons and called, "Angela?"

Preacher turned to see a woman climbing out the back of one of the canvas-covered vehicles. She was in her twenties, he judged, and looked tired. She pushed back strands of honey-colored hair from her face as Peter and Roger hurried toward her. Her slender figure made it clear she wasn't about to give birth, and Preacher figured she hadn't done it recently or she wouldn't look as spry as she did. This had to be Peter Galloway's wife, who had been helping Roger's wife Dorothy.

Along with Preacher, the older men trailed after Roger and Peter. Roger gripped Angela's hand and said eagerly, "Is it over? Do I have another son or a daughter?"

Wearily, Angela shook her head. "It was a false alarm," she said. "Dorothy's not ready to give birth yet. I'm sorry."

"Not ready?" Roger repeated. "But I . . . I don't understand. She was in labor. . . ."

"False labor. It's not uncommon, and it feels like the

real thing. Sometimes it can take all day to pass, and Dorothy had an unusually strong bout of it. She's all right now, though."

"I don't believe it," Roger muttered. "I was so sure it was time. . . ."

Angela smiled and patted her brother-in-law's arm. "Babies come when they're good and ready," she said, which was pretty much the same thing Preacher had said earlier. "Don't fret, Roger. I'm sure everything will be fine." She looked over at Preacher. "Who's this?"

Preacher took off his broad-brimmed hat and nodded to her. "Ma'am," he said. Angela Galloway was the first white woman he had seen in over a year.

"This is Preacher," Jonathan said. "He helped us when those Indians attacked us earlier."

Angela smiled. "I heard the shooting, but I was too busy at the time to see what was going on. Thank you, sir, for your help."

"I'm just glad I came along when I did," Preacher said, and somewhat to his surprise, he realized it was true. He didn't have any use for movers, especially ones that were dumb as rocks, but likely they would all be dead by now if he hadn't come along, including those kids. He had buried enough innocent folks in his life and figured he would bury more before it was over, but at least he didn't have to today.

"Preacher's going to help us get back," Roger said.

"Get back? I thought we were going on to Oregon as soon as Dorothy delivers."

"Evidently there's no way to get there the way we were going," Peter said to his wife, "and if we don't return to what passes for civilization out here as quickly as possible, we're all going to die in a blizzard."

Angela pressed a hand to her breasts and stared at Peter. "My God! You . . . You can't be serious."

Peter nodded toward Preacher. "Ask him. He was the one who said it."

Angela turned toward Preacher again. "Is it true? Are all our lives in danger?"

Preacher told her the truth. Something in her blue eyes told him she could handle it.

"Ma'am, y'all were in danger the first day you set foot west of the Mississippi."

FIVE

When he awoke, Nah Ka Wan fully expected to find that he had died and was ready to be welcomed into the spirit world by Neshanu Natchitak, the Chief Above. His physical body would be taken into the earth by Mother Corn, who had dominion over all things in that fleshly realm, and used to help make the grass grow and the flowers bloom when spring came once again to the land.

Instead, he was alive. He knew that because pain worse than any he had ever experienced now filled him. A groan escaped from his mouth.

"He lives," a voice said in the tongue of the Sahnish.

The words came from above him, somewhere close by. Nah Ka Wan forced his eyes open and saw the grave, painted face of Badger's Den, the medicine man who had accompanied Swift Arrow's war party. The face of Badger's Den went away and was replaced by the fierce features of Swift Arrow himself.

"Nah Ka Wan," Swift Arrow said. "Where are the others?"

Nah Ka Wan struggled to make his mouth work. His lips parted, but at first only husking sounds came out. When at last he was able to form words, he said, "Dead . . . all dead."

"How?" Swift Arrow demanded.

"Killed by . . . the whites we sought . . . except one . . .

a wolf got him . . . the wolf was with . . . a hair-faced white man . . . He killed all the others. . . ."

"One man killed five Sahnish warriors?" Swift Arrow sounded as if he could not believe such a thing.

Nah Ka Wan nodded weakly.

Swift Arrow turned and spoke to Badger's Den. "There was no hair-faced white man with them when they came near our village. He has joined them since then."

"You think it could be the one called Preacher? He has hair on his face and travels with a wolf."

"I do not know. But if Preacher is with them, is it bad medicine?"

"Preacher is never good medicine for his enemies," Badger's Den said.

Nah Ka Wan closed his eyes to rest. He had heard of this Preacher; most who lived on the plains and in the mountains had heard of him. Among the Indians he was famous because of the grizzly bear he had slain with only a knife, almost losing his own life in turn to the great beast.

The Sahnish revered the bear. Many warriors slew them in order to take their skins. Swift Arrow himself wore a robe made from the skin of a bear, with the head left on so that it sat atop Swift Arrow's own head. Nah Ka Wan hoped to have a robe of bearskin someday, when he was a mighty enough warrior.

First, though, he had to recover from his ordeal. He roused from his half sleep and murmured, "How did you find me?"

"We followed the sounds of the bear," Swift Arrow replied. "We came upon him standing over you, rolling you around on the ground with his paws. You did not move, and we feared that the bear had slain you. So we killed the bear and took his skin, and then we saw that you still lived, though your arms and legs are dead."

Nah Ka Wan did not know what Swift Arrow meant by that. He tried to move his arms and legs and found that he could not. Crying out, he asked that his arm be lifted so that he could see his hand. The flesh was white and had no feeling in it, like that of a corpse.

The cold had done it, Nah Ka Wan thought, the cold of the stream and then the greater cold of the air. His arms and legs had died and would never return to life, so the rest of him might as well have died too. He could no longer hunt or fight or even take care of himself.

"Slay me!" he cried. "Slay me!"

"We cannot," Swift Arrow said solemnly. "To do such would be an insult to Neshanu Natchitak, who governs all. It must be his hand who takes you. It must be the will of the Chief Above." He added, "But I say this to you: You will not live. The bear wounded you."

Nah Ka Wan closed his eyes and turned his head to the side, grinding his teeth together and fighting back tears.

"We must go on," Swift Arrow said after a moment. "Tell us where to find the hair-faced one and the rest of the whites."

Nah Ka Wan swallowed hard. The war chief was right. Vengeance was all that mattered, and now the blood debt was greater than ever before, because of the warriors who had died today. He opened his eyes again and forced himself to tell Swift Arrow that they should find the stream and follow it. That would take them to the whites.

Swift Arrow gave orders that Nah Ka Wan should be lifted and propped against the trunk of a tree, so that he could look around and see the place in which he was going to die. It was on the side of a hill, with trees all around and a mountain rising before him to a snow-crested peak. To the right, the land fell away in a series of valleys so that Nah Ka Wan could see for miles and miles. It was a good place to die, he decided.

He looked down at himself and saw that he had been wrapped in the skin of the bear. His chest and stomach burned where the bear had ripped them open while rolling him on the ground. The beast had not been trying to hurt him, only to decide what he was. But the harm had been done anyway, and along with the damage he had suffered from the cold, it was all too much to be overcome. He knew that the time remaining to him could be numbered in heartbeats. The sun slipped below the peak as he watched, and the air began to grow colder.

"We leave you now," Badger's Den said as the war party walked away. "Soon you will be with Neshanu Natchitak. Tell him that you were a brave warrior, and he will welcome you."

Nah Ka Wan nodded but could not speak, because his teeth had begun to chatter again. For a time, a slight warmth had come into his body, but it was gone now. The deep cold had returned.

Badger's Den joined the others, and soon they vanished into the trees. Nah Ka Wan was alone on the hillside as the light faded from the sky. The bearskin was tucked snugly around him, but it did nothing to counter the frigidness that consumed him from within.

As the stars began to come to life in the darkening sky over the mountains, Nah Ka Wan—whose name meant He Who Is Fortunate—died, wrapped in the skin of the bear.

The first thing Preacher did was to get a bucket from one of the wagons and use water from the creek to put out that damned fire. It gave off enough smoke to announce their presence for miles around. Then he showed the others how to dig a fire pit, bank rocks around it, and build a fire that gave off warmth but little smoke or light.

"That fire's not big enough to provide enough heat," Peter complained. "It gets cold out here at night."

"I never would've guessed," Preacher said dryly, making an effort to control his temper. "Everybody'll just have to bundle up a mite more."

"Do you think any more Indians will attack us?" Roger asked.

"No way of knowin' just yet. Could be the ones who jumped you were renegades and there ain't any more of them around here. But if they were from a larger war party . . ." Preacher shrugged and left the rest of it unsaid.

He was still mighty puzzled by the whole thing, he thought as he hunkered by the fire and put some coffee on to boil. The 'Rees shouldn't have been here. The Arikara were more agricultural than a lot of tribes, and actually seemed to like farming. Though they hunted as well, they also traded the grain and other crops they grew to other tribes for meat. Because of their farming, they were more tied to the land and tended to wander less. Originally from farther south, most of them now lived on the plains between the North Platte and the Missouri Rivers. There must have been a mighty good reason for a war party to pick up and head west a hundred miles into the edge of the mountains.

Unless, as he had mentioned, the warriors were renegades who had been forced to leave the tribe for some reason. In a case like that, there was no telling where the exiles might roam. Preacher actually hoped that was what had happened. If there was a larger war party on the loose in these parts, odds were their path would cross that of the wagon train, and probably sooner rather than later.

Roger Galloway sat down beside Preacher. "When we make it to this Garvey's Fort, will you spend the rest of the winter there too?" he asked.

"Ain't decided yet. Dependin' on the weather, I might come back up here so's I can get an early start on my trappin' come spring."

Roger hesitated. "I was, ah, hoping that we might persuade you to spend the winter there and then lead us on to the Oregon Territory in the spring."

"I never signed on to be no wagon train guide."

"I know that. But we've all heard of you, Preacher. Nobody knows the Rocky Mountains as well as you do. Why, you were one of the first men to explore this wilderness!"

Preacher grunted. "One of the first white men, you mean, and even that ain't right. There was French trappers up here even before Lewis and Clark came traipsin' through on their way to the Pacific, and Jesuit missionaries too. Black Robes, the Injuns call 'em. For a while there was even a settlement of sorts not far from here, a place called New Hope. Long gone now, of course. So there's lots of fellas who know their way around. You can find somebody to guide you."

"Well, I'll accept that for now," Roger said. "I reserve the right to hope that you change your mind, though."

"Reserve all you want," Preacher said as he used a thick piece of tanned buffalo hide to protect his hand as he picked up the hot coffeepot.

The party had plenty of supplies, so he didn't feel bad about sharing their food and coffee. Angela Galloway, Peter's wife, carried a plate of food in to Dorothy, who was resting in Roger's wagon. Preacher had learned that Roger and Peter each had a wagon, and Geoffrey and Jonathan drove the other two vehicles. Simon rode pretty much wherever he could.

The kids wanted Preacher to tell them stories about living in the mountains, so he obliged by spinning a cleaned-up version of some of the incidents that had happened to him. He told them about fighting the grizzly with a knife, but didn't go into detail about the terrible wounds he had received from the critter's claws. He told them about some of the Indians he had known, concentrating on the friendly ones and leaving out any mention of the grisly tortures he had seen meted out by the unfriendly ones. He supposed that he made the frontier sound like a nicer, safer place than it really was, but he was talking to young'uns after all. Time enough for them to know the truth when they was growed.

It was their parents' responsibility—and now, by extension, his too, because he had agreed to help them—to see to it that they got a chance to grow up.

Eventually the kids grew sleepy and turned in. So did all three of the old-timers. Roger went off to sit in the wagon with his pregnant wife. That left Peter and Angela to sit by the fire with Preacher, and Peter had made it clear that he didn't care for the mountain man's company. After just a few minutes, he stood up and said, "I'm going to bed. Come along, Angela."

"I'll wake you up in a couple of hours," Preacher said.

Peter stared at him for a second and then asked, "Whatever for?"

"To stand your turn on watch, of course. You fellas post a guard and take turns standin' watch, don't you?"

"We haven't found it necessary so far to do so," Peter said.

Lord, how had they stayed alive this long? Preacher asked himself. Aloud he said, "Well, it's necessary now. It's a whole heap necessary. You'll stand two-man guard shifts, switchin' out every couple of hours."

"Who's going to stand guard with you?"

"I'll be all right by myself. I ain't likely to doze off."

Angela Galloway said, "I could keep Mr. Preacher company. I'm tired but not really sleepy."

"Absolutely not!" Peter exclaimed.

Preacher smiled at Angela. "I'm obliged for the offer, ma'am, but it ain't needful. You go on with your husband and get some rest."

"You're sure?" Angela asked.

"Yes, ma'am."

She got to her feet and said, "All right, then," but she didn't look all that happy about going off to their wagon with Peter. Preacher frowned as he watched them go. Ever since he had run into these folks, he had gotten the feeling that something was wrong. He wondered if the obvious tension between Peter and Angela was part of it, or if there was more going on.

He sipped coffee from the tin cup in his hand, relishing the strong black brew, and listened to the night around him. He had a brace of pistols tucked in his belt, and both Hawkens lay on the ground beside him. He was ready if trouble came at him from the darkness.

It might be a different story, though, if the trouble came from within the camp. That was going to be harder to guard against.

SIX

The snow that Preacher thought he had smelled the day before never materialized. He remained convinced, however, that winter was still on the verge of busting wide open. The only question was when that would happen.

The night passed peacefully. Peter Galloway grumbled some more about being waked up to stand guard, but he did his part, taking one side of the camp while his uncle Geoffrey took the other. Roger and Jonathan took the next shift, and by the time that was over, Preacher was up and about again and stood guard while everyone else got a little more sleep. Since he was up anyway, he started breakfast cooking, frying some bacon and then using the grease to help make some johnnycakes. The coffee was perking and bubbling cheerfully when Angela climbed down out of the wagon and came toward him, rubbing the sleep out of her eyes.

"Cooking is my job," she said as she walked up to the fire.

"And good mornin' to you too," Preacher said.

She laughed. "I'm sorry. I guess I'm just not really awake yet. Usually I'm more polite. Thank you for preparing breakfast."

"I figure you got enough jobs around here right now, what with midwifery and all." *And putting up with that jackass of a husband,* Preacher added to himself. He poured coffee in a cup and handed it up to her. "Here you go."

She took the cup and sipped gratefully from it as she sank down on a nearby log. "That's good," she said. "Not quite as strong as I usually make it, but still good."

"Out here you got to stretch things and make your supplies last as long as you can. Ain't like back East where you can just walk down the street to a store and buy more of just about anything. It's usually a hundred miles or more to the nearest tradin' post."

She smiled at him. "You know everything there is to know about living on the frontier, don't you, Preacher?"

"Not hardly. A man who don't learn something new every day is a man who just ain't payin' attention. And that's true no matter where you are, not just on the frontier."

"Have you learned anything so far today?"

Just that you're mighty pretty, even early in the mornin' like this, with your hair still a mite tangled and your face all soft . . .

Preacher clenched his jaw and clamped down on his thoughts. That there was a married woman and he had no right to be thinking such things . . . no matter if her husband *was* an ass.

"No, I reckon I'll have to keep on lookin'. But I'll learn something before the day's over. You can count on that." He used his knife to turn the johnnycakes as they sizzled in the pan.

"Were you born out here?" she asked abruptly.

"No. My family lived back in Ohio. Still does, I reckon. I ain't seen 'em since I was twelve."

"You left home when you were that young?" She sounded astonished.

"Way I saw it, a twelve-year-old boy was next thing to a man. I had to do my growin' up sorta quicklike, but I managed. Worked for a spell on a keelboat."

And fought river pirates alongside Pete Harding, the

man who had become his friend and mentor. Captain Harding, once the war with the British started. He had commanded the company in which Preacher found himself. Unfortunately, Harding hadn't survived the war. That had left Art, as he was called then, to carry out alone their plan to come west to the Rockies.

Angela Galloway didn't want to hear about all that, though, he told himself. The lady was just making polite conversation, that was all.

"Grab a plate and get you some o' this bacon and johnnycake," he said gruffly. "Time I was roustin' out the rest of the bunch. We got to do a heap o' travelin' today."

The kids were the easiest to rouse. Being young, they popped up out of their bedrolls in the wagons, bright-eyed, bushy-tailed, and ready to face the new day. That was a heap better than being bright-tailed and bushy-eyed, Preacher thought with a grin.

Getting the adults started was more difficult. Clearly, they were accustomed to laying abed until the sun was well up. Roger didn't complain much, but Peter did, as usual, and Geoffrey and Jonathan were dragging too. Simon Galloway seemed to be hungover, and looked as if he felt utterly miserable.

Preacher didn't feel any sympathy for the man. He liked a drink of whiskey every now and then, and he had even been drunk a few times in his life, mostly when he was younger and not accustomed to handling liquor. But in Preacher's opinion, a man who spent most of his time in a jug was just hiding out from the world, and Preacher wasn't the hidin' sort.

After everyone had eaten, the men got to work hitching up the mule teams to the wagons. Preacher saddled his dun. As he led the horse over to the wagons, he saw Angela climbing out the back of the one where Dorothy was resting. "How's the other Mrs. Galloway this mornin'?" he asked.

"She spent a fairly restful night," Angela said as she moved away from the wagon. She cast a worried glance back at the vehicle. "She's weak, though. This confinement has been hard on her. If the baby isn't born soon, I'm not sure that Dorothy will be strong enough to handle the delivery."

Preacher couldn't help but frown in disapproval. "Sounds to me like she ain't got no business bein' way out here in the middle o' nowhere."

"No, she doesn't," Angela agreed, keeping her voice pitched quietly so that none of the others would overhear. "But Roger and Peter were insistent that we start on in spite of everything. It was so late in the year when we reached St. Louis, I was sure we would spend the winter there and start west next spring."

"That's what you should have done. Where are you folks from anyway?"

"Philadelphia." Angela smiled. "I wouldn't mind being back there right now either."

Not Preacher. He had heard about those eastern cities like Philadelphia and New York and Boston. They were huge, larger even than St. Louis, and St. Louis was plenty big for him. Big enough so he felt a mite crowded every time he visited there. When there were too many people around, Preacher just couldn't seem to breathe right, like there wasn't enough air to go around. That was crazy, of course, and he knew it, but he felt like that anyway.

When the mules were hitched up and the wagons turned around so that they pointed east instead of west, Preacher went from wagon to wagon, checking to make certain the men had loaded pistols close at hand in case of trouble. "Your wagon will lead off," he told Jonathan Galloway.

"I've been leading," Roger objected.

"You got a lady in a delicate condition ridin' with you," Preacher pointed out. "I want a wagon in front of you and a wagon in back of you, for extra protection. Peter, you'll be third in line, and Geoffrey, you'll bring up the rear."

"Fine with me," Geoffrey said with a smile. Peter nodded his agreement, not seeming to care where in line his wagon traveled.

Preacher would take the point, but he would also have to cover their back trail since he was the only one with a saddle horse. He would scout out the best route, get the wagons started on it, then fall back for a spell to watch behind them. Then he could gallop back to the front and make sure everything was all right there. He was going to be busy, riding back and forth like that, but he couldn't see any other way to do it.

He called Nate, Mary, and Brad aside just before the wagon train was ready to leave and told them, "I'm countin' on you kids to help out and not cause any trouble. You do what your folks tell you, and don't give 'em no sass. Stay in the wagons, and when we're stopped, don't wander off. You need to stick mighty close to the grown-ups. You understand?"

All three of the young'uns nodded gravely. Preacher knew that even though they liked him and were fascinated by him, they were a little scared of him too. So much the better, he thought. They were more likely to mind him that way. Kids who weren't a little afraid of their elders usually turned out to be little hellions, and a lot of the time they grew up to be pretty sorry adults too.

Preacher took the dun's reins and swung up into the saddle. Everyone who wasn't already on one of the wagons climbed aboard. Preacher walked the horse to the head of the line and waved an arm over his head. He didn't call out "Wagons ho!" or any such silliness. He just motioned for them to follow him and headed east.

The sun was up, though it wasn't doing much to warm the chilly air, and the sky was a deep blue, dotted with puffs of white clouds. A light breeze blew out of the north. It was a pleasant morning, especially for this time of year on the fringes of the high country.

But as Preacher led the wagons along the creek, the wind began to blow harder, and the temperature, instead of rising as the sun climbed higher in the sky, started to drop. Preacher looked to the north, saw the grayish-blue bank of clouds lying close to the horizon, and bit back a curse. He knew the clouds meant they were in for trouble. The only question was whether or not the storm that was on the way would be the first of the season's full-fledged blizzards, or just another teaser that would drop only a powdery dusting of white snow.

Time would tell, Preacher thought. Probably before the day was over, in fact . . .

By noon, most of the blue sky had been gobbled up by the onrushing clouds. The heavens were gray and ominous now, and when Preacher rode alongside the wagons, he saw that the men on the driver's seats were all huddled in thick coats, with their hats pulled down tightly on their heads. The two women and the kids were all inside the vehicles. Preacher hoped they were wrapped up good in blankets and quilts.

"Is it going to get much worse?" Roger called to him.

Preacher turned the dun so that he was riding alongside Roger's wagon. "Yeah, it'll get worse," he replied. "I don't know how much worse, though. Right now it's just cold, so we'll keep movin'."

"We could stop and build a fire," Roger suggested.

Preacher shook his head. "Keep 'em movin'," he said curtly.

Roger seemed to have forgotten that they had more to worry about than just the weather. There was still the little matter of that Arikara war party. So far today, in his ranging back and forth, ahead of and behind the wagon train, Preacher hadn't seen any sign of Indians, hostile or otherwise. But his gut told him they were still around somewhere.

And if the 'Rees were holding some sort of grudge against these white pilgrims, for reasons that the Galloways didn't want to admit, they wouldn't give up their vengeance quest just because a storm was blowing in. Now there would be even more of a blood debt to settle because of the six warriors who had died in battle the day before. True, Preacher and Dog had killed them, not any of these immigrants, but the other members of the war party wouldn't know that.

Assuming there *was* a war party, Preacher reminded himself. He still didn't know that for sure. He wasn't going to argue overmuch with his instincts, though. They had kept him alive this long, so they had to be right more often than not.

The creek turned and angled northeastward, but Preacher kept the wagons moving almost due east. Their water barrels were full, so they didn't have to worry about running out of water any time soon. Not only that, but there were other streams up ahead where they could refill the barrels if they needed to. Inexperienced travelers might have to follow a creek or a river to get to where they were going out here, but Preacher didn't need that. He could strike out across country and his internal compass would keep him going in the right direction.

They stopped for a short time in early afternoon to rest the mules and eat a cold meal from the leftovers of breakfast. Preacher sought out Angela and asked, "How are you holdin' up, ma'am?"

She had a scarf wrapped tightly around her head so that only a single strand of honey-colored hair escaped, and she was bundled up with a blanket around her shoulders in addition to her coat. She summoned a weak smile and said, "I'm fine, Preacher. Cold, of course, but we all are."

"What about your sister-in-law?" This would be a hell of a time for Dorothy Galloway to go into labor again, for real this time, but Preacher knew it was sort of inevitable.

"She's all right." Preacher sensed that Angela wanted to say more, so he stood there in silence for a moment. Hesitantly, Angela went on. "She was a bit out of her head for a while. She seemed to think we were back in Philadelphia. She asked me to build up the fire in the stove. Then she said some things . . . well, they made even less sense than that."

Preacher frowned. Having a pregnant woman to deal with had the potential for enough trouble by itself; having a *crazy* pregnant woman on his hands could be even worse.

"Keep an eye on her," he said to Angela. "I know in her condition she probably couldn't get out of the wagon very easy, but we sure don't want her runnin' off and gettin' lost, or anything like that."

"Don't worry," Angela assured him. "Someone will be with her at all times. Peter brought her something to eat just now."

Preacher nodded. He was going to be mighty glad when they got to Garvey's Fort. . . .

"Someone's coming!" Jonathan Galloway shouted.

SEVEN

Preacher had one of his rifles in his hand as he talked to Angela. At Jonathan's shout, he wheeled around and trotted toward the lead wagon, priming the Hawken as he went. Roger and Geoffrey joined him. The four of them gathered by the mule team hitched to Jonathan's wagon and looked to the north, where Jonathan was pointing.

Two men on horseback, leading a pack mule, rode toward the wagons. There was a little draw not far behind them, and Preacher figured that was where they had come from. He hadn't seen them earlier, which meant they had probably stayed out of sight in the draw until they got close enough to take a good look at the wagons. Then they had emerged, figuring that these immigrants didn't represent any threat. The evident wariness told Preacher that the newcomers had at least some experience on the frontier.

As they came closer and Preacher could make out more details, he decided that they were both mountain men. One wore a broad-brimmed hat, the other a fur cap with flaps that came down over the ears. Both were swathed in heavy capotes and buffalo robes, and they had rifles balanced across their saddles. Their bearded features looked vaguely familiar, which meant Preacher had probably seen them at Rendezvous or some trading post, but he didn't know them personally.

He said to the others, "Stay here," then moved out in front of the group to stand there patiently, the Hawken cradled in the crook of his arm. The two riders reined to a halt about forty feet from him. "Howdy," one of them called. "All right to come into your camp?"

"Ain't really a camp," Preacher replied. "We're just noonin' a mite late today. But you're welcome if you ain't lookin' for trouble."

"Farthest thing from it, mister." The two men walked their horses slowly forward.

The one wearing the hat was heavyset, with a round face and a ginger-colored beard. The one with the cap was leaner, and his black beard was shot through with gray. They dismounted, and Ginger-beard nodded to Preacher and said, "Mart Hawley's my name. This here's my partner, Ed Watson."

"They call me Preacher."

Hawley and Watson exchanged a quick look. Hawley said, "I told Ed it was you. We seen you at Rendezvous, back in the spring. Never got introduced, though." He thrust out a gloved hand.

Preacher shook it, then shook hands with Watson, who seemed to be the quiet type. Some men acted like they forgot they ever knew how to talk after they'd spent some time in the mountains. The high country just had that effect now and then.

"Where you boys headed?" Preacher asked.

Hawley scratched at his beard. "Well, now, that's a mighty good question. We been debatin' whether to go south, east, or west. Got to go somewheres, though, 'cause winter is nigh upon us."

"It surely is," Preacher agreed.

"I got to say, we didn't expect to run across no wagon train at this time of year, even a little one like this."

Preacher waved a hand at the immigrants behind him. "These are the Galloways. They didn't make it through the mountains in time, so I'm helpin' them get back to Garvey's Fort."

"That'll be a hard run, what with them wagons," Hawley said. "Closest place for some pilgrims to winter, though. They's a few cabins up in the mountains, but none big enough for a whole flock of folks like this."

"That was my thought."

Hawley looked at his partner again. "What do you say, Ed? Want to head for Garvey's, spend the winter there?"

Watson gnawed at the thick mustache that hung over his lips for a moment, shrugged, and then nodded.

"Sounds good to us," Hawley said to Preacher. "Onliest thing is, I just now realized you didn't ask us to come along. We ain't in the habit o' pushin' in where we ain't wanted."

The same thought had occurred to Preacher: These two men hadn't been invited to join their party. He didn't know them, didn't know what sort of fellas they were. On the other hand, both Hawley and Watson were armed and were probably good shots. If they ran into any more Arikara warriors out for blood and scalps, two men might make the difference. For now, at least, Preacher was willing to run that risk.

"You can ride along with us," he said. "You got to know, though, that there's a chance we got trouble followin' us. There was a ruckus yesterday. 'Ree war party jumped these folks just as I came along. The Injuns wound up dead."

"How many of them?" Hawley asked with a frown.

"Six."

"You kill 'em?"

"Me and Dog," Preacher replied as he jerked a thumb at the big wolflike animal, who sat nearby watching the humans, his face as inscrutable as ever.

Hawley grinned. "Yeah, you're Preacher, all right. Folks say you're a dangerous man."

"All o' them tall tales you hear about me ain't true."

"But some of them are?" Hawley persisted.

Preacher shrugged and turned away. "We got a few johnnycakes left. You boys hungry?"

"As b'ars," Hawley said.

That morning the war party led by Swift Arrow had backtracked Nah Ka Wan to the creek. The young warrior had walked for a long way before collapsing and becoming prey for the curious bear that had ultimately provided his death shroud. The Sahnish then followed the creek to the west, as Nah Ka Wan had indicated. It was the middle of the afternoon before they reached the spot where the whites had camped the night before.

"Look at the size of the fire the foolish white men built," Badger's Den said as he pointed at the large pile of ashes and partially burned wood. "No wonder Nah Ka Wan and his companions were able to find them."

"They left here and headed east," Swift Arrow mused. "Are they fleeing back to their homes?"

"And why did we not meet them on our way here?" the medicine man asked. "Our paths should have crossed."

"Unless they left the creek," Swift Arrow said. He waved a hand as if brushing away worry. "We will follow them. Their wagons are slow. They cannot escape from us."

"So far they have," one of the warriors said. Like most of the others, he was young and his blood ran hot in his veins. He was called Runs Far, because he never seemed to tire.

Swift Arrow scowled at this show of disrespect, slight though it was. "We will find the whites, and their scalps will be ours," he declared, glaring around at the other members of the war party as if daring any one of them to disagree with him. None did, and Runs Far looked worried that he had invoked the war chief's displeasure.

"Good," Swift Arrow went on after a moment. "We go now." He started trotting along the creek, following the double lines of tracks left by the wagon wheels. The others fell in behind him.

Only when the others could not see his expression did Swift Arrow allow any doubt to show on his face. He glanced at the sky, which was covered with gray clouds scudding down from the north. The wind was biting cold. There would be snow by nightfall. Swift Arrow was sure of it.

But he was equally sure that he and the warriors with him would stay on the trail of the white men until justice was done, until the blood debt had been paid and the scalps of the transgressors hung from the lances of the Sahnish.

Now that he had some experienced men to side with him, Preacher was able to stop spreading himself so thin. When the wagon train got under way again, he told Hawley and Watson to scout out ahead while he covered their back trail.

"You know the way to Garvey's, don't you?" he asked before they started.

"Yeah, we been there," Hawley confirmed. "We keep hittin' due east till we get out o' these foothills, then we angle just a mite south."

Preacher nodded. "That'll get us there. You see any signs of trouble developin', one of you light a shuck back here and fetch me while the other one gets the wagons ready."

"In a circle, you mean?" Hawley asked.

"If that's what it needs." Different sorts of trouble called for different responses.

Hawley nodded and he and Watson rode off. Preacher went the other direction, trotting the dun alongside the wagons as he headed for the rear. As he passed Peter Galloway's wagon, the three youngsters called to him from inside the canvas-covered vehicle and waved. Nate was riding in that wagon with his cousins, since his mama was in such a delicate condition in the wagon just ahead.

With Dog loping along beside him, Preacher dropped back a good half a mile behind the wagons and then rode a ways both north and south, looking for any sign that the Arikara were pursuing them. He didn't see anything, but even though they were getting out of the mountains now, this was still pretty rugged country. He reined the dun to a halt and let his keen eyes scan the landscape, knowing even as he did so that there were dozens of hiding places where the Indian warriors could be concealed.

He didn't see anything out of the ordinary. As he turned the horse, intending to close up the gap a little between him and the wagons, something touched his face. It turned instantly to moisture, only a tiny drop but enough to let Preacher know what was going on. He tipped his head back and looked up to see several more snowflakes swirling down out of the gloomy sky. They were small, and he saw only a few of them. But where there was one snowflake, there were usually millions more, just waiting to grow heavy enough to fall.

Preacher said, "Come on, Dog," and heeled the dun into a trot again. He rode after the wagons, watching as the snowflakes fell more frequently. They were still light, and this was a long way from a blizzard, but it was a start.

The wind was blowing harder by the time he came in sight of the wagons, still a good quarter of a mile in front of him. The tiny white flakes danced and darted in the air now, instead of drifting down slowly to the earth. Here and there, small patches of white had already begun to appear on the ground. If the snow didn't get any heavier than this, there would be only a dusting of it, but Preacher knew they couldn't count on that.

The thick clouds meant that darkness would fall very early on this night. It wasn't too soon to start looking for a place to stop. They would need at least a little shelter. Maybe the lee of a bluff, or even better, a cave. Preacher hoped that Hawley and Watson had the sense to keep their eyes open and call a halt if they found such a place.

A short time later, the wagons rolled around a hill and went out of sight. Preacher increased the dun's pace, not liking it now that he couldn't see the wagons anymore. But when he rounded the shoulder of the hill a few minutes later, he saw that the wagons had been driven down into a hollow. A cliff overhung it at an outward angle, providing some shelter. The place wasn't a cave, but it would have to do. They weren't likely to find anything better between now and nightfall.

Hawley walked over as Preacher dismounted. "Figured you'd want us to stop, since it's started to snow. It'll be dark 'fore much longer too."

Preacher nodded. "That's fine. I don't reckon I could've done any better myself."

Hawley grinned, exposing worn-down brown teeth. "That's mighty high praise comin' from the famous Preacher."

"Why don't we forget about that famous business? Just call me Preacher."

"Sure."

Preacher walked among the wagons, checking on the pilgrims. Everybody seemed to be all right, cold and worn-out but otherwise none the worse for the long day on the trail. Angela Galloway smiled at him, and her husband Peter scowled, so that hadn't changed since the morning.

"Is this that blizzard you warned us about?" Angela

asked as she held out a hand and let a couple of snowflakes fall on her palm.

"It might be by mornin'," Preacher said.

"I hope not."

Preacher just grunted noncommittally. He didn't know what to hope for anymore. A high country blizzard could be a killer, but on the other hand, if the storm dumped a few feet of snow on the ground, it would sure cover up their tracks if the Arikara were looking for them. Preacher supposed that was what they called a mixed blessing.

One thing was certain: The weather would do whatever it wanted to, and there wasn't a blessed thing this puny group of humans could do about it.

EIGHT

Preacher built a bigger fire tonight than he had the night before. For one thing, the temperature was considerably colder, and they needed the warmth. For another, the overhang of the cliff would disperse the smoke to a certain extent, so there was less of a threat that someone could track them by it.

Mart Hawley had the wagons parked in a half circle at the base of the cliff. Preacher built the fire inside that circle. The heat rose and was radiated back from the rocky face of the cliff. After a while the camp was almost warm, and everyone was grateful for that after spending the day in that biting, frigid wind.

Night fell suddenly while the camp was being set up, and as darkness mantled the sky, the snowfall increased. Preacher looked at it and shook his head. Maybe not a sure-enough blizzard, it was too soon to tell about that, but for damn certain, more than a dusting was due.

He went over to Roger Galloway's wagon and called softly, "Miz Angela?"

A moment later, she parted the canvas flap at the rear of the wagon and looked out at him. "What is it, Preacher?" Her cheeks were rosy from the cold, but other than that her face was pale and drawn.

"How's Miz Dorothy doin'?" As Preacher asked the question, it occurred to him that so far he hadn't even laid eyes on Dorothy Galloway. If not for the fact that he had heard her yelling her head off when she was going through that false labor, she might as well not have been a member of the party, at least as far as you could prove it by him.

Angela shook her head wearily. "Not very good, I'm afraid. She's even weaker tonight. She doesn't want anything to eat or drink, and I'm worried that she might be coming down with a fever."

"What'll you do if she is?" Preacher asked with a frown.

"The best I can," Angela said. "But there won't be much anyone can do for her."

Preacher lowered his voice. "Does her husband know about this?"

"Roger knows. He's trying to keep up a brave front, but he's very frightened."

Preacher nodded. "Well, if there's anything I can do . . ."

"I'll let you know right away," Angela promised. "Thank you, Preacher."

He nodded again and turned away from the wagon. Over by the cliff, the three kids were trying to scrape up enough snow to make snowballs they could fling at each other. Even when they were mighty tired and cold, it was hard to keep a young'un's spirits down for very long.

The mules had been unhitched and herded together, then tied to stakes driven into the ground. Wouldn't be able to do that for much longer, Preacher thought. The ground would be frozen too hard for the stakes to penetrate. Roger, Peter, and their father Simon stood together, talking quietly. Geoffrey and Jonathan were using buckets to water the mules. Hawley and Watson stood apart from the others, apparently unsure what to do.

As Preacher walked over to them, Hawley said, "Ed

and me can move outside the circle and have our own campfire if you want."

Preacher shook his head. "No, that ain't necessary. We asked you to travel with us, and that means you share our fire."

"We got a mite of grub we'd be glad to throw in. Ain't nothin' but some jerky and pemmican, but these folks are welcome to share in it."

"Hang on to it for now," Preacher advised. "Might need it later if rations run short before we get to the fort."

Hawley nodded. "All right, that makes sense. We feel a little bad, though, like we ain't contributin' anything."

Watson jogged Hawley's arm with his elbow and gave him a meaningful look.

"We, ah, got some jugs o' whiskey on that pack mule," Hawley went on. "Be glad to share that too, even if it is just rotgut."

"Keep it," Preacher said quickly. If he was right about Simon Galloway, the man already had his own stash of Who-hit-John, and none of the others seemed to need it.

"Well, if the time comes, it's there, and we'd be glad to share."

Preacher nodded in acknowledgment of the offer, then moved toward the fire. Somebody needed to start getting supper ready, and it looked like he was elected.

He fried more bacon, got some biscuits baking in a Dutch oven he found in the back of one of the wagons, and put a pot of beans on to cook. A skim of ice had formed on the water in which the beans had been soaking all day. Preacher didn't think the water barrels would freeze up overnight, not with the heat of the fire warming the camp, but if it got much colder that was a possibility. They might have to chip ice out of the barrels and melt it, or melt snow for water instead. That might be inconvenient but wouldn't pose a major problem.

When the food was ready he called everyone over and doled it out. For the most part the Galloways ate in silence, and the two mountain men who had joined them were quiet as well. Preacher thought Roger Galloway looked haggard. The strain of worrying about his wife and unborn child was beginning to wear heavily on the man. Preacher figured he wished he had never come west. If anything happened to Dorothy or the baby, Roger would probably blame himself . . . and he'd be more right than wrong in doing so.

When supper was over and everything had been cleaned up, Angela got the children settled down for the night while Roger sat with Dorothy. That left Preacher, Hawley, Watson, Peter, Simon, Jonathan, and Geoffrey sitting around the fire, warming themselves. Hawley said to the group in general, "You fellas ever do any card playin'?"

"You mean poker?" Jonathan asked.

"Yes, sir." Hawley reached inside his thick coat made of buffalo hide and took out a stack of greasy cards. "I got a deck. I've found that it's relaxin' of an evenin' to play a few hands."

"I'm more partial to whist myself," Geoffrey said.

Hawley shook his head. "Don't reckon I know how to play that. But I like a good game o' stud poker."

"I'll play," Peter said. "I could use something to keep my mind off the chill that's still in my bones from that wind."

Jonathan spoke up. "Count me in too. But I'm afraid I'm not very good at cards. I won't give you much of a game."

"Aw, hell, don't worry about that," Hawley said. "It's just somethin' to pass the time."

But even as Hawley spoke, Preacher thought he saw an unpleasant gleam in the man's eyes. Could be Hawley thought these pilgrims were ripe for the pickin' . . . and chances were, he was right. Preacher resolved to keep an eye on the game, even though he didn't plan to take part in it himself.

Simon and Geoffrey played too, along with Peter, Jonathan, Hawley, and Watson. The six of them sat around a blanket that Jonathan spread on the ground. They used pebbles gathered at the base of the cliff for chips. Hawley dealt first, since the cards were his. Watson could talk after all, Preacher discovered, although the man in the fur cap asked for his cards only in curt grunts. The shuffle of pasteboards, the click of pebbles together, reminded Preacher of the sounds he had heard in many a tavern and trading post. It was comforting in a way. The wind had died down with the coming of night, although the snow still fell, the flakes sizzling into oblivion when they hit the flames of the campfire. The night began to have a peaceful feeling to it.

But Preacher knew how deceptive that could be. They had to remain alert and would need guards posted again tonight. For the time being, he felt like taking a look around. He picked up one of his rifles and said softly, "Dog." The big wolflike creature followed him, padding through the snow as Preacher walked quietly out of camp, away from the wagons. No one seemed to notice him leaving.

He had been careful not to look directly into the fire too much, so he still had his night vision. He ranged out several hundred yards from the camp, pausing every few moments to listen intently for any telltale sounds of someone moving in the night. Everything was quiet except for the faint hiss of the snow falling. Some folks had tried to tell Preacher that snow didn't make any sound when it fell, but he knew good and well that it did. You just had to know how to listen for it.

When he was satisfied that no Arikara war party was

sneaking up on the camp, he turned and walked back to the hollow under the looming cliff. The glow from the fire was partially blocked by the encircling wagons, but it was still visible. If anyone was abroad in the night, they would be able to see it too. All the more reason to keep guards posted all night. With kids and a sick woman in the party, they couldn't do without the fire, though.

When he got back, he found Angela Galloway pouring herself a cup of coffee. "Get the young'uns settled down for the night?" Preacher asked her.

"Yes, they were exhausted. They went right to sleep."

"You look about done in yourself."

Angela smiled wearily. "Don't worry about me. I'll be fine."

Over in the circle of cardplayers around the blanket, Peter laughed triumphantly. Preacher inclined his head in that direction and said, "Sounds like luck's on your husband's side, at least for now."

Peter Galloway was a damned lucky man, Preacher thought, in more ways than one.

"They seem to be enjoying themselves," Angela said. "People have a way of finding amusement, even in trying circumstances."

"It don't do no good to sit around moanin' and cryin' and feelin' sorry for yourself. That's just a plumb waste of time."

Angela smiled at him. "You've probably never felt sorry for yourself in your life, have you, Preacher?"

He thought about Jennie and the pain he had felt when he found out she was dead. He had grieved for her, of course, but part of his sorrow had been for his own sake, for the loss he had suffered.

"I wouldn't say that," he replied softly. "I just figure it's better to try to do somethin' about whatever's wrong." In his case, he had taken vengeance on the men responsible for Jennie's death. It hadn't helped much, but it was better than nothing.

"There's an old saying about how it's better to light one candle than to curse the darkness," Angela said.

Preacher nodded. "Yes, ma'am, I reckon that's just what I'm talkin' about."

They stood there quietly for a few moments after that while Angela sipped her coffee and Preacher leaned on the rifle, grasping the barrel of the Hawken while its buttstock rested on the ground. He had taken a shine to Angela Galloway as soon as he saw her, but he knew it was wrong and he would never act on the feeling. For one thing, and most importantly, she was a married woman, and Preacher respected the sanctity of marriage. Even though he had left home at an early age, his parents had given him a good moral grounding and the ability to tell right from wrong. For another thing, he didn't want to be disloyal to Jennie's memory, even though it had begun to fade. Someday, Preacher figured, he would be ready to let go of the pain and just remember the good things, but that day wasn't here yet.

A deep chuckle drew his attention to the men playing cards. "Looks like this pot is mine," Jonathan Galloway declared as he leaned forward to rake in the pile of pebbles in the center of the blanket.

"Not so fast." The words, surprisingly, came from Ed Watson. "That pot ain't yours."

"What?" Jonathan exclaimed. "Why not?"

"Because you cheated, you son of a bitch!"

NINE

Preacher knew trouble when he heard it a-bornin'. He straightened from his casual stance as Peter Galloway said angrily, "Damn you, you can't talk to my uncle that way! A Galloway never cheats!"

"Well, he did," Watson insisted in a reedy voice. "I seen him deal a card off the bottom of the deck."

"That's preposterous," Geoffrey said. "Jonathan, tell him."

"Of course. I never cheated at cards in my life," Jonathan said. "And I'm insulted that you think I did tonight."

Watson glared at him. "I don't think it—I know it. I seen it with my own eyes. He ain't the onliest one neither. It ain't no coinseedence that ever since we started playin' for money, one o' you boys has won ever' hand."

"They're playin' for money?" Preacher muttered to himself. "I thought they was playin' for pebbles."

"It was you and your friend who wanted to 'make things more interesting,' as you put it," Peter said to Watson. "We just went along with you, even though I didn't think it was really that good an idea. If you're too stupid to win, don't blame us and claim we're cheating."

For once, Preacher couldn't blame Peter Galloway for being hotheaded, even though Peter might have phrased his argument a mite more discreetly. If a man was honest and came from an honest family, he couldn't just let it pass when somebody accused him or his kin of cheating.

"I ain't stupid," Watson shot back, "which means I don't believe you. You're all a pack of cheaters and liars!"

Peter threw his cards down on the blanket and started to get to his feet. "Take that back or I'll thrash you!" he said.

"Oh, my God," Angela said softly. "Peter, don't—"

Watson had no intention of taking back his harsh words. Preacher knew that just by looking at the man's face. He started forward, intending to intervene in the argument, but it was too late. Watson launched himself across the blanket, uncoiling from the ground like a striking snake. His fist lashed out and crashed into Peter's jaw. Peter sprawled backward on the ground, scattering the powdery, new-fallen snow.

"Peter!" Angela cried.

Watson continued his attack, lunging at Peter and drawing back his leg for a kick. "Thrash me! Go ahead and thrash me, why don't you!"

Simon, Geoffrey, and Jonathan were all too stunned by the sudden vicious assault to do anything to help Peter. Preacher could have gotten there in time to stop Watson from kicking Peter, but he held back, wanting to see what the young man would do, how he handled himself. Might come a day when Preacher would have to depend on Peter Galloway to save his life or the life of someone else.

Although stunned by the punch, Peter still had his wits about him enough to see Watson's booted foot coming at him. He rolled to the side, avoiding the kick, and reached up to grab Watson's leg. He heaved on it, toppling the mountain man and sending Watson crashing to the ground.

Hawley started to his feet, reaching for the pistol be-hind his belt as he did so, and Preacher finally stepped in. He swung the Hawken up so that its barrel was pointed in Hawley's general direction and growled, "Stay out of it, mister. Let them settle it."

Hawley stopped reaching for his gun and settled back down on the ground, but his face was taut with anger. He didn't like having a rifle pointed at him. Preacher didn't much care what Hawley liked or didn't like.

Peter tried to press his momentary advantage. He leaped at the fallen Watson and swung a couple of wild punches at the man's face. Watson blocked them both, brought a knee up, and planted his foot against Peter's chest. A hard shove sent Peter flying through the air.

"Can't you stop them?" Angela said worriedly to Preacher.

"I could, but there ain't no need to."

"No need? Peter could get hurt!"

Preacher shook his head. "Not too bad, as long as it's just fists. Better to let them hash it out amongst them-selves."

Watson had the advantage now. He threw himself on top of Peter Galloway and tried to lock his fingers around Peter's throat. Peter was younger, taller, and heavier, but Watson knew all the tricks of rough-and-tumble, bare-knuckles brawling. He got a stranglehold on Peter and bore down, cutting off his air.

That grip didn't last long. Peter bucked up off the ground and threw Watson to the side. Gasping, he rolled away and came up on his hands and knees, then stag-gered to his feet. He rubbed his sore throat where Watson's fingers had dug into it.

A few feet away, Watson struggled up as well. By now the other men had drawn back, giving the combatants some room. The blanket was wadded up, and the cards and pebbles were scattered. Clearly, the game was over for the night.

With angry shouts, the two men came together and started slugging it out, fists flying and thudding into flesh and bone. Again, Watson's greater experience helped him. His punches were short and compact but had all of his strength behind them. Peter gradually had to give ground. As he backed up, Watson's foot suddenly shot out, hooked behind Peter's ankle, and jerked. Peter went over backward.

Watson reached into his coat and pulled out a knife. With a savage grin on his face, he lunged at Peter, the blade poised to strike down into the younger man's chest.

The Hawken in Preacher's hand roared as he fired without seeming to aim. The heavy lead ball struck Watson's knife hand, shattering bone and shredding flesh. The knife went flying harmlessly into the air. Watson screamed and fell to his knees, clutching the wounded, blood-spouting member to his chest.

"You shot him!" Hawley shouted accusingly. "You said we ought to stay out of it!"

"That was when it was just fists," Preacher said. "Watson made it a heap different when he pulled that pigsticker."

Watson glared up at him from his knees. "You bastard! You've ruined me!"

"You're lucky I didn't kill you," Preacher said coldly.

"We ain't gonna forget this," Hawley warned.

Preacher nodded and said, "I sure as hell hope not. Tend to your friend."

Hawley got up and went to Watson's side. He helped Watson to his feet and led him over by the cliff. Working quickly, Hawley bound up the wounded hand with a strip of cloth he cut off Watson's shirt. Both of them sent frequent, hate-filled glances toward Preacher and the Galloways.

Angela hurried over to Peter as he climbed shakily to his feet. "Are you all right?" she wanted to know.

He nodded. "I'm fine." Amazingly enough, the look he gave Preacher was resentful. "I could have handled him. I was doing all right."

If that was what the damn fool wanted to believe, Preacher wasn't going to waste breath or energy arguing with him. Preacher knew, though, that Peter Galloway would have been dead in another few seconds if he hadn't shot Watson.

The shouting and the gunshot had roused everyone else in the camp. The kids looked out from the wagon where they were sleeping, full of questions and wide-eyed with fear. Once Angela was satisfied that her husband was all right, she went to reassure the young-sters that everything was fine and tell them to crawl back into their bedrolls and go back to sleep.

Meanwhile, Roger Galloway climbed down from his wagon and came over to join the others. He had a pistol in his hand. "What is it?" he asked anxiously. "Is it the Indians? Are we under attack?"

"Nope," Preacher said.

Simon said, "Peter got in a fight with one of those mountain men."

"A fight?" Roger repeated. "About what?"

"The man said I was cheating at cards," Jonathan explained, "but I never did. You know I wouldn't do that, Roger."

"Of course not." Roger looked at his brother and asked the same question Angela had. "Peter, are you all right?"

"I'm fine," Peter said again, more disgustedly this time. "We should have known not to trust those ruffi-ans." He cast a meaningful glance Preacher's way.

Preacher figured that if any cheating had been going

on, more than likely Hawley and Watson had been doing it. He had reserved judgment on the men, but now he decided that they had planned to fleece the pilgrims at cards all along. But they had gone up against stiffer competition than they had expected. All of Jonathan's talk about not being any good at poker had been a ruse, designed to draw in Hawley and Watson. They had played along without even realizing it, even to the point of suggesting that they play for money instead of pebbles, which was no doubt what Jonathan had wanted all along.

But despite that con, Jonathan had been winning fair and square. Preacher hadn't seen Jonathan or any of the other Galloways cheating.

Well, it was over now, and nobody had gotten killed. There was that to be thankful for anyway, Preacher thought as he reloaded the Hawken.

Hawley walked over to him. "What are you gonna do about this?" he asked, knowing that Preacher was in charge here.

"Come mornin', you and Watson will go your way and we'll go ours."

"You're not goin' to kick us out of camp tonight?"

"Nope, not in weather like this. Not that I care overmuch whether the two of you freeze. I just don't want to have to mess with your stiff carcasses come mornin'."

"This ain't fair," Hawley blustered. "You said we could travel together."

"That was before your pard tried to kill somebody."

"We'll stand a lot better chance of gettin' to Garvey's Fort if we stay together."

"You will, you mean," Preacher said.

"Might come a time when you'll need our guns."

"Well, we'll just have to get along without 'em, I reckon. Get back over there by the cliff, and the two of you stay there. Somebody will be keepin' an eye on you all night, so don't try anything."

"Ain't fair," Hawley muttered again as he turned away. "Just ain't fair." He went back over to Watson and told him what Preacher had said. Watson was still in pain. He cradled his injured hand against his body.

The Galloways all began to move toward their wagons. Now that the trouble was over, they were ready to turn in. Except for Roger, who started toward Preacher and said his name.

Preacher half-turned to see what Roger wanted, so it was only out of the corner of his eye that he saw Watson pull a pistol from under his coat with his good hand. In an instinctive reaction to the threat, Preacher pivoted back toward the cliff and fired from the hip. Watson had lifted the pistol and pointed it at Preacher, but he fumbled for an instant before pressing the trigger, probably because he had the gun in his left hand. That second of delay was enough to prove fatal for him. The ball from Preacher's Hawken smashed into his chest and lifted him backward off his feet as it plowed all the way through his body and burst out his back in a shower of blood and pulped flesh. He hit the face of the cliff and bounced off, pitching forward and leaving a smear of crimson on the rock.

Like lightning, Preacher lowered the rifle and pulled one of the pistols from behind his belt. He covered Hawley, who was reaching for a gun, and said, "Don't do it."

Hawley froze, then slowly lifted his hand away from his pistol. "Don't shoot," he croaked, knowing just how close he had come to dying. "Don't shoot, Preacher. I ain't gonna cause any trouble. What Ed did, that was on his own head. I didn't have nothin' to do with it."

"You were reachin' for a gun," Preacher snapped.

"Well, hell, a man sees his partner shot down, he just naturally tries to do somethin' about it."

That was true enough, Preacher supposed. Instinct had sent Hawley's hand toward his gun, and instinct had come near getting his head blowed off. But nobody else had to die, not tonight.

Preacher said, "Come over here, take all your guns and knives out, and put 'em down on the ground. Then back off."

"You can't take a man's weapons away," Hawley whined.

"I ain't takin' 'em permanent. You can have 'em back in the mornin' after we've left. But for now just do what I tell you."

Grudgingly, Hawley complied, shedding himself of two pistols, a hunting knife, and a dirk.

"That all?" Preacher asked as Hawley backed away from the weapons.

"That's it."

"You better not be lyin' to me."

"I ain't as big a damn fool as you seem to think I am," Hawley said bitterly. "But I ain't gonna forget about this neither, Preacher."

"No," Preacher said, "I don't expect you will."

TEN

The sound of the distant shots came faintly through the frigid night air, first one, and then a few moments later another. Swift Arrow heard them and grunted. "Perhaps the whites are killing each other," he said to Badger's Den.

The medicine man frowned. "It will not satisfy the blood debt they owe the Sahnish if they kill each other."

"True. But there will be at least one left on whom to take our revenge, if Neshanu Natchitak wills it." Swift Arrow smiled. "Who is the only white man who speaks the truth to our people?"

"A dead white man, because he says nothing," Badger's Den replied, and the other members of the war party laughed at the old joke.

They sat around a tiny fire built in the lee of a rock, trying to ignore the cold. Every man there, if he was honest with himself, missed the warmth of his lodge and his woman. When they had left their village, following Swift Arrow on his quest of vengeance against the white men, they had expected to be back before the first real snowfall. But the white men had been fortunate and had somehow stayed ahead of their pursuers for long enough so that that goal was no longer possible. The first real storm of winter was here, and the warriors had no choice but to pull their bear and buffalo robes tighter

around themselves and take no notice of the bad
weather.

Swift Arrow worried, however, that the snow would
make it more difficult for them to locate the wagons.
The white mantle would obscure any tracks left by the
wheeled vehicles. Again, the Sahnish would be reduced
to splitting up into search parties, such as the one that
Nah Ka Wan had been a member of.

At least they knew the right direction in which to
begin their search. The shots had told them that much.
When morning came, Swift Arrow thought, they would
take up the trail once more, and they would not stop
until all the hated whites were dead.

Hawley didn't try anything else during the night. He
sat beside the corpse of his friend and stared darkly at
the rest of the party until exhaustion finally overcame
him and he fell asleep, leaning against the cliff.

Preacher made sure they all understood that one man
on every guard shift would have to watch Hawley.
Preacher didn't trust the surly mountain man as far as
he could throw him. The smart thing to do would be to
go ahead and shoot the son of a bitch, but Preacher
couldn't bring himself to do that. He couldn't just kill a
man in cold blood.

The snow stopped during the night. Away from the
camp, the ground was covered with four or five inches of
the white stuff, Preacher saw as he looked around the
next morning. That wasn't enough to cause the wagons
any trouble, although it was possible there were some
deeper drifts they would have to contend with. It was
pretty to look at too, that white blanket spread over the
ground, as well as the caps of snow that nestled on the
branches of the pine trees.

The kids could make good snowballs now, and they

fell to it with a vengeance, a-whoopin' and a-hollerin' as they ran around and flung the hard-packed missiles at each other. While they were doing that, the adults fixed breakfast and got ready to travel again.

Preacher shadowed Mart Hawley as Hawley tended to his horses. "You don't have to watch me so blasted close," the man snapped. "I ain't gonna cause any trouble. I told you, pullin' a gun was Ed's idea, not mine."

"Indulge me," Preacher said dryly. "I'll feel a mite easier if I keep an eye on you, Hawley. What do you plan to do with your partner?" Preacher inclined his head toward Watson's body.

"Find a ravine, I reckon, and pile some rocks on him after I dump him. Unless you want to help me dig a grave for him."

"Not likely," Preacher said.

Hawley glared at him. "Ain't you got a ounce o' human compassion in you? Sure, he lost his head and got hisself kilt, but he really weren't that bad a feller."

"I'll take your word for it."

"When do I get my guns back?"

"We'll leave 'em a half mile or so up the trail after we've pulled out. Just follow the wagon tracks in the snow and you'll find 'em. I'll even wrap 'em up in some cloth to protect 'em from the weather."

"What if I need to shoot somethin' before then?"

"My advice would be not to need to," Preacher said. "You wait until we're gone and well out of sight before you leave here. And I sure won't take it kindly if you decide to come after us."

"Well, damn it, what if we just happen to be goin' the same direction? I still thought I might try to winter at Garvey's place."

"Just don't come ridin' up our backside. If I see you betwixt here and there, I plan on shootin' first and askin' questions later."

"You're mighty damned touchy," Hawley muttered.

"I get that way when folks try to kill me."

Preacher went back to the wagons. Roger and Peter had built up the fire until it was blazing brightly again, and Jonathan was cooking breakfast. Preacher said to Roger, "How's your wife this mornin'?"

"A little better, I think," Roger replied. A haunted look in the young man's eyes told Preacher that he wasn't really convinced of what he was saying, however. Maybe he was trying to make himself believe it.

"No baby yet, though," said Preacher.

Roger shook his head. "No. No baby."

Preacher could do a lot of things, but he couldn't make a baby be born when it wasn't good and ready. He put a hand on Roger's shoulder for a moment and gave him a reassuring nod. That was about all he could do.

A short time later, after everyone had eaten breakfast—except for Hawley, who would have to make do now with the jerky and pemmican he already had—and the wagons had been hitched up, Preacher said, "Climb up there and let's get movin', folks. Got a lot of ground to cover today."

He swung up into the dun's saddle and rode out of the hollow. Dog went with him and then bounded ahead, kicking up snow with his paws as he ran. He looked more like a wolf than ever in these surroundings. Preacher reined in and turned to watch as the wagons climbed out of the hollow and began rolling across the relatively level ground to the east. There were still some more hills to cross before they would reach the actual plains, but the going would get a little easier with each mile they put behind them.

Hawley stood near the cliff with his horses. Ed Watson's corpse lay nearby. Preacher remembered how the first man he had been forced to kill had haunted him for a long time. He had seen the face of that river pirate in his dreams, and even sometimes when he was awake. Now, so many violent years had rolled past that he could no longer even make an accurate estimate of the number of men who had gone down to death at his hands. But he had never murdered anyone, never taken a life unless he was forced to it, and never killed anybody who didn't need killin'. His conscience was clear and he slept just fine at night.

Some folks just never understood. They prattled on about how every human life was sacred and how nobody had the right to kill somebody else. That was all well and good, and Preacher supposed there was a kernel of truth in what they said. But they seemed to forget that man was an animal, and an animal will always fight to save its own life or the lives of those it holds dear. From the grizzly bear and the mountain lion down to the smallest of field mice, something inside every critter on the face of the earth made it strike back when it was threatened. You'd never catch an animal hesitating and pondering moral questions when it ought to be fightin' for what was right. The greatest morality was survival.

At least it would be, Preacher thought, until so-called civilization bred that out of folks and they got in the habit of just sittin' back and taking whatever evil the world dished out at 'em. He shook his head and hoped he never lived long enough to see it come to that.

"Keep headin' straight on thataway," he called to Jonathan Galloway as Jonathan's wagon rumbled past. Preacher pointed where he meant, and Jonathan nodded that he understood. Preacher waited off to the side on the dun as all four of the wagons rolled by. He sat there watching Hawley until the wagons had a good long lead. Then finally he turned the dun and rode after them. Dog growled one last time at Hawley and then loped after Preacher.

Preacher had fashioned a makeshift bundle out of a

piece of an old blanket and tied up Hawley's weapons in it. When he judged he had gone far enough, he set the bundle on top of a rock where Hawley couldn't miss it, and then rode on. He hoped he wasn't making a mistake by leaving Hawley alive. If the man was filled with enough of a thirst for vengeance, he might creep up on the wagons at night and take a potshot or two at them.

If that happened, Preacher would deal with it. He wouldn't hesitate. He'd just go out and hunt down Hawley and kill him on sight.

The sky was still overcast, but no more snow fell during the morning. The wagons pushed on steadily and actually made pretty good time. If they could keep this up, Preacher thought, they might reach Garvey's Fort before winter really closed down and clamped its icy grip on the landscape.

Yep, they still had a chance to salvage this disaster of a trip.

Mart Hawley stood above the ten-foot-deep gully where he had dumped the body of his friend and partner. Watson's corpse had been stiff with both cold and rigor mortis, and Hawley had had a hell of a time wrestling it into the gully. Now he stood there with a large chunk of rock in his hand and looked down at Watson.

"Ed, you stupid bastard," Hawley said. He raised the rock above his head and then threw it down with all his strength into Watson's face, which was still contorted from the man's death agonies. The rock struck with a dull thud.

"If you hadn't lost your head, we could'a strung along with them pilgrims until we had a chance to kill Preacher," Hawley went on as he picked up another rock. "Then them wagons would've been ours, and that pretty woman too. Course, we'd'a had to kill the rest of 'em, but I don't reckon that'd have been too hard."

He flung the rock at Watson's corpse with all the fury he could muster. "Stupid damn bastard!"

For several minutes, he kept cursing Watson and throwing rocks into the gully. By all rights, he should have left the body uncovered so that wolves and other varmints could get at it. That's what Watson deserved for being so dumb as to lose his temper and try to kill Preacher. Everybody in the Rocky Mountains knew that killing Preacher would be one hell of a chore. It would have to be planned out ahead of time. That's what he would do, Hawley told himself. He would take his time and make a plan, and then stick to it until he had Preacher in his sights and could blow his damn head off. That would be a fine day, yes, sir, one fine day.

Hawley threw one more rock into the gully and then turned away. That was good enough. He had tried to cover up Watson, because after all, they had been partners and had ridden and trapped together for a couple of years, but if it wasn't good enough, then too bad. Hawley had wasted enough time. He wanted to get after those wagons, retrieve his guns—assuming that sumbitch Preacher had left them as he'd said he would—and get started on his plan.

It would take a while, Hawley thought as he rode off, leading Watson's horse and the pack mule. But he could afford to be patient.

Preacher didn't know it yet, but he was already a dead man. Yes, sir, a . . . dead . . . man.

ELEVEN

The afternoon passed as peacefully as the morning had. Preacher kept the group moving at as fast a pace as possible. He spent more time behind the wagons than he did in front of them today, since now he had not only the Arikara war party to worry about but also Mart Hawley as well. Preacher didn't believe Hawley would just let it go. Hawley would want vengeance for his partner.

Nobody suggested cards after supper that night, if there was even a deck anywhere amongst the party's belongings.

The sky had begun to clear late in the afternoon, and the winds were light. They were in for the coldest night yet, Preacher knew. There was no cave, no bluff, no cliff to shield them. They stopped beside a creek that had ice beginning to form along its edges. They had to build their fire out in the open, and the terrain was flat enough so that it could be seen for a long distance. Preacher didn't like it, but he had no choice in the matter. Without the fire, they would all be frozen by morning.

The temperature dropped as sharply as he expected. By morning the air was so cold it took the breath away and seemed to chill a man all way to his marrow. But at least no one had attacked them during the night. That was something to be grateful for, Preacher thought.

Everyone was sluggish and slow to get moving because of the cold, even the young'uns. Preacher hustled them up as best he could. They would feel better once their blood was pumping faster. Preacher boiled coffee, fried bacon, hitched up the mules, and said impatiently, "Let's go, let's go."

Peter Galloway scowled in irritation as he cupped his gloved hands around a cup of hot coffee. "What's all the damned hurry?" he complained. "Everybody's cold. Give us a little time to get warmed up."

"You'll warm up a whole heap faster if you're doin' something," Preacher told him. "And you can bet if there are more o' them Arikara after us, they ain't loafin' around this mornin'. They'll be on the move already."

"Do you think there are more hostiles pursuing us?" Jonathan asked.

"I sure wouldn't rule it out."

Not only that, Preacher thought, but if the Arikara were back there, there was a good chance they would have seen the fire last night, and they could be closing in at this very moment.

"Dog, take a look around," Preacher went on, and Dog trotted off to scout the area around the camp.

Geoffrey stared after the animal. "It's like he understood every word you said," he commented to Preacher, sounding surprised.

"Well, I don't reckon he understood the words so much as he figured out what I wanted. We been together for quite a few years now, so we know each other pretty well."

"Can you communicate with any other woodland animals?"

Preacher couldn't help but grin, even as worried as he was. "It ain't like I sit around havin' deep conversations with squirrels . . . although I've knowed a few fellas who didn't draw the line at talkin' to critters. But you can learn something from almost every creature that lives in the wild, if you just pay attention to 'em. They'll nearly always tell you when somebody's skulkin' around and is up to no good. Animals got a way o' sensin' that. You just got to learn how to look and listen right."

Jonathan asked, "Could you teach us?"

Preacher frowned at him. "Teach you to be frontiersmen, you mean?"

"That's right," Jonathan said with an eager nod. "If we're going to live out here, we need to learn how to get along properly in the wild."

Preacher shrugged and said, "I reckon I could teach you a few things. Mostly, though, it's just a matter of payin' heed to what's goin' on around you."

And the frontier was the best teacher of all, he added to himself. Only problem was, it was also a harsh teacher, and anyone who failed to learn its lessons usually wound up dead before very long. But those who survived learned a hell of a lot, that was for damned sure.

Dog came loping back a little later, and his attitude told Preacher that he hadn't found anything suspicious. If the Indians were out there—and Preacher's instincts still told him they were—they hadn't closed in yet.

The wagons finally got rolling, a good half hour after Preacher thought they should have. The sky was clear as a bell and achingly blue. The sun shone on the snow-covered ground and glittered on the snow and ice in the trees. The breath of men and mules and horses plumed in front of their faces. Preacher pointed the wagons toward a saddle of ground between two hills, and then dropped back a ways to look over the country behind them.

He had seen very little of Angela Galloway this morning, and he was glad of that. She was pretty and nice and he didn't need to be reminded of that. He made up his mind that when they got to Garvey's, he would move on and winter somewhere else. If he stayed around Angela for months, he would just get more uncomfortable. And although he was no expert when it came to women, he thought she was a mite interested in him too, and he didn't want her to have to feel the same vague guilt and unease that he was experiencing. Better for him to just go on his way and leave her to her husband and her kids, where she belonged.

The sun climbed higher, but didn't do much to warm the frigid landscape. Once, Preacher thought he saw a lone rider far behind them, but even with his keen eyesight, he couldn't be sure. Hawley, he thought, trailing them but not getting too close. Either the trapper had taken Preacher's warning to heart . . . or he was being cagey and biding his time before he tried to get his revenge. Either way he wasn't an immediate concern.

Mart Hawley was nervous. He didn't know if that was because of the cold, or the isolation, or something else that he couldn't pin down. He wasn't used to riding alone, and despite the anger he had felt toward Ed Watson, he wished the son of a bitch was still around. Ed hadn't been very bright, and except when he lost his temper he talked only a little more than a rock, but by Godfrey, he'd been better than nothing as far as companions went. Maybe not much, but still better.

Hawley asked himself if he really wanted to try to kill Preacher. The man had quite a reputation, despite his relative youth. He was mean as a he-coon and strong as a grizz, quick as a panther and sharp-eyed as an eagle, and he just flat out had not an ounce of back up in him. He was pure pizen. Was avenging Ed Watson's death really worth it?

Hawley shivered in his capote and his thick buffalo robe as his horse plodded along. He was following the tracks of the wagons because he didn't know what else to do. He'd spent a miserable night huddled by a tiny fire, convinced he was going to freeze to death before morning. Maybe if he waited another day or two and let Preacher and the others get over being mad at him, they would allow him to rejoin their party.

Or more than likely, Preacher would just shoot him out of the saddle as soon as he got within rifle range.

Hawley might have to take that chance. He wasn't convinced he could make it to Garvey's Fort on his own. And his resolve to kill Preacher was wavering a whole heap. Hawley knew that he had a streak of pure meanness inside him and wasn't afraid to admit that about himself. He would have enjoyed watching Preacher die, and if things had happened differently, if he had been able to seize the chance to do it, he would have gladly jumped on that Miz Galloway, with her pretty face and that hair the color of honey. He had raped women and girls before, although only Injuns, and one white whore back in St. Louis, and they didn't hardly count in his mind. But despite all that, he was a practical man, and he could put the urge for vengeance and all them other urges away for the time being, if it was a matter of either behaving himself or freezing and starving to death. Hell, just give him a chance, and he'd be as sweet and innocent as any angel.

Hawley was so lost in thought he didn't see the buckskin-clad figures until they seemed to rise up out of the very ground all around him. But as his horse whinnied in fear and shied away from them, he saw the dark, stony faces with their daubs of war paint and knew that no matter how you looked at it, he was in the worst fix of his life.

He had time to utter one heartfelt "Shit!" before the Injuns pulled him out of the saddle.

The cold didn't let up all day, but Preacher knew it was only a matter of time. Tonight or tomorrow, the wind would shift back around to the south and the icy grip of the storm would be broken. The snow would begin to melt. Of course, it might not be but a day or two before another cold snap blew through, but at least there would be a little respite.

"How many more days before we get out of the foothills?" Roger Galloway asked him that afternoon as Preacher rode for a while alongside Roger's wagon.

"We'll probably reach the plains day after tomorrow, or maybe the day after that," Preacher said. "I never traveled through these parts with wagons before, so I ain't rightly sure how long it'll take."

"You could move a lot faster if you were on your own, couldn't you? Helping us has really slowed you down."

"Well, that's one thing about bein' a fella like me, who drifts around a lot. I ain't generally in a hurry to get where I'm goin'. One place is about the same as another, far as I'm concerned. As long as I ain't too crowded, I'm happy."

"You don't like people very much, though."

"I never said that. I like people just fine. Got lots of friends up here in these mountains, like ol' Jeb Law. I always enjoy goin' to Rendezvous and catchin' up with what ever'body's been doin'. But I don't have to have people around to be happy. I got a good horse and a good dog, and there's places I ain't been yet, and places I been but want to go back to. That's all it really takes for a man like me."

Roger shook his head. "I envy you. You live a life of almost perfect freedom, with no one to tie you down or make a claim on you."

And that need for freedom, Preacher thought, was what had always stood between him and Jennie and kept them from being together for more than a short time. Preacher had known even then that he could never settle down, and Jennie had deserved more than a man who was never home.

"You got a wife and a young'un and another on the way," Preacher pointed out. "Some fellas would be envyin' you."

"I suppose." Roger glanced back over his shoulder into the wagon. Lowering his voice, he said, "I'm worried about Dorothy. She's sleeping now, but this has been a terrible ordeal for her. I . . . I can't help but hope that once the baby is born, things will be easier for her."

Since Roger seemed to be in a talkative mood, Preacher indulged his curiosity and asked, "Why were you and your brother so all-fired anxious to get to Oregon that it couldn't wait until spring?"

"We just . . . We thought there would be time, I suppose. We knew we'd be cutting it close, but we thought that if we were lucky, we'd get there and have our choice of the land to settle. Do you know what's going on back East?"

"Not really," Preacher said. "We don't get much news out here, and when we do, it ain't recent."

"Interest in immigration and settling the West is growing rapidly. Next year you're liable to see wagon trains like you've never seen them before. There's speculation that thousands of families will start west. Within a year or two, there should be a well-marked, well-traveled trail all the way from Missouri to Oregon."

The Indians wouldn't be too happy if that happened, Preacher thought, and neither would some of the fur trappers. "And you folks wanted to get a jump on that," he said.

"That's right. I suppose that makes us greedy."

Preacher shrugged. "I ain't in the business o' passin' judgment on anybody. I reckon you had your reasons, and they were good enough for you. You should've thought twice about it, though."

"I know that now," Roger said.

Preacher heeled the dun into a trot and moved out in front of the wagons. He wasn't sure he believed what

Roger had told him. That story about getting to Oregon before the rush and claiming some prime land was probably true as far as it went, but Preacher sensed there was still something unsaid, some other reason why the Galloway brothers, their father, and their uncles had started west at the wrong time of year. Greed just wasn't a strong enough motive.

But fear might be.

Question was, what were they afraid of?

TWELVE

Mart Hawley had never been so scared in all his borned days.

At the same time, he was utterly astounded that he was still alive, but the fright overwhelmed him and kept him from being grateful that the Indians hadn't killed him yet.

The Arikara warriors had bound his hands and feet and tossed him back on his horse, only belly-down across the saddle so that he was sick as a dog by the time they finally stopped. They dumped him on the ground then, and he lay there in the snow retching his guts out, convinced that at any moment they would crush his skull with a war club or chop his head open with a tomahawk or drive a lance right through him and pin him to the ground or pincushion him with arrows. The terror just made him sicker, until there was nothing left inside him to come out. After that he had the dry heaves for a while.

Night had fallen by the time he realized they weren't going to kill him, at least not right away.

He lay huddled against a rock. Now that the fear had subsided a little, he was aware of the cold seeping into his bones. The Injuns hadn't made a fire. How could they survive in weather like this without a fire? It just went to prove what he had long suspected, that Injuns weren't really human like white folks. They were a whole different species. They didn't even seem to feel the cold. They just sat around gnawing on dried meat like animals.

Starlight glittered on the snow and provided enough illumination for Hawley to see one of the warriors stand up and walk toward him. This was it, he thought with a soft moan. The Injun was gonna kill him now.

Instead, the man hunkered on his heels in front of Hawley and spoke. His English was broken, but he supplemented it with sign talk, which was pretty much universal among the tribes. Hawley understood well enough to know what the Injun was getting at.

"You know . . . Preacher?"

"Preacher?" Hawley repeated as he goggled at the Indian. "You mean like a minister, or . . . or the man *called* Preacher?"

"You know Preacher?" the Indian asked again, and this time he sounded a mite impatient.

Hawley heard that and knew he couldn't afford to give the wrong answer. He nodded his head and said emphatically, "Yes, I know Preacher."

"Preacher . . . friend?"

Hawley thought back desperately to everything that had been said while he and Watson were in camp with the immigrants. He recalled that they had had some Injun trouble, and Preacher and that damn wolf-dog of his had wiped out a whole scouting party by their lonesomes. If *those* Injuns had been part of the same bunch as *these* Injuns . . .

"No," he said even more vehemently than before. "Preacher not friend."

The Indian grunted. Hawley wasn't sure what that meant, but the fact that they still hadn't killed him had to be good.

"Hate Preacher," Hawley went on. "Want to watch Preacher die."

"You not friend to other white men?"

Hawley thought back again. Preacher had said that the Indians he'd killed were 'Rees. Hawley was no expert at telling the tribes apart, and besides, it was too dark to make out some of the details, but he thought he recognized the way these savages wore their hair.

"Hawley friend to Arikara," he said, knowing that he was taking a big chance. If his captors weren't 'Rees, if they were some of that tribe's traditional enemies, then he had just signed and sealed his own death warrant.

After a moment, the big, ugly fella, who was probably the chief of this bunch, nodded. "You know where find Preacher and other white men?"

"I know right where they're goin'," Hawley answered without hesitation, seizing on this opportunity to maybe save his life. "I can take you right to 'em."

"You help kill?"

"Just give me a chance. I'll scalp that sumbitch Preacher my own self, if you'll just take me with you."

"We talk," the Indian said. "Decide whether you live or die. Swift Arrow say you live."

Hawley knew what that meant. He wasn't out of the woods yet. Swift Arrow, this redskin here, thought they ought to keep him around to help them catch up to the immigrants and take their vengeance on Preacher. But even if he was the chief as Hawley suspected, he would still have to talk the matter over with the others and get them to agree with him. He couldn't just decree that they weren't going to kill this captive.

But Hawley still felt so relieved he almost pissed himself. He wasn't going to die, he just knew it.

And even better, he was going to get to take his revenge on Preacher after all.

Preacher found a gully for them to camp in that night, a dry wash about ten feet deep and twenty yards across.

The banks were caved in here and there, and one of those places allowed the wagons to get down into the wash. Preacher wouldn't have camped in such a location at a different time of year, because a big rainstorm could cause a flash flood that might wash them all away, but that wasn't going to happen now. They couldn't get out in a hurry either, because it would take time to work the wagons back up those caved-in banks, but he had to admit that they couldn't do *anything* in a hurry when dealing with wagons.

More importantly, the walls of the gully gave them some shelter from the wind and they could build a bigger fire without it being seen.

While Jonathan and Geoffrey unhitched the teams and tended to the mules, Preacher sought out Peter Galloway and said, "Let's you and me go get some wood."

"Can't somebody else do that? I'm tired."

"So's ever'body else," Preacher pointed out, trying not to sound as irritated as he felt at Peter's attitude. "Your brother needs to spend the time with his wife, I reckon, and I don't know where your pa is." Simon was hiding out in one of the wagons, dodging chores as usual, Preacher suspected. "And I sure ain't sendin' the young'uns out on their own."

"All right, all right," Peter said grudgingly. "Let me get my rifle, just in case any more savages show up."

Preacher figured that was only a matter of time. The Arikara were still behind them somewhere. But he didn't think they were close yet.

A few minutes later, Preacher and Peter walked out of the gully and headed toward some nearby trees where they could probably find enough broken branches for the fire. Each man carried a rifle, and Preacher had a brace of pistols tucked behind his belt. Dog bounded ahead of them, always energetic. It was late in the day, with the sun only barely above the mountains to the west. Darkness would fall quickly.

"My wife talks about you all the time," Peter said.

The blunt statement took Preacher a little by surprise. "What?"

"She's very impressed by you, Preacher." There was a friendly tone in Peter's voice, but Preacher could tell it wasn't genuine. "She thinks you're quite a man."

"I'm sure Miz Galloway's a fine woman."

"And a fine-looking woman too, don't you think?"

"I ain't paid that much attention," Preacher lied.

"Oh, surely you have. You're a man, after all. You couldn't help but notice an attractive woman."

"I don't go around lookin' at other fellas' wives," Preacher said stiffly.

Peter's voice took on a hard edge as he said, "Well, she looks at you. A great deal, in fact."

Preacher shook his head. "I wouldn't know nothin' about that."

"No, and you wouldn't even think about stealing a kiss from her, would you?"

Preacher stopped short and turned to look at Peter, saying curtly, "If you got somethin' you want to say, mister, best you go ahead and just spit it out."

"All right, I will," Peter said as he stopped and turned to glare at Preacher. "Stay away from my wife. Stop talking to her. And if you lay one hand on her, I swear I'll kill you."

"You oughta be more careful who you go around threatenin' to kill. Folks tend to take that serious out here."

"I'm completely serious," Peter said. "Dead serious."

Preacher's whole body was taut with anger. Peter Galloway put his teeth on edge under the best of circumstances. The way the man was acting now just made it worse.

But in the back of his mind, Preacher was all too aware of how he had reacted to Angela Galloway, and the way she had reacted to him. No matter how much Preacher disliked the fella, Peter was just acting as any normal man would who thought his marriage was threatened. With an effort, Preacher reined in his temper and said, "You ain't got anything to worry about, Galloway. I ain't got no designs on your wife, and I reckon a fine lady like her could never be interested in a scruffy ol' mossback like me."

"You're not old. Hell, you're not much more than thirty, are you?"

"It ain't the years," Preacher said with a faint smile. "It's the miles."

For a long moment, Peter still glared at him, and there was a tense silence between the two men. Then Peter nodded and said, "All right, I'll take your word that there's nothing going on. But remember what I said about staying away from Angela."

Preacher couldn't resist commenting in return. "You pay her enough attention and you won't have to worry about such things."

For a second he thought that was going to start the argument all over again, but then Peter nodded a second time and stalked toward the woods without looking back at him. Preacher followed, shaking his head. As far as he was concerned, they had just wasted several minutes of the daylight that was left.

"Slow down a mite," Preacher warned as they neared the trees. "It ain't smart to go chargin' in some place when you don't know what might be hidin' there."

"You mean there might be Indians in there?"

"Or a bear. Old Ephraim and most of his kin are hibernatin' at this time of year, but there could still be a few roamin' around, lookin' to fill their bellies 'fore they go to sleep for the winter."

"Who the hell is Old Ephraim?"

"That's what some fellas call any grizzly bear, I reckon

because somebody once saw a grizz and thought it looked like somebody he knew named Ephraim."

"I don't want to run into a bear," Peter said, casting a wary glance toward the trees.

"Could be panthers or wolves too."

"My God! Is there something lying in wait to kill you every time you turn around out here?"

"Now you're startin' to understand," Preacher said solemnly.

A minute later, after Dog had run into the woods and then back out again, Preacher went on. "It's safe enough, else we would'a heard Dog carryin' on in there. Gather up the biggest armload of wood you can carry, and let's get back to camp quick as we can."

They went to work, picking up broken branches that had fallen on the ground. Preacher tucked his Hawken under his arm and gathered up a sizable load of firewood. Peter followed his example, and after a few minutes, they were ready to start back.

They had covered only about half the distance to the gully when in the fading light Preacher saw someone emerge from the wash and start toward them at a run. The figure was too small to be any of the men, and after a second, Preacher realized it was the oldest boy Nate, the son of Roger and Dorothy.

Peter recognized him at the same moment. "That's Nate!" he exclaimed. "Something must be wrong!"

Preacher thought the same thing. He had given the children strict orders to stay near the wagons and never to venture off by themselves. Something important must have happened to make Nate disobey that command. They hurried forward as Nate continued running toward them, kicking up snow from his heels.

"Preacher!" he called. "Uncle Peter! Come quick!"

"What is it, Nate?" Preacher asked sharply as the youngster pounded up to them.

"It's my ma," Nate replied breathlessly. "She's about to have that darned baby, and Aunt Angela says it's really gonna be born this time, come hell or high water!"

THIRTEEN

"Oh, my God!" Peter exclaimed. He seemed quite shaken by what he had just heard.

Preacher doubted that Angela had really used the phrase "come hell or high water," but that wasn't important. What mattered was that their group was about to increase by one. He said, "Let's hustle on back and get that fire built. I don't know much about birthin' babies, but I do know we're liable to need plenty o' hot water!"

They hurried on to the wash and slipped and slid down the caved-in bank. Roger Galloway, his father, and his uncles were all gathered around the wagon where Dorothy Galloway was. Roger looked quite agitated, and the older men seemed worried too. Unlike the first time, when Dorothy's screams hadn't unnerved them, this time they were taking it harder, probably because they were already on edge from the Indian attack and the strain of not knowing when the Arikara would strike again.

Peter dumped his load of wood where Preacher indicated; then Preacher added some of the branches he was carrying and put the others aside to be used later. He laid the Hawken on the ground and knelt beside the pile of wood. Getting busy with flint, steel, and tinder, he had a tiny flame flickering within a minute. He leaned over, blew on it, and watched it grow. Some of the wood caught, but the fire spread slowly. Preacher was patient and worked with it, keeping at it until the flames leaped and glowed brightly.

Inside the wagon, Dorothy gave a piercing cry that made the men gathered outside jump. Preacher straightened from the fire and said, "Somebody get a pot and start some water boilin'." He looked around and spotted Nate. "Go check on your cousins," he told the youngster.

Nate scurried off while Preacher climbed out of the wash again and looked back toward the west. The light was almost gone, but he didn't see anything moving. He wasn't confident, though, that there was nothing out there. Nobody was better than an Injun at not being seen when he didn't want to be seen.

Dorothy screamed again.

It was going to be a long night, Preacher thought.

Nate had last seen his cousins Mary and Brad in the wagon belonging to their ma and pa, Nate's Uncle Peter and Aunt Angela. He went there first, proud that Preacher had entrusted him with a job, and pulled the canvas flap at the rear aside to look in. He didn't see the two younger kids, but that didn't mean they weren't here. The interior of the big wagon was heaped with goods the family was taking to Oregon, along with their bedrolls and several pieces of furniture. Mary and Brad could be hiding somewhere, or they might have crawled into a hole and gone to sleep.

"Mary! Brad!" Nate hissed. "Are you in here?"

There was no answer.

Nate frowned. His cousins looked up to him; he was older, after all, and a natural leader. He didn't think they would ignore him.

Unless they were playing some sort of game with him. That was possible, even though this wasn't a good time.

"Consarn it, if you're in here you better speak up,"

he said. "Preacher told me to find you, and we got to do like he says."

Still no response from the dark interior of the wagon. Muttering under his breath, Nate climbed in and started to look around. He knew all the good hiding places, of course, since he was a kid too. But Mary and Brad weren't in any of them.

That meant they were either outside or in one of the other wagons. Nate hadn't seen them outside when he got back with Preacher and Uncle Peter, and he knew for darn sure that they wouldn't go anywhere near the wagon where his ma was a-hollerin', so that left the wagons belonging to his Uncle Geoffrey and Uncle Jonathan. Nate knew the two older men were really his great-uncles, since they were Grandpa's brothers, but he still called them uncles.

They were good about not being bothered by young-'uns, not like some grown-ups, so Nate thought it was possible his cousins were poking around in one of their wagons. He dropped to the ground and hurried over to check the two vehicles.

He didn't find Mary and Brad in either of them.

Now he was starting to get a mite worried. It wouldn't be like them to run off, but with the superiority of his years, Nate thought that you never could tell with kids. They were liable to do most anything. He glanced toward his ma and pa's wagon, where the adults were gathered around talking in low tones, all except for Ma and Aunt Angela, who were inside the wagon, of course. Nate looked up and down the wash as far as he could see in either direction. He didn't spot Mary and Brad anywhere.

He saw something else, though, and when he looked closer he felt his heart sinking. Small footprints in the snow led away from one of the wagons over to the western edge of the wash, which ran north and south. When the tracks reached the bank, they turned and started north, following the course of the wash. The old stream that had carved out the gully sometime in the dim past had twisted and turned, so the wash didn't run straight. It had a lot of bends in it. The first one to the north was about a hundred yards from the camp. Mary and Brad could be right around that bend, Nate told himself, hiding from the others and thinking it was all a grand joke.

He turned his head, looking from the footprints to the grown-ups and back again. It was getting dark, but he could follow those tracks in the snow. Once the stars came out, it would be fairly light, and the moon would be up in a while too. Nate knew he ought to go get Preacher and tell him that the kids were gone, but if he did that, they would get in trouble. Uncle Peter was a tempersome man, and if he got mad at Mary and Brad for running off, he was liable to blister their butts. Even if it was just a joke on their part.

I can find them, Nate thought. *I can find them and bring them back before anybody even knows they're gone.*

Besides, Preacher had given him this job. Go check on your cousins, the mountain man had said. Nate had been watching Preacher for several days, ever since he'd joined up with them, and he thought Preacher was just about the grandest fella he had ever seen. He was tough enough to fight Injuns and smart enough to live on the frontier, and although Nate looked up to his father, in the space of only a few days he had decided he wanted to be just like Preacher when he grew up. Preacher would be proud of him if he went and found the two younger kids and brought them back, Nate thought.

That was all it took to convince him. None of the grown-ups were paying any attention to him at the moment. He went over to where the tracks led off to the north and started following them.

In a matter of moments, he was out of sight of the wagons.

* * *

Not surprisingly, Dorothy Galloway did not have an easy time of this birth. She was already weak and sick, and a long, hard labor might be enough to do her in, Preacher thought as he talked quietly with the Galloway men. They winced every time Dorothy let out a yowl inside the wagon, and Preacher knew exactly how they felt. At a time like this, men were about as much use as tits on a boar hog.

He couldn't afford to forget about their situation. Life had to go on, and Preacher was nothing if not a practical man. After a while, he said, "We better get some supper started, and somebody needs to stand guard."

"I'll do that," Simon Galloway volunteered, surprising Preacher. So far, the man had had to be nudged into doing anything useful. The glance Simon cast toward the wagon, though, told Preacher that he just wanted to get away from what was going on in there.

"Take a rifle and go up on the edge of the wash then," Preacher said to him. "Find you a place to hunker down where you won't be too visible, and listen as hard as you can. Keep your eyes open too. If you see anything worrisome, don't holler. Just get back down here on the double and tell me about it."

Simon nodded. "I can do that. It's going to be cold away from the fire, though."

"It ain't like you got to stay up there all night long. We'll spell you after a while."

"All right." Simon took a rifle out of one of the wagons and climbed out of the wash.

Jonathan and Geoffrey offered to fix supper. That left Roger and Peter to talk together and be responsible for feeding wood into the fire, as well as for fetching Angela anything she needed. Preacher and Dog moved up on the eastern rim and roamed north and south several hundred yards. Preacher didn't expect any trouble to come at them from that direction, but you never could tell. Death could be lurking just about anywhere on the frontier.

He didn't get so far away that he couldn't hear the cries from the wagon. By the time he got back, they had stopped again, and he saw Angela Galloway standing with Roger and Peter. She was bundled up in a heavy coat with a shawl around her head, covering her hair. As Preacher walked up, she said to him, "I was just telling Roger that it looks like this may take quite a while. I don't expect the baby to be born until sometime along toward morning, if that soon. We may have to stay here for several days. Dorothy will be too weak to travel when this is over."

Preacher frowned. "The longer it takes us to get to Garvey's Fort, the bigger the risks we're runnin'. That snowstorm a couple of days ago was just ol' man winter gettin' warmed up."

"I can't help it," Angela replied, shaking her head. "I'm just telling you the way things are. Too much strain on Dorothy is going to kill her."

Roger's face grew even more haggard at his sister-in-law's blunt declaration. Peter looked concerned too. He said, "If we need to stay here, we'll stay, and that's all there is to it."

What they were liable to do, Preacher thought, was sit there until the rest of that Arikara war party caught up. Then they would be in for even worse trouble than if a blizzard caught them on the plains.

At the same time, he understood how the others felt. They didn't want to risk Dorothy's life . . . at least not any more than they already had by bringing her out here in her condition.

"I reckon we'll stay as long as we need to," he said. "But when we do get movin' again, we'll have to push mighty hard. If you think the pace has been fast up till now, it's gonna get even faster."

Roger and Peter nodded, but Preacher figured they didn't fully understand. Angela said, "I need to get back in the wagon and see to Dorothy. She'll probably have more contractions any time now."

"You're sure her water broke?" Roger asked. "This isn't another false labor?"

Angela smiled wearily and laid a hand on his arm for a moment. "This is the real thing, Roger. You'll be a father again, sometime in the next twelve to eighteen hours."

Birthin' was sure a long, painful process, Preacher thought. He was mighty glad he would never have to go through it. Having fought a grizzly bear and lived through it, he wasn't sure but what he would rather do that again than endure what Dorothy Galloway was going through now.

After he had eaten the supper that Jonathan and Geoffrey prepared, Preacher climbed up on the western bank of the wash and quietly called Simon's name. Simon answered, and Preacher walked over to the clump of rocks where the older man had posted himself.

"Anything unusual goin' on out there?"

"Well, you have to remember that I'm not all that familiar with what's usual out here," Simon replied. "But to answer your question, no, I didn't see or hear anything alarming."

"That's fine. Go on down and get you a surroundin'."

"What?"

"Somethin' to eat," Preacher explained. "Get some supper."

"Oh. Thank you." Simon moved off into the darkness,

and a moment later Preacher heard him climbing down into the wash.

Preacher settled down on one of the rocks and peered into the night. The stars shone brightly overhead and cast enough light for him to be able to see the trees and the hills, and farther away the mountains. His breath fogged in clouds in front of his face. It was cold tonight, but not as frigid as it had been the past two nights.

The Galloways might make it, he thought. Really, for a bunch of greenhorns, they had been damned lucky so far, but there was nothing saying that their luck wouldn't hold. They might even make good settlers if they ever reached the Oregon Territory. He liked the two old-timers, Geoffrey and Jonathan, because they seemed willing to learn, and Roger might be all right once he grew up a little more. Peter and Simon, well, Preacher didn't know about them. A frontiersman had to have a bit of a reckless streak in him, or he would never come out here in the first place. But Peter was hotheaded and acted before he thought, and that was a good way to get killed. Simon was just weak, the sort who would one day crawl into a jug of whiskey and never come out.

As for Angela, she was Peter's best chance. He would need her intelligence and level-headedness if he was going to get by.

Preacher's senses were still razor sharp, even while he was musing about the ultimate fate of the Galloway family, so he was aware of it when someone climbed out of the wash and hurried toward him. The urgency of the footsteps told Preacher that something must have gone wrong again.

It was even worse than he expected. Jonathan Galloway came up to him, puffing and blowing, and gasped, "Preacher! Preacher, the children . . . They're gone!"

FOURTEEN

Preacher swung around, alarm growing rapidly inside him. "Gone?" he repeated. "Hell, they can't be gone! I done told 'em to stay close to the wagons. Maybe they're just hidin' somewhere."

Jonathan shook his head and said, "No, we looked everywhere, in all the wagons. I tell you, Preacher, they've vanished! I called them for supper, and they . . . They just aren't there!"

"Did you check for tracks?"

"Tracks?"

"In the snow," Preacher said, trying to hang on to his patience. He had to remember he was dealing with folks who knew blessed little about the frontier and its ways of life.

"Good Lord, I don't think we did! I . . . I never even thought of it."

"Come on," Preacher said grimly. "Let's go have a look."

When Preacher got back to camp with Jonathan, he found the place in an uproar. The men were running up and down the wash, calling the children's names. Angela stood at the back of Roger and Dorothy's wagon, looking worried, as well she might since two of her kids were out there somewhere in the night, unaccounted for.

"Preacher!" she exclaimed when she saw him coming.

She ran to him and clutched his arm. "Preacher, the children are gone!"

"I know," he told her, then tried to make his voice reassuring as he went on. "No need to worry, I reckon we'll find 'em mighty quicklike. They can't have gotten too far in the time they've been gone."

"That's just it," Angela said. "No one remembers the last time they were here. They could have been gone for hours!"

Preacher's jaw tightened as he realized he was guilty too of not keeping a close enough eye on the young'uns. Of course, he'd had a lot on his mind, but that was no excuse.

"We'll find 'em," he promised again, then turned and called to the others, "Everybody stop runnin' around! You're liable to stomp out the tracks they left."

He told Angela to return to her job of tending to Dorothy, then motioned for the others to gather around him. When the men were all there, Preacher picked up a burning brand from the fire and used it as a torch. "Let's have a look around," he said.

It took him only a few minutes to find the small, kid-sized footprints on the other side of the wagons. The tracks led off up the wash and evidently disappeared around a bend. From the looks of them, Preacher figured Mary and Brad had taken off first, and then later Nate had followed his younger cousins. He recalled telling Nate to check on them.

Nate had found them missing and had gone to look for them, Preacher thought. He was as sure of it as if he had seen the whole thing.

"All right, it won't be no trouble to follow these tracks," he said. "I don't expect to run into any trouble, but I'll take a couple of you with me just in case."

"Geoffrey and I will go," Jonathan volunteered immediately.

"Yes, that's a good idea," Geoffrey added without hesitation. "The rest can stay here and guard the camp."

Preacher nodded. "That's what I had in mind. You fellas get rifles and pistols. Sooner we get after them young'uns, the sooner we can bring 'em back."

Roger and Peter were both worried. Peter began, "Preacher, I know we've had our differences—"

Preacher stopped him. "That don't mean nothin' at a time like this. We'll get 'em back. You boys who're stayin' here best be on your guard all the time. Don't let up."

"We won't," Roger said. He looked as if he had been driven almost to distraction, what with the troubles his wife was having giving birth and now the disappearance of his son, but he was holding it together somehow. He gave Preacher a solemn nod.

Jonathan and Geoffrey were well armed when they came back from their wagons. Each man carried a rifle and a pair of pistols. Preacher nodded to them and said, "Let's go." They started up the wash, following the footprints that they could see by starlight. Dog tried to run ahead of them, but Preacher called him back. He didn't want Dog messing up the tracks that the young'uns had left.

The children had gone farther than Preacher expected. He and his two companions followed the trail for a good mile up the wash, and then the prints climbed another caved-in section of bank and started off to the west, toward the higher foothills. Preacher wondered where in blazes those sprouts thought they were going.

A three-quarter moon was rising, and the silvery light it cast threw the landscape into sharp contrasts. The shadows of the trees stood out starkly against the thin snow cover on the ground. The moonlight also made the footprints easier to see. Preacher moved quickly, trusting to Geoffrey and Jonathan to keep up. The older men were soon huffing and puffing, but they persisted gamely in their efforts. Preacher slowed the pace a little only when he became worried that they were breathing so hard their approach might be heard too easily if any danger was lurking in the dark. Geoffrey and Jonathan were grateful for even that much of a respite.

The trail entered a dense stretch of woods and became harder to follow due to the thick shadows under the trees. Preacher slowed even more. He had to be careful now. If he lost the trail, in all likelihood he wouldn't be able to find it again until morning.

And even though it wasn't as cold tonight as it had been, the air still had quite a chill in it. Would it be enough to freeze some little kids to death if they had to stay out here all night?

Preacher had to admit that he didn't know, and that uncertainty ate at his insides and made him want to go faster. He had to hold himself back, take it slow, and be certain what he was doing and where he was going.

He just wished he could stop thinking about how, no matter where they were, those kids had to be mighty scared right about now.

Nate prodded Mary and Brad along, saying, "We've got to keep going. If we stop, we might freeze to death."

"But I'm cold," Mary whined, as if she hadn't heard him just say that he was trying to keep them from freezing to death.

"I wanna go back to the wagon," Brad added.

"That's what we're trying to do," Nate said. "We'll be back soon."

He wished he could be as sure of that as he hoped he sounded. To tell the truth, he wasn't sure they were even going toward the wagons. Out here in the woods, it was easy to get turned around. Once he'd caught up to the two younger children, Nate had tried to turn right around and follow his own tracks, because he knew that would take him back to the wash where the wagons were. Unfortunately, he had somehow strayed from them, and even though he *thought* he was going in the right direction, he couldn't be certain of that.

Each step could be taking them farther away from safety and deeper into the wilderness. He didn't like to even think about that possibility.

If they got back safely—*when* they got back safely, he amended the thought sternly—he was going to ask Preacher to teach him how to tell where he was going by looking at the stars. Nate knew Preacher could do that, and he figured the mountain man could teach him too. If he knew now, he could find his way back.

It occurred to him to look for the moon. The moon rose in the east, didn't it, and he and Mary and Brad were west of the campsite. Therefore, if they walked toward the moon, they would get where they were going.

The moon was already pretty high, though, and as he gazed at it, Nate wondered where exactly it had risen. He took a guess, and since it matched the direction they were already going, he figured that was good enough and kept plodding along.

"I'm tired," Mary said suddenly. "I'm not going any farther. I'm going to sit down on that log."

She marched over to the log, a good-sized fallen pine that had probably been struck by lightning sometime in the past, and sat down just as she had threatened. Nate stood in front of her and said, "We got to go on. We can't stop. They're bound to be lookin' for us by now, and the longer we're gone, the more trouble we'll be in."

"I didn't want to go," Brad said as he came up beside Nate. "She made me."

"Did not!" his sister said sharply.

"Did too!" Brad shot back. "I told you we'd get in trouble if we left the camp!"

"You wanted to go exploring even more than I did," Mary said accusingly.

"Did not!"

"Both of you hush up," Nate told them. "It doesn't matter whose idea it was. We just gotta get back, that's all."

"We'll walk some more in a little bit," Mary said. "I just want to rest a while first."

"Well . . ." Maybe it would be all right, Nate thought. They were all tired. If he could rig some sort of shelter, maybe it wouldn't hurt anything to let his cousins rest. They were younger and smaller than him, after all. He couldn't expect them to be as strong as he was.

"Let's get some of these branches and put them against the log," he said. "We can make a little lean-to."

"You do it," Brad said. "I'm tired."

"We'll *all* do it," Nate insisted. "Come on. Then we can rest for a while."

Grudgingly, the two younger children pitched in to help. Within a few minutes, they had several pine boughs leaning against the fallen tree, forming a little cavelike hollow. All three of the youngsters crawled in. Nate felt better immediately since they now had at least a crude shelter. He broke several smaller sticks off the branches and made a pile of them, then reached into his coat.

"I got some flint and steel and tinder," he said. "I'll see if I can make a fire."

"You're not supposed to play with fire," Mary said. "You're not even 'sposed to have that stuff."

"Hush up," Nate ordered again. "I know what I'm doin'."

This was what Preacher would do if he was here, Nate thought as he began trying to strike sparks with the flint and steel. Preacher would build a fire, because they needed a fire to warm them on a cold night like this. He fumbled with it, since he didn't have much experience at such things, and it seemed like every time he struck a spark, it failed to fall into the little pile of tinder that he had poured out in the middle of the pile of sticks.

But finally one of the sparks fell properly and the tinder caught. Nate leaned closer and blew on the tiny flame. It grew larger and curled around one of the sticks until the stick began to smolder and then burn. The fire spread, and its reddish-yellow glow grew brighter inside the little makeshift shelter. That made Nate feel better too.

"We'll just sit here and warm up for a while, and then we'll finish walking back to camp," he told the others. They all held out their hands toward the fire to warm them.

After a few minutes, Mary leaned her head against Nate's shoulder. Brad crawled closer on the other side and rested his head in Nate's lap. Nate braced himself against the trunk of the fallen tree. His eyelids grew heavy. He knew he was getting drowsy and tried to fight it off, thinking that it would be much better if he could stay awake, but the urge was just too strong. His eyes drooped closed. The last thing he was aware of was sliding his arms around his cousins as they huddled next to him, and then all three young'uns were sound asleep.

FIFTEEN

Preacher eventually located the spot where Nate had caught up to Mary and Brad, and from that point on, the three youngsters had traveled together. Unfortunately, one of the things Preacher had worried about appeared to have come true: The tracks led in huge circles. The kids were wandering around and around in the foothills, utterly lost.

"What are we going to do, Preacher?" Jonathan asked. "If we follow the tracks, won't we get lost too?"

Preacher shook his head. He knew he could rely on his inner sense of direction to point out the right way back to the camp any time he wanted to return there. He didn't intend to go back, though, without the children. If they were abandoned out here, their lives could be measured in days, if not hours.

He reminded himself that he had been only a few years older than Nate when he first came to the Rocky Mountains, but that was different. Life had hardened him to the point that he could take care of himself, at least to a certain extent. Nate had no experience at surviving in the wilderness, and he had the two younger kids to look after, on top of everything else.

"We've got to try to figure out where they're going to wind up and then head straight for that spot," Preacher said.

"How are we going to do that?" Geoffrey asked. "It looks to me like they're just wandering aimlessly. They could be anywhere."

"Maybe not." Preacher let his eyes rove over the moon-lit landscape. "Folks just naturally tend to go certain ways and avoid certain things. If you know the country, you can sort of figure where somebody would be likely to go. And I know the country."

"But you're still talking about an educated guess," Jonathan pointed out.

Preacher nodded. "Yep, but I've got the education. These mountains have been my school for years now. I know the obstacles those young'uns are likely to come across, and I know how they probably got around 'em."

"But what if your guess is wrong?" Geoffrey asked.

"It won't be," Preacher said flatly.

Because if it was . . . well, he wasn't going to think too much about that. Not yet anyway.

The three men trudged on into the night.

Angela Galloway had been through three labors: Mary, Brad, and a couple of years earlier another girl who had been stillborn. That last delivery had been difficult, difficult enough so that Angela had known something was wrong as soon as it started, and the two previous ones were painful as well. But despite that, Angela knew she had never gone through anything like what her sister-in-law Dorothy was enduring now.

Angela sat beside the thick bedroll where Dorothy lay and brushed back several strands of brown hair from the sweat-beaded forehead. The fact that Dorothy could sweat when the weather was as cold as it was spoke volumes for the pain she was in. Dorothy wasn't aware of the cold. She probably wasn't aware of anything except the overwhelming need to get that baby out of her body.

But the baby, bless its heart, sure didn't want to come.

Of course, helping Dorothy through this ordeal wasn't the only thing on Angela's mind. Her two children were out there somewhere in the cold and dark, and there wasn't a thing she could do to help them or comfort them. The feeling of helplessness that gripped her made her sick at her stomach if she thought about it too much. Fear gnawed at her nerves. She loved Mary and Brad, loved them dearly, and the thought that she might never see them again was almost too much for her to grasp. She knew she had to keep herself busy and distracted, or else she might give in to the panic that tried to well up inside her.

"Peter," Dorothy murmured.

That was odd, Angela thought. Dorothy had just called her brother-in-law's name, not her husband's. And that wasn't the first strange thing Dorothy had said during the past few days, when she seemed to be out of her head more often than not. Of course, Dorothy had mentioned all of the Galloways at one time or another during her ramblings, so her saying Peter's name now didn't have to mean anything. . . .

Another wave of contractions gripped Dorothy. She threw her head back and screamed. Cords of muscle stood out on the sides of her neck. Angela held her hand and spoke to her, trying to calm her and get her to push. Dorothy was trying, but the baby just wouldn't come. If a doctor or an experienced midwife had been here, they might have been able to tell if the baby was turned wrong in the womb or if there was some other problem. But Angela just didn't know, and didn't know what else to do either.

The contractions passed. Dorothy subsided, her arched back easing down onto the bedroll. When she was breathing easier again, Angela thought it was safe to stand up and get a breath of fresh air. She went to the rear of the wagon and moved the canvas flap aside. She was shocked to see the gray light of dawn filling the camp.

It was nearly morning. The children had been missing all night.

Before Angela could think about that, another scream ripped from Dorothy's throat, and this one had a different sound to it than any of them before. Angela jerked around sharply and hurried to her sister-in-law's side. She lifted the blankets draped over Dorothy's upraised knees and then gasped as she saw the blood.

The baby had to come now, or both mother and child were going to die. Angela was sure of it.

Hawley woke up with his teeth chattering and his bones aching from the cold that had seeped into them during the night. The Injuns hadn't given him any robes or blankets to help ward off the chill. All he'd had to warm him were his buckskins and his capote.

But he was still alive, by Godfrey! He hadn't frozen to death, and the lightening of the sky overhead told him that dawn wasn't far away. The sun didn't provide much heat at this time of year, but any warmth was better than none.

And every minute that he remained alive was a blessing, even though he was still in the hands of the savages.

Hawley wondered if they had decided yet whether or not to kill him. He had fallen asleep the night before while they were still talking. The warriors had been ringed in a circle around a small fire, and they had taken turns speaking with the long-winded eloquence common to Injuns. Hawley understood only a few words of the Arikara tongue—mostly words that had to do with drinking and screwing—so he hadn't really been able to follow the discussion that well. The big ugly buck who seemed to be the war chief was called Swift Arrow, and he wanted to keep Hawley alive and use him to help find that bunch of immigrants. Another Injun, one called Badger Something-or-other, thought it would be best to go ahead and kill him, the sooner and the more painfully the better. The others seemed about equally divided on the question, and if anybody had told Hawley that he could doze off while his very fate was being debated, he would have told them they were crazy. That was exactly what had happened, though. Exhaustion had caught up to him.

Did the fact he was still alive mean that Swift Arrow had prevailed in the argument? Hawley didn't know. He turned his head and looked around, hoping to find out.

He was still lying against a tree with his hands and feet bound. He could barely feel his extremities, a condition due to the cold as well as to the tightness of his bonds. Not far away, the Injuns were up and about, gathered around the campfire. He might have been wrong, but Hawley thought there were fewer of them in the bunch now.

Swift Arrow was still there, though. Noticing that Hawley was awake, he stood up and walked over to the trapper, stalking over the snow-covered ground like a mountain lion.

"You live," he greeted Hawley.

"Yeah," the trapper croaked, his voice rusty and uncomfortable in his throat. "Am I gonna keep on livin'?"

"You help us find Preacher."

It wasn't a question, but Hawley nodded eagerly anyway. "That's right," he said. "I'll help you find Preacher. I'll even help you kill him."

"Swift Arrow kill Preacher."

There was no room for argument in that flat statement, and Hawley no longer cared who killed Preacher as long as the son of a bitch wound up dead. He said, "Sure. Swift Arrow kill Preacher."

The chief nodded emphatically. He returned to the fire, then came back to Hawley a moment later. He put a piece of jerky in Hawley's mouth. Hawley chewed eagerly on the tough strip of meat as he realized how ravenously hungry he was.

"I'll show you today where those wagons went," he said around the jerky. "It won't take us long to find them pilgrims. A day or two, that's all."

"Swift Arrow send out scouts."

Hawley figured out after a second what the chief meant. Swift Arrow had already sent out some of the warriors to have a look around. That's why there were fewer of the Injuns gathered around the fire.

"That's fine, but you don't have to worry," he said. "I can find them you're lookin' for."

Swift Arrow smiled thinly. "Not worry. White man worry."

"That's right," Hawley said, bobbing his head in agreement and smiling back at the savage. He was damned worried.

And he would be until the man called Preacher was dead and these bloody-handed redskins were in his, Mart Hawley's, debt.

Nate dreamed about his home back in Philadelphia and the kids who had gone to school with him. They had been envious and impressed when he told them his family was forming a wagon train and going west to live in the Oregon Territory. It sounded like such a grand adventure . . . and it had been, up to a point.

Then everything had started going wrong.

But in his dream, Nate was back in the classroom at the academy he attended. His pa and his Uncle Roger and his grandpa Simon all had money, and they could afford to send Nate to a fancy school. Folks tended to think of immigrants as poor people, but the Galloways had money, no doubt about that. Nate dreamed he was there again, only instead of the clothes he had usually worn to school, he was garbed in fringed buckskins and wore a big hat. He had a powder horn slung over his shoulder and carried one of those long-barreled rifles like Preacher carried. In real life, a Hawken was so heavy he could barely pick one up, let alone cradle it in the crook of his arm like it was a part of him, but he didn't have any trouble with it in his dream. All the kids stared wide-eyed at him, especially when he slid the long-bladed hunting knife from the beaded sheath on his belt and showed it to them. And when they asked him where he had been, he just grinned and said, *Why, I been to the mountains, boys. I'm a mountain man now.*

It was the best dream Nate had had in a long time.

But like all dreams, it came to an end.

He wasn't sure what woke him; all he knew was that he was cold and stiff and hungry, and he needed to pee really bad. Mary and Brad still leaned on him in their crude shelter underneath the pine boughs they had propped against the fallen tree. They were still asleep.

Light peeked through a couple of gaps in the branches above Nate's head. Was it morning already? Had they made it through the night? Evidently so, and Nate felt his spirits lift at that realization. Now that it was light again, they could see where they were going. He was confident that they could find their way back to camp in no time.

Of course, when they got there they were going to be in a whole heap of trouble, as Preacher would say. They'd been gone all night, and their parents were bound to be worried sick. When grown-ups got scared, they also got mad. They'd hug a fella's neck when they saw he was all right, then paddle his butt. Then hug some more and likely paddle some more. But whatever happened, Nate and his cousins would just have to take their medicine. They had it comin'.

And it would be worth it to be warm again, and to get something to eat.

First, though, he had to get out of here and relieve the insistent pressure on his bladder. He took hold of Mary's shoulders and eased her down until she was lying on the ground. She didn't wake up. Then he carefully slipped his leg out from under Brad's head.

His muscles were so stiff he could barely move as he tried to crawl out of the pine-bough lean-to. He wanted to grunt and groan with the effort, but he held the sounds back so he wouldn't disturb his cousins. Nate had heard his grandpa and his uncles make noises like he wanted to make now when they had to get up out of their chairs, and he wondered if they felt like this all the time. It must be horrible to be old, he thought.

He blinked as he emerged into the light. Even though the sun was barely up and the light was still watery and dim, it seemed bright to him. He pushed himself to his feet and stumbled over to a nearby tree. With fingers stiff from the cold, he fumbled at the buttons of his trousers and finally got them open. He closed his eyes in relief as he started to pee into the snowdrift on the other side of the tree.

That was when he heard a branch snap and opened his eyes to see an Indian standing no more than a dozen feet away, a tomahawk in his hand and a savage grin on his red, paint-daubed face.

SIXTEEN

Corn Man was not a proper name for a Sahnish warrior, or at least so the warrior known by that name had always believed. But though the Sahnish could be warlike when called upon to do so, they also took great pride in the skill with which they tilled the land and coaxed crops from it. They grew more corn than anything else. It was a staple of their diet, and they also traded it to other tribes for meat and buffalo robes. Corn Man was very good at the growing of corn, and so that name had been bestowed upon him. In a way it was a source of pride, since it connected him directly to Mother Corn, the Great Spirit who ruled the earth and was second only to Nishanu Natchitak, the Chief Above. In times of peace he had not minded being called Corn Man. His hope was that one day he would take the place of Badger's Den as the tribe's medicine man and would be entrusted with the care of the sacred bundle.

That day would be long in the future, though, and when it was time to take up arms and exact vengeance on those who had harmed the Sahnish, then it was better to be called Swift Arrow or Runs Far or some more fitting name for a warrior. Not *Corn Man* . . .

Still, it looked as if he would be the first to spill the blood of the whites. There stood one of them now, gaping at him. A young one, to be sure, but still one of the white interlopers in the land of the Sahnish. The boy had emerged from a crude shelter as Corn Man watched, then gone over to a tree to make his morning water. That came to an abrupt end as terror cut off the stream in mid-splash.

Corn Man lifted his tomahawk and bounded toward the fear-frozen youth.

A shrill scream cut through the cold air. It came not from the boy but from the shelter, where a young girl had just stuck her head out from behind the pine boughs.

Corn Man stopped, unsure what to do. The girl scrambled out from the shelter, still screaming, followed by a smaller boy, who also cried out in fear. The noise would bring the other members of the scouting party Swift Arrow had sent out before dawn that morning, and unless he acted quickly, Corn Man would be denied the honor of killing all three of these white children by himself. He snarled and swung back toward the oldest one. . . .

Who had stooped and picked up a branch from the ground, and now he threw it as hard as he could, right at Corn Man's face. The short but heavy piece of wood flew straight and true and smashed across Corn Man's nose. Tears of pain sprang into his eyes, blinding him. He stumbled and almost fell, but caught his balance.

Any hesitation he might have felt at killing children was now gone. They were white, they had caused him pain, and they deserved to die.

"Run!" the boy shouted. "Run for your lives!"

Corn Man did not understand the words, but through the tears in his eyes, he saw the young ones flee. The oldest boy caught hold of the girl's hand, and then she used her other hand to grab the younger boy. Together they ran away from Corn Man.

He gave chase, vowing that they would not get away from him. Perhaps he would keep the two younger ones alive, so that Swift Arrow could decide what to do with them.

But the boy who had struck him, that one would die, and before the sun rose much higher in the sky. This Corn Man vowed.

Preacher had called a halt a couple of hours before dawn. The moon had set, making it more difficult to see where they were going, and Jonathan and Geoffrey were so played out they couldn't go on without some rest. They had found a spot under some trees where not much snow had fallen. The two older men had curled up on the ground, while Preacher sat down and leaned his back against a tree trunk. What he did then couldn't actually be called sleep, since all his senses remained alert, but it was a form of rest, and he felt somewhat re-freshed when he got to his feet and told Jonathan and Geoffrey it was time for them to be moving again. The sun was up, and Preacher intended to move faster now that they could all see where they were going.

Both of the older men groaned as they climbed awk-wardly to their feet. Preacher could have told them that they would get mighty stiff sleeping on the cold ground like that, but they would remember it better for having gone through it. And their muscles would loosen up quickly enough once he got them moving.

"Are we going to have any breakfast?" Jonathan asked as he stretched.

Preacher handed him a strip of jerky. "Gnaw on that while we're going. That's all we got time for." He pointed to a hill in the distance. "See that knoll over yonder? That's where we're headed. I think the young'uns ended up somewheres around there."

"How in the world do you know that?" Geoffrey asked.

"Well, they kept makin' bigger and bigger circles. Sooner or later they're gonna come to a ravine that's too deep and too wide for them to cross, so they'll have to move northwest along with it."

Jonathan said, "Why couldn't they go back southeast?"

"They could," Preacher said, "but that'd mean turnin' around and doublin' back on their trail, and I don't reckon they would do that because they think they're goin' the right direction. They were movin' along steady-like, without stoppin' much, so Nate must've been convinced he was on the right track."

"Well . . . maybe. I hope you're right."

"So do I," Preacher allowed. "Anyway, that ravine'll take 'em toward yonder knoll, and then they'll come to a good-sized creek that'll force 'em even more toward it, since I don't reckon they'll want to go swimmin' in weather this cold."

Both Geoffrey and Jonathan shivered at the very thought of plunging into the icy-cold waters of a creek.

"We're gonna cut across country straight toward the hill," Preacher said, "so I think we stand a good chance o' gettin' there either before they do or just about the same time."

"I pray that's so," Geoffrey said.

"Well, a mite of prayin' never hurt, that's for sure." Preacher picked up his Hawken. "Let's go."

They moved out at a brisk pace. As the sun rose higher, Preacher felt a wind from the south touch his face and knew it was going to be warmer today than it had been for several days. The snow on the ground would probably melt before the day was over, leaving a muddy mess in places. That could make things tricky when the wagons rolled out again, but it was jumping the gun to worry about such things now. For the moment, he had to concentrate on finding those kids and getting them back to their families.

He wondered briefly how it was going back there at camp, and if Dorothy Galloway had finally had her baby.

* * *

Angela had never seen so much blood in her life. She wasn't sure how Dorothy could still be alive after losing that much of the vital fluid, let alone be conscious and struggling to give birth.

"I've got to . . . turn it," Angela said. As she had suspected, the baby was oriented incorrectly inside Dorothy's birth canal, and that was why the labor and delivery had been so difficult. But now that she was certain what was wrong, Angela hoped she could save them. All she could do was try.

From the back of the wagon, Roger asked, "Is there anything I can do?"

"No!" Angela practically shouted. "Just stay out of here, Roger."

She heard Peter talking to Roger, no doubt trying to draw his brother away from the wagon. She used a rag to wipe away blood and mucus, and tried to slip her hand further into Dorothy's body to get a grip on the baby. It would have helped, she thought a bit wildly, if she had ever lived on a farm and helped deliver calves. This baby was as slippery as a newborn calf, that was for sure. And she had to be careful not to get the cord wrapped around its neck, or it could strangle before it got out.

Dorothy screamed and strained, and Angela felt the baby's head against her hand. She cupped it as gently as possible and urged it toward the outside world. "Push, Dorothy, push hard!" she urged, and suddenly she saw the top of the baby's head. "It's coming! A little more, just a little more!"

Another shrill scream, and the rest of the head emerged, then a shoulder and an arm and another arm . . . It was a magnificent sight for all its grotesqueness. A new life coming into the world, born in blood and pain, strife and desperation, but at the same time filled with undeniable promise.

"Yes," Angela said in a half whisper, as much to herself as to Dorothy, because it was doubtful that Dorothy could hear much of anything now. "It's coming, it's coming. . . . It's a boy! He's beautiful, Dorothy, just beautiful!"

Angela eased the baby the rest of the way out and placed him on a clean blanket. She used a corner of the blanket to wipe mucus away from his mouth and nose, and he took a deep, quavery breath and blew it out in a loud squall that brought a smile to Angela's mouth and tears to her eyes. Now the cord had to be cut and the afterbirth delivered. She tended to that quickly, then wrapped the blanket around the crying baby. As she tucked it in, she paid attention for the first time to the full head of wispy hair.

It was jet black.

That was odd, since Roger had sandy hair and Dorothy's was only slightly darker, a light brown. But the color of the baby's hair didn't really matter now. His lungs were healthy enough—he was proving that with every howl—and he had ten fingers and ten toes. Angela had done a quick count before she wrapped him up. Everything else could wait.

She stepped to the back of the wagon, pushed the flap open, and called, "Roger! Roger, come quick and get your son!"

Roger ran over, followed closely by Peter, and scrambled into the wagon. Angela placed the baby in his arms and said, "Hold him while I tend to Dorothy. Not too tightly now. You don't want to drop him, but don't squeeze him too much either."

"I'll be careful," Roger promised. Peter looked on from outside the wagon, an odd expression on his face, almost as if he were jealous of his brother while being happy for him at the same time.

Angela turned back to Dorothy, and had a bad moment when she looked at her sister-in-law's face. Dorothy's features were so pale and drawn that for a second Angela was afraid she was dead. But then she saw Dorothy's chest rising and falling slightly, and a moment later the new mother's eyes flickered open.

"My . . . my son . . . ?" she asked in a whisper.

"He's fine," Angela said as she leaned over Dorothy and wiped her face. "A strong, healthy boy. He's fine, Dorothy, and you will be too."

"His name is . . . John . . . John Edward . . . Galloway . . ."

"The name fits him," Angela said with a smile. "It's a very distinguished name."

"Promise me . . ." Dorothy's fingers caught hold of Angela's hand and held it with surprising strength. "Promise me . . . You'll take care of him. . . ."

"I won't have to," Angela said. "You're his mother, dear. You'll take care of him and do a wonderful job of it."

Dorothy's head moved weakly from side to side. "N-no. You've got to . . . promise . . ."

"I'll always do everything I can for you and your children."

"Swear . . ."

"I give you my word," Angela whispered.

With a sigh, Dorothy closed her eyes. Her head leaned back. Angela's heart leaped in fear, but again she saw that Dorothy was only asleep.

"Angela . . ." Roger said from behind her. "Angela, is she going to be all right?"

Angela stood up and turned to face her brother-in-law. "I won't lie to you," she said quietly. "Dorothy lost a great deal of blood. It seems to have stopped now, but she was so weak to start with . . . I'll do everything I can, Roger. That's all I can promise you."

Tears rolled down Roger's cheeks and dripped on the blanket wrapped around his newborn son. "You have to save her," he said. "I can't live without her."

"If you have to, you will." Angela put a hand on his shoulder and squeezed. "You have Nate, and now you have another son, John. You have to live for them, Roger, no matter what else happens."

"John," Roger repeated softly, looking down at his son.

"John Edward Galloway," Angela said, "this is your father."

And as she saw the way Roger looked at the baby, she thought again of her own children, lost in the wilderness, perhaps by now even . . .

No. She would not allow herself to even think it. Preacher was out there looking for them.

Preacher would bring her children home.

SEVENTEEN

Nate threw a terrified glance over his shoulder as he tugged Mary and Brad along with him. The Indian was still chasing them, waving that tomahawk around and looking like he wanted to scalp all three of them. Nate knew they couldn't fight him. The Indian was too big and too strong, and he looked more frightening than anything Nate had ever seen, with those bones sticking up in his hair like he had grown them himself and was some sort of devil.

Deep down, Nate knew they couldn't outrun the Indian either. But they had to try. They couldn't just stop and wait for him to catch up and kill them.

There wasn't even time to think about what Preacher would do. There wasn't time for anything except sheer, panicked flight.

The kids had stopped screaming. They didn't have enough breath for that anymore. All of them were panting in the cold air, their breath visible in plumes and streamers around their heads. Nate saw a tree-covered slope in front of them and headed for it. Maybe they could throw off the Indian if they got in the trees. Maybe they could hide from him.

Those were forlorn hopes, Nate knew, but right now, any hope was better than none.

The Indian was so close when they reached the hill and

started up it that Nate could hear him huffing and blowing. Nate hoped he wouldn't run into a tree or dash his brains out on a low-hanging limb. It would be all right, though, if something like that happened to the Indian.

"Nate!" Brad suddenly shrieked. "He's got me!"

Nate felt the tug as Brad was pulled away from him and Mary. He tried to stop and turn around, but he stumbled and fell instead, letting go of Mary's hand as he went down. She screamed too. Nate rolled over and saw that the Indian had hold of Brad by the neck with his free hand. The other hand swung the tomahawk at Mary's head. She dropped underneath the swing as the lethal weapon went over her head. It was more by accident than design, though. She tried to scramble away on her hands and knees, but the Indian planted a moccasined foot in the middle of her back and shoved her to the ground, pinning her there. He picked up Brad by the neck so that his feet swung and kicked in midair.

Nate knew Brad would choke to death if the Indian held him like that for very long. He scooted a little closer, moving as fast as he could, and lifted his leg in a kick, driving the heel of his boot between the Indian's legs. The Indian howled in pain, dropped Brad, and forgot all about scalping them or bashing their heads in with his tomahawk. He doubled over in agony, clutching himself.

Nate scrambled up, grabbed his cousins, and hauled them to their feet. He started climbing again, heading higher on the hill. When he looked back, he saw that the Indian was stumbling after them, although he was still bent over and wasn't moving very fast now.

For the first time, Nate dared to really hope that they might get away.

Of course, there might be other Indians around nearby. Where there was one savage, there might be more. But he couldn't worry about that now. They had to get away from this Indian first.

A strong, red hand shot out from some bushes and clasped itself around Nate's arm. He gasped in pain and surprise as the cruel grip tightened even more and swung him off the ground. Without him to pull them along, Mary and Brad tumbled off their feet.

Nate found himself staring into the face of another Indian. This one was even bigger and uglier than the one who had been chasing them. To Nate's surprise, the Indian said something in English, disgustedly spitting out the word "Children!"

Even more shocking, a vaguely familiar voice answered in English. "That's right, Chief, children. But they come from the wagon train you're after. I recognize the little brats."

Nate turned his head and stared in horror at the face of the man called Hawley. He looked the same as he had the last time Nate had seen him, with that bristly, ginger-colored beard. Only his eyes were different now. Last time, Hawley had been scared of Preacher, and it showed.

Now the man leered at Nate and his cousins with an expression of pure evil, and although Nate wouldn't have thought it was possible, he discovered that he was even more frightened of this white man than he was of the Indians.

This was a mighty fine stroke of luck, Hawley thought as he looked at the kid squirming in Swift Arrow's grasp. Swift Arrow and the rest of the war party, along with the now-freed Hawley, had followed the scouts sent out earlier by the war chief. Hawley planned on leading them to a spot where they could pick up the trail of the wagon train. But now, lo and behold, the three pesky young'uns from the immigrant party had been chased right into their laps by one of the scouts.

That redskin came trotting up, moving carefully and hunched over a little like he was hurt. Swift Arrow spoke sharply to him, and Hawley caught something about "making war on children." The other Injun argued back—respectfully, since Swift Arrow was the chief—and his main point was that when had the whites ever hesitated about making war on Injun children. Swift Arrow couldn't dispute that at times, redskinned little ones had died in fights with white men. Even more often, previously unknown sicknesses brought to this land by the whites had killed many more, striking indiscriminately at men, women, and children. Sometimes, shameful though it was to contemplate, white folks had infected the Injuns a-purpose, in hopes of wiping them out.

Hawley thought that actually wasn't that such a bad idea, only it hadn't worked well enough, at least not yet. Right now, though, he didn't want the Injuns wiped out. Unexpected as it might be, the savages were now his allies.

"Swift Arrow," he said, "you better hang on to them kids."

The war chief turned to him. "What good children?"

Hawley licked his lips and said, "Bait. I'll bet you anything Preacher's out lookin' for them sprouts right now. You keep the kids, and they'll bring Preacher right to you. You can kill him, and then you won't have near as much trouble killin' the other folks when you catch up to the wagons."

"No!" That was the oldest boy yelling at him. "No, you can't hurt Preacher!"

Swift Arrow still had hold of his arm. He shook him until the boy cried out in pain.

"Boy be quiet," Swift Arrow ordered. He looked down at the other two kids, who were huddled on the ground sobbing in fear. "All be quiet!"

Hawley hunkered so that he could speak directly to

the younger kids. "You two best be quiet, or the chief'll scalp you. You hear me?"

Biting back whimpers of pain, the older boy said, "Mary, Brad, hush now. It's going to be all right."

Hawley knew better, but he didn't say as much. Instead, he put a false note of cheer in his voice and told them, "That's right. Ain't nothin' bad gonna happen to you kids. You just settle down and stop cryin', and nobody will hurt you."

The little girl sniffled and looked up at him. "You . . . You promise, mister?"

"Sure," Hawley lied. "Hell, I'm a white man, ain't I? You can trust me. I'll look after you."

Swift Arrow dropped the older boy, who fell beside the other two. He clutched his arm and whimpered, and Hawley wondered briefly if Swift Arrow had pulled the arm right out of its joint. Not that he really cared.

"You keep children," Swift Arrow said. "We use to trap Preacher."

Hawley nodded. "Damn right."

And once Preacher was dead, they wouldn't have any more use for these sniveling little kids.

Jonathan and Geoffrey kept up better than Preacher expected after this long a time. The men were moving on very little rest and even less food, but they kept going somehow. Preacher supposed it was because they loved those kids.

He found himself wondering if he would ever have any kids of his own. If things had been different for him and Jennie, then maybe . . .

But no, it didn't do any good to think about that. Maybe one of these days, when he was older and more settled down, he would meet another woman . . . somebody like Angela Galloway maybe . . . but not Angela, of course, since she already had a husband and kids . . .

Older and more settled down, Preacher thought again. As if that was likely to ever happen.

All those thoughts vanished in an instant from his head as he saw the sun strike a momentary reflection off something on the hill that was their destination. In the blink of an eye, he was once again focused on the chore at hand. The reflection was there and then gone, but it had been enough to tell him that somebody was up there on the hill. He put out a hand to stop Geoffrey and Jonathan.

"Those kids carryin' anything metal on them?" Preacher asked.

"Metal?" Jonathan repeated. "You mean like a knife or a gun?"

"Anything the sun might strike a glint off of."

Geoffrey said, "Nate has a folding knife. And Mary probably has some little geegaws that might shine in the sun. Did you see something, Preacher?"

"The sun flashed on something up yonder on the hill. Don't know what it was, but it couldn't have been anything natural."

"You said they might go up there," Jonathan said excitedly. "Could they have gotten there ahead of us?"

"Sure, anything's possible," Preacher allowed. "They could've moved a mite faster than I expected."

"Well, let's go get them! Do you think if we shouted their names, they could hear us from here?" Jonathan lifted his hands and got ready to cup them around his mouth.

Preacher made a sharp, slashing motion. "Don't go to hollerin', damn it! We don't know if it's them, and even if it is, we don't know if they're alone."

"Who else could it be?" Geoffrey asked.

"What about that Arikara war party?"

The two older men exchanged a glance that Preacher couldn't read. "I thought you weren't sure there even *was* a war party," Jonathan said.

"Didn't you say those Indians who attacked us were probably renegades?" Geoffrey put in.

"I said they might be. My gut tells me that ain't the whole story, though. I think there's more o' those 'Rees, and I think they're after you folks for a reason."

"That's crazy!" Geoffrey insisted. "We never saw those Indians before."

"What about Indians like them?"

Both men shook their heads. "No, of course not," Jonathan said.

Preacher's uneasy instincts warned him the men might be lying. He was convinced they were. And yet he knew that getting to the bottom of it would have to wait. First they needed to find those kids. Preacher hoped they weren't in too much trouble.

"Let's go," he said. "Watch me, and try not to make too much noise."

He set out with the older men trailing him. An occasional glance over his shoulder told him that they were trying their best to imitate him as he moved soundlessly through the woods toward the knoll. They made a little racket, but not too much. Preacher thought again that with time, they might turn into decent frontiersmen.

He just wished they would tell him the damn truth about any grudge that the Arikara might have against them.

They came to a gully that ran all the way to the base of the hill. Preacher motioned them into it and then led the way closer. When they reached the bottom of the hill, he raised a hand to call a halt. He listened intently, hoping to hear childish voices drifting down the slope.

Instead, he heard the faint whisper of stealthy footsteps, followed by something alarming: a whimpering sound that might easily be a young child crying. Preacher glanced at Geoffrey and Jonathan and saw that they had heard it as well. Their eyes were wide, and he could tell they were both ready to blurt out questions. He stopped them with another curt gesture and a finger held to his lips. He motioned for them to lie down at the edge of the gully behind some brush. Preacher stretched out beside them and parted the branches a tiny bit so that he could peer through them.

In a matter of moments he saw a sight that would haunt him for all his borned days. A dozen or more Arikara warriors strode quietly through the woods. Behind them came a familiar buckskin-clad figure: Mart Hawley. Hawley had hold of Mary and Brad by the arms and jerked them along roughly. Nate was with them too, being tugged along by one of the Indians. The kids looked scared to death, as well they might be. They were in the hands of a war party that obviously had a grudge against their folks, and even worse, a white man who had evidently turned renegade and thrown in his lot with the Arikara.

The job of fetching those kids back to the wagons had just gotten a hell of a lot harder.

EIGHTEEN

Preacher and his two companions watched the Indians and their captives until they got out of sight. Preacher could tell that Geoffrey and Jonathan were about bustin' at the seams from wanting to go after the kids. He motioned for them to take it easy and hoped that they could restrain their impatience.

Finally, when the Indians were out of earshot, Preacher came to his feet and said, "Let's go."

"Go? Go where?" Geoffrey practically exploded. "The Indians are gone!"

"And they got away with the children!" Jonathan said. "We just sat here helpless and let them go!"

Preacher shook his head. "If we had jumped them here and now, we wouldn't have done anything except get us and probably the kids killed. There were too many of those Injuns to take on in a straight-up fight. Plus they got that son of a bitch Hawley with 'em."

"I saw that," Jonathan said. "It looked like he was their friend, for God's sake!"

"I reckon he's thrown in with 'em," Preacher agreed. "I don't know how come 'em to be together, but he's on their side now, that's for sure."

Geoffrey asked, "Why are we standing around talking? Shouldn't we be going after them? If we delay too long, they'll get away, and then we might never find them again!"

"We can find 'em," Preacher assured his companions. "Even though they're redskins, a bunch that big will leave tracks we can follow. Besides, from the looks of it, they're headin' toward the wagons. Hawley must be leadin' the way for 'em."

"That bastard," Jonathan said in a low, angry voice.

Preacher nodded again. "You won't get no argument from me on that score."

"Will they hurt the children?" Geoffrey asked.

"Injuns are notional folks," Preacher said with a shrug. "I won't lie to you. They're capable of killin' those kids if the whim strikes 'em. More than likely, though, they'll keep 'em alive, at least for a while. Hawley may figure he can use the young'uns as hostages when him and the Injuns catch up to the wagons. Maybe try to trade them for me."

Jonathan frowned. "Why would they place so much importance on . . . Oh, I see. You're the most dangerous member of the party. They might think that if they get rid of you, the rest of us won't put up much of a fight."

"I'm afraid they might be right about that," Geoffrey said gloomily.

"From what I've seen, you fellas don't have a lot of back up in you," Preacher told them. "You'll do just fine when it comes down to the nut-cuttin'. Now let's get after that bunch. Keep it as quiet as you can."

"You can count on us, Preacher," Jonathan said.

Preacher thought that was probably right. He would have felt a lot better about things, though, if he'd had Jeb Law or some of his other mountain man friends there to side him.

A man made do with what he had, he told himself.

Right now that was a couple of old-timers from Philadelphia.

Preacher hoped that would be enough.

Nate was scared, but he tried not to show it. His arm and shoulder hurt too, but he wouldn't allow himself to cry. Crying was for babies, and right now he had to be a man, despite the fact that he was only ten years old. It was all right for Mary and Brad to sniffle a little every now and then; they were kids, and they were scared.

Nate forced his brain to look past the fear he felt and consider the situation. The three of them were still alive, and that was something. The Indians hadn't killed them out of hand. Nate didn't trust Hawley as far as he could have thrown the trapper. Hawley hated them just like the Indians did. So Nate knew better than to hope that Hawley would protect them and somehow get them out of this trouble.

As long as they were alive, though, they still had a chance. Nate wasn't going to give up.

He sure wished he could hug his ma right about now, though. He wondered too if he had a little brother or sister yet. They should have stayed in the camp. The two younger ones shouldn't have wandered off to go "exploring," darn it. . . .

Thoughts like that didn't do any good, he told himself. What he should be doing was watching for a chance for him and Mary and Brad to escape. He bit his lip against the pain in his shoulder and kept moving. If he lollygagged along, the Indian who had hold of his arm would give it a jerk, and that would just make him hurt even worse.

The Indians moved through the woods for what seemed like hours, even days. The sun rose higher in the sky, and when Nate looked at it, he knew it wasn't even noon yet, no matter what it felt like. After so long a time, though, the Indians stopped to rest. Along with Mary and Brad, Nate slumped gratefully to the ground, stretching out on some pine needles.

Hawley hunkered beside them and said, "How you kids holdin' up?"

"I'm tired," Mary whined. "Can't we go back to the wagons?"

"That's what we're doin'. I reckon you'll see your ma and pa again 'fore too much longer."

"I want Mama," Brad whimpered.

Hawley snapped, "Shut up. Don't go to pulin' and poutin', or them Injuns are liable to lift your hair." He looked at Nate. "Which one are you, boy? Who you belong to?"

"My parents are Roger and Dorothy Galloway," Nate replied, trying to sound dignified and not the least bit scared of the smelly mountain man in his greasy buckskins.

"It's your ma who's havin' the baby?"

"That's right." Again Nate felt a fierce longing to know how his mother was doing.

"What about them two?"

"They're my cousins, Mary and Brad. Their parents are my Uncle Peter and Aunt Angela."

Hawley grinned. "Angela . . . She's the purty one with that long blond hair, ain't she? Lord, I'd like to get me some o' that."

Mary blinked up at him and said, "You want to have long blond hair like my mama?"

Nate wasn't exactly sure what Hawley had meant by his comment, but he was certain the man hadn't been talking about Aunt Angela's hair. Before the trapper could make some crude response, Nate said, "Shush, Mary. We probably won't stop for long. Save your breath and rest."

"That's good advice, kid. I reckon it'll take most of the

day to catch up to them wagons, so the Injuns can't afford to wait around for very long. We'll be up and hustlin' again 'fore you know it."

True to Hawley's prediction, within minutes the big, ugly Indian called Swift Arrow barked some commands in the guttural Arikara tongue, and the warriors resumed their swift march, dragging their young prisoners along with them.

Nate wanted to see his parents again, wanted it more than anything he could think of in the world, but at the same time, he knew that when the Indians caught up to the wagons, they would try to kill the rest of his family. He started thinking desperately, trying to come up with some way he could slow them down or maybe even throw them off the track. . . .

Dorothy slept most of the morning, and Angela was grateful for that. It gave her a chance to rest as well. There was a rocking chair in the wagon, so Angela sat in it, her lap covered with a blanket and the new baby wrapped up and cradled in her arms. As she looked down at John Edward's red, scrunched-up face, she took note again of his black hair. Her own children had had hair that dark when they were born, although in both cases it had lightened up some over the years.

She remembered when Nathan had been born. His hair had been fair, almost blond, though it had darkened to the same shade as Roger's. A vague sense of unease stirred inside her. Something wasn't right here, but she couldn't put her finger on what it was.

She dozed off, exhausted from the night-long ordeal. If she was this tired, she couldn't imagine how Dorothy felt, having gone through the lengthy, difficult labor, along with being sick on top of it. And then the birth, and losing all that blood . . .

The baby woke her with its crying. For a second, disoriented from sleep, she looked down at John Edward and thought he was one of her own. But of course he wasn't. She knew what he wanted, but she couldn't give it to him. She said softly, "Just you wait a minute, honey. I don't know if your mama is up to it, but we'll see what we can do."

She stood up and went over to the thick pallet where Dorothy lay. The bloodstained, sweat-soaked bedding underneath her had been changed. Dorothy seemed to be sleeping more peacefully now, and Angela hated to disturb her. She had no choice, though. The baby had to eat.

"Dorothy . . ." Angela said quietly. She set the infant aside on a pillow and slipped an arm under Dorothy's shoulders. Carefully, she raised her sister-in-law to a half-sitting position and stayed there, supporting her. Pushing back the robes that were wrapped around Dorothy, she bared a breast. She reached over with her other arm and even more carefully picked up the baby, cradling him in the crook of her elbow and keeping the palm of her hand under his head to prevent it from lolling loosely. He was so tiny, she thought, so helpless.

Dorothy murmured, only half-conscious. That was all right; she didn't have to be fully awake for this. Angela brought the baby to his mother's breast, and as soon as the nipple nudged his lips, he opened them, took it in, and began to suckle.

Angela sat there holding both mother and child. She wished she could take on the chore of feeding John Edward, but she had no milk. Nor would she ever again, she thought as dampness misted her vision for a moment. Ever since that stillborn child, Peter had avoided touching her. Truth to tell, that was the way she had wanted it at first. She had pushed him away enough times so that he had gotten in the habit of not coming near her in bed, she supposed. Most of the time that was all right, but on occasion she missed his touch so badly she could barely stand it.

But life went on and everyone had crosses to bear, and right now her mind was occupied with helping her sister-in-law and her new nephew, as well as with worrying about the fate of her own children. She had hoped that Preacher would be back with them by now.

"Angela . . . ?" Dorothy whispered.

"Right here," Angela replied quickly, bending her head to bring it closer to Dorothy. "You're fine. The baby is eating."

"The . . . baby . . ." Somehow, Dorothy found the strength to reach up and stroke the black hair on John Edward's head. "So beautiful . . ."

"Yes, he is," Angela agreed with a smile.

"He looks just like . . . his father . . ."

The smile on Angela's face turned to a frown. She didn't see how Dorothy could say that. The baby looked almost nothing like Roger. If anything, he looked a lot more like—

My God, she thought. *No. It can't be.*

But she knew it was, and she wondered how she could have been so incredibly, stupidly blind.

She was just human. She had seen what she wanted to see and ignored what she didn't want to see. Some things could not be ignored, though, and the pain of that realization shot through her.

"Angela . . ." Dorothy said in a voice filled with the weakness and sickness that threatened to consume her. "I have to tell you. . . . You deserve to know . . . about the baby . . . and Peter . . ."

"Don't say anything else," Angela told her shakily. "Please, don't say anything."

"I . . . I can't die . . . with this burden on my soul . . ."

Angela put a false heartiness in her voice as she said,

"You're not going to die. Just stop thinking about that. You're going to be just fine."

Dorothy's head moved slowly from side to side. "No. You have a right . . . to know . . . Peter and I . . . Peter is the baby's . . . father . . ."

There it was, in undeniable, incontrovertible words. A wave of dizzy sickness hit Angela, as if the world had suddenly started spinning in the wrong direction. A shudder went through her. But other than that, she didn't move. She couldn't move. She had her arms around Dorothy and . . . John Edward.

Her husband's child, with another woman.

A tear welled from Angela's right eye and trickled down her cheek.

NINETEEN

The Indians didn't give their captives any food at midday. Nate figured they would be forced to go hungry, but Hawley grudgingly let them have some jerky from his pack. Mary and Brad whined about it, of course, but they took the strips of tough, dried meat and gnawed on them anyway. Nate didn't waste his time complaining. He was just glad he had something to put in his empty stomach.

As the group cut through the heavily wooded foothills, Nate realized just how badly he and his cousins had been lost the night before. They must have spent hours going around and around in ever-widening circles. It was doubtful they would have ever gotten back to the wagons. If the Indians hadn't captured them, eventually they would have collapsed and died of starvation . . . if they hadn't frozen to death or been eaten by wolves first.

Of course, there was always the chance that Preacher would have found them. Nate couldn't shake the feeling that the mountain man was out here somewhere, searching for them.

As the afternoon went on, he began to see things that looked familiar to him: a massive, lightning-blasted pine; a peculiar rock formation that looked like an old man; a stream that tumbled some thirty feet down a cliff in a foaming waterfall. Nate knew he had seen these landmarks the day before. Did that mean they were getting closer to the wagons? He thought it must.

"When are we gonna get back to camp?" Brad asked with a sniffle.

Without thinking about what he was doing, Nate said, "Never, the way they're going." He pitched his voice low, but he made sure it was loud enough for Hawley to overhear him.

He realized a second later that his instincts had guided him correctly. Brad let out a wail, and Hawley turned sharply toward them. "What the hell did you say?" he demanded of Nate.

Before Nate could answer, Brad yelled, "He said we're never gonna get back!"

Hawley's hand shot out and grabbed Nate's wrenched shoulder. Nate cried out in pain as the cruel grip made pain stab through him. "What are you talkin' about?" Hawley asked as he gave Nate a hard shake. "We're right on the trail o' them wagons!"

"Y-yeah," Nate stammered. "Yeah, sure we are. We'll be there soon. Please stop shaking me!"

Hawley grabbed Nate's other shoulder and brought his face close to the boy's. Snarling, he said, "You better be tellin' me the truth!"

"S-sure I am. I swear!"

The Indians had come to a halt as the commotion broke out, and now Swift Arrow stalked over and said, "What wrong?"

Hawley shook Nate again, drawing a whimper from him. "This little bastard said somethin' about us goin' the wrong way, and now he won't tell me what he meant by it!"

"Honest, Mr. Hawley, I just got mixed up and made a mistake," Nate said through his tears. "I didn't mean nothin' by it."

Swift Arrow pointed eastward and said to Hawley, "You say wagons go this way."

"They did," Hawley insisted. "They're headin' for Garvey's Fort, I tell you, and that's the way they'd be goin'. Unless—" Hawley broke off his words and looked at Nate again. "Did Preacher decide to go some other direction? Maybe head down toward the Platte? There's a few tradin' posts down there."

Nate shook his head. "I . . . I don't know anything about the Platte. We were still goin' the same way as when you left us."

Hawley snorted. "When Preacher killed my partner and run me off, you mean. I ain't sure I believe you, you little shit. Preacher's just tricky enough to have hit off in some other direction, just to throw me off his trail. I reckon he knew I'd come after him and was afraid of me."

Not on his worst day would Preacher ever be scared of the likes of you, Nate thought, but he kept it to himself. His hastily formed plan appeared to be working.

Swift Arrow put his hand on the handle of the knife sheathed at his waist. "You take us to wagons," he said to Hawley. There was no mistaking the threat in his voice and in his stance.

Hawley bobbed his head and said with obviously false confidence, "Sure, I'm takin' you to the wagons. We're goin' the right way."

"Boy say not." The war chief jerked his hand in a curt gesture at Nate.

"The boy don't know what he's talkin' about. Anyway, he said we *are* goin' the right direction."

"Boy lie," Swift Arrow said with a contemptuous look.

Nate just looked as guilty as possible and wouldn't meet the eyes of either Hawley or Swift Arrow.

"I reckon he must be lyin', all right," Hawley finally acknowledged. "Preacher and those wagons have changed directions. I figure they're headin' for the Platte River. I can take you there—"

"Swift Arrow know where Platte River is."

The implication in the flat statement was obvious: If Swift Arrow knew where the immigrants were going, why did he need Hawley? For that matter, Nate wondered why they hadn't killed the trapper before now if they thought the wagons were headed for Garvey's Fort. They didn't really need Hawley to show them the way.

They must have something else in mind for Hawley, Nate thought. And he would have been willing to bet that it wouldn't be anything good. Hawley seemed to think he had the redskins wrapped around his little finger, but Nate figured he was in for a bad surprise sooner or later.

"Listen," Hawley said quickly. "You still need me. I can come up on those wagons without those folks suspectin' anything. I'll get 'em off their guard, and then you can take 'em without any trouble."

"You help kill whites?"

"Sure, I'll help kill 'em. I told you that. Whatever you say, I'll sure do it."

Mary and Brad started crying harder at that. Even they knew now that they were doomed, that Hawley's promise to protect them had been just a big lie.

"Not kill you yet," Swift Arrow said after a moment. "We take you with us."

"I'm much obliged for that. I'll guide you to the Platte—"

"Not know that Preacher go there," Swift Arrow cut in. "Must search again."

"You mean split up the war party?" Hawley looked a little skeptical about that idea.

"Find quicker that way. Whites may still go Garvey's Fort."

Hawley rubbed his bearded jaw and frowned. "Yeah, I reckon you're right," he said after a moment. "All we got to go on is this dumb kid's word. He might not have even known where the wagons were when he wandered off."

"Did so," Nate muttered under his breath, but Hawley and Swift Arrow heard him. Both of them glared.

Let them look at him like that, Nate thought. He didn't care. All that mattered was that he had slowed down their pursuit, and he had even gotten them talking about splitting their forces. He couldn't have hoped for a much better result from his little acting job.

But he couldn't get the rest of his hopes up either. He had bought a little time. . . . That was all. Their future, his and his cousins', was still in the hands of a bunch of savages and a white renegade.

"What are they doing?" Jonathan asked anxiously as Preacher shinnied down from the pine tree he had climbed a few minutes earlier so that he could spy on the Arikara war party, which had halted about half a mile away on the other side of a little valley. The Injuns didn't know there was anybody behind them, so they weren't looking in that direction.

Preacher landed lithely on the ground and grinned at the two older men. "Looks like they're splittin' up into two or three different bunches," he said.

Geoffrey and Jonathan stared at him in surprise. "Why would they do that?" Geoffrey asked.

"I ain't got no idea," Preacher admitted. "They've got a good strong force. No need that I can see for them to split up. But maybe the war chief in charge of the bunch knows somethin' that we don't . . . or at least thinks he does."

The group of 'Rees they had seen that morning had been joined by others until the war party was at least forty members strong. A bunch that big would be hard to fight off if they all attacked the wagon train at the same time. Anything that broke them up into smaller groups was a good thing, Preacher thought.

"What about the children?" Jonathan asked.

"I saw 'em," Preacher nodded. "They looked like they were still all right."

"Thank God," Geoffrey said fervently.

Jonathan said, "If they split up, how will we know which group the youngsters go with?"

"We'll be able to tell from the tracks," Preacher assured him. "There's still enough snow here and there to pick up some prints, and when the snow's all melted, there's bound to be mud. Maybe Dog can help us too."

The day had warmed up considerably as the southern breezes continued to blow, and the landscape was more green again than white. This break in the weather wouldn't last, though. Preacher's bones told him another storm was coming. It was just a matter of when.

Preacher whistled, and Dog came out of the woods. The big wolflike creature had been ranging far ahead of them most of the day. Preacher ruffled his fur between his ears and said, "Let's go, fella. You ain't no bloodhound, but I reckon you might be able to pick up a scent if we had somethin' that belonged to one of those kids."

Jonathan cleared his throat. "As a matter of fact . . ." He reached inside his coat and brought out a small rag doll. "This is Mary's. There's a tear in it, and I was going to try to mend it for her since Angela has been so busy taking care of Dorothy these days. I can sew a bit, you know. An old bachelor skill."

Preacher nodded in understanding. "A man who can't sew a mite is up the creek if he needs somethin' mended and the nearest woman is nigh five hundred miles away."

"Indeed. Anyway . . ." Jonathan held out the doll. "Do you think Dog could track them from this?"

Preacher took the doll. "We can give it a try. That way we won't lose the trail for sure."

He held the doll under Dog's nose and told him to go find Mary. As usual, Dog seemed to understand what Preacher wanted. He turned and trotted off, tail wagging. The three men walked quickly after him.

The tracks Preacher found on the other side of the valley confirmed what he had seen from up in the tree. The war party had broken up into three groups, and they had fanned out to the east, southeast, and south. From the looks of it, Preacher thought that the Indians had decided they might not be going in the right direction. In fact, they had been, but something must have happened to cause them to doubt that. Preacher couldn't figure out that part of it, but the why didn't really matter. What was important was that the bunch holding the kids prisoner now numbered around a dozen again.

Four-to-one odds weren't good, but at least they were tolerable. Preacher and his companions had a chance now to get the kids away from those Injuns.

They pressed on, moving a little quicker. Preacher felt a growing urgency. This opportunity might be the only one they would get.

TWENTY

Angela was sitting in the rocking chair again when Roger looked in the back of the wagon. The baby was sound asleep, nestled next to Dorothy, who was also asleep. Angela stared straight ahead, and Roger had to speak to her twice before she came out of her reverie with a little start.

"I'm sorry to bother you," Roger said. "I know you must be exhausted. I just had to find out how they're doing."

Angela managed a tired smile. "They're both asleep. The baby ate a little while ago."

Roger stepped up into the wagon. "Dorothy is . . . all right?"

"She seems to be resting comfortably. But she's still awfully weak, Roger. She needs proper medical attention."

"We're a long way from that," Roger said, a bitter edge creeping into his voice.

"Yes, we are." There was no point in denying it, Angela thought. "We should have waited for spring. The baby could have been born in St. Louis."

"I know." Roger's eyes were haunted. "I know. But we just couldn't wait."

From the start, there had been something wrong about this journey. Angela had known that, had sensed the urgency with which Roger and Peter and their father had organized everything. She and Dorothy, along with Geof-

frey and Jonathan, had been swept along with the preparations, and their questions about why they had to leave
Philadelphia so suddenly had been brushed aside with
vague answers or sometimes even no answers. But the secret, if indeed there really was one, was still unknown to
her.

A lot of secrets had been kept from her lately, she
thought wryly.

Roger moved past her and knelt beside his wife and the
baby. "Can I . . . sit with them for a while?"

"Goodness, you can do whatever you want, Roger. This
is your wagon, and Dorothy is your wife." Angela left the
rest of it unsaid, but Roger didn't seem to notice.

"Why don't you step outside and get some fresh air?" he
said. "It might make you feel better."

Angela nodded. "Thank you. I'll do that." Roger was a
considerate man, a good man. She had always liked him
because of his devotion to his family, not just to his wife
and son but to his brother and father and uncles too. He
tried to do what was right and best for all of them. At least,
he had until this fateful and ill-advised journey west.

She moved to the back of the wagon and climbed out.
The sun almost blinded her. It seemed awfully bright to
her after being cooped up inside the wagon all day. And
the air was even warm, a far cry from the icy temperatures
of the past few days. Most of the snow had melted, and
what was left was dripping.

She knew what Preacher would say if he were here:
"Prob'ly be another one o' them blue northers in a day or
two." Preacher seemed to know such things, no doubt
because he had lived in the wild for so long and was somehow connected with nature to a greater extent than those
who had spent all their lives in civilization.

Where *was* Preacher? And where were the children?
The fact that Preacher had been gone for so long had to

be a bad sign. The children hadn't just wandered off. Something had happened to them. Angela was sure of it.

Someone called her name, and she turned to see her husband hurrying toward her. Peter had a rifle in his hand and a worried expression on his face.

"Aren't you supposed to be standing guard?" Angela asked him as he came up to her.

"My father is watching for trouble," Peter replied. "How are Dorothy and the baby?"

It would be so easy. She could look right at him and say, *Your mistress and your bastard son are sleeping.* At this moment, she would have enjoyed seeing the shock on his face if she said that to him.

And yet for some reason she held back. If she told Peter, she would have to tell Roger too, and she found that she didn't want to hurt him that way. There was enough trouble plaguing the family right now without all the added strain that such a revelation would bring. To be honest, she was so worried about the children that she simply couldn't summon up the strength to hate Peter right now.

"They're asleep," she said in reply to his question.

"The baby is all right?"

Angela nodded. "He seems to be fine."

"Well, that's good. I'm happy for Roger. But what about Dorothy?"

"I don't know. She came through the birth, and it was bad. But she could still take a turn for the worse."

"God, I hope not! That would be terrible. Terrible for Roger."

And for Dorothy's lover too.

Angela shoved that thought out of her head. "I hoped that Preacher would be back by now," she said, changing the subject, but not to a more pleasant one. She was more worried about her children than she was about the fact that Peter had cheated on her.

A grim look came over his face. "He should have let

Roger and me go with him, instead of taking those two old men."

"Those two old men are your uncles," Angela reminded him. "They happen to love you, and the children, very much."

"I know that. But if it comes down to a fight with Indians or something like that, how much help will they really be?"

"Enough," Angela said softly. She had to hope so anyway, for the sake of Mary and Brad and Nate. For the sake of all of them really, because if Preacher got killed trying to bring the children back, there was a good chance that none of the immigrants would ever see civilization again.

The sun was lowering over the peaks to the west. Its rays cast dappled shadows under the aspens and cottonwoods that thickly lined the banks of the creek. Shadows through which Preacher glided like he was one of them, insubstantial, fleeting, there and then not there.

As he approached the spot where the Indians had stopped, apparently for the night, he hoped that Jonathan and Geoffrey were in position. He had carefully pointed out where they were to go, told them what to do, and then had given them time to get there, but that didn't mean the old-timers couldn't have been delayed somehow. If they weren't ready, Preacher was walking straight into big trouble.

He had considered waiting until night fell to make his move, but had decided that the warriors would actually be more on their guard then. They were less likely to be expecting trouble now, so now was when Preacher was going to try to snatch those young'uns away.

He bellied down and crawled, gliding noiselessly through the brush. He was close enough to hear the Indians talking among themselves. He also heard some miserable whimpering that came from one or more of the children. Probably the two younger ones, Preacher thought. He had seen enough of Nate to know that the younker had sand. Nate might feel like crying, but he would try to hold it back if he could.

Preacher had two pistols, both double-shotted, tucked behind his belt, and he carried his Hawken, sliding it carefully along the ground as he crawled. Dog followed, also on his belly. Jonathan and Geoffrey were armed with rifles and pistols. Preacher wished he'd had more time to work with the older men on their marksmanship during the first few days of this ill-fated journey. Once the ball started, every shot would have to be a true one.

Preacher came to a halt and parted some brush. He saw the Arikara warriors gathered on the bank of the creek. A couple of them were getting ready to build a small fire. The others were talking amongst themselves. Off to one side, Nate sat with his back against a rock. His younger cousins were on either side of him, and he had his arms around them as if to protect them. The rock had shielded the ground beside it from the sun during the day, so not all the snow had melted. There was still a thin layer of it where the youngsters sat. Had to be mighty cold on their behinds, not that any of their captors would give a damn about that.

Mart Hawley stood near the prisoners, close enough to be guarding them without really paying that much attention to them. He was busily engaged in digging a wad of chewing tobacco out of a pouch and packing it into his cheek. Preacher wouldn't have minded putting his first bullet into the son of a bitch, but the 'Rees were more of a threat. He had to deal with them first.

The sun was behind the mountains now. Dusk began to settle over the landscape with its usual swiftness. In the brush near the creek, Preacher came up into a crouch, then slowly straightened to his full height. Even though he was now in plain sight, the Indians didn't notice him until he stepped through the brush with a crackle of branches and said in a loud voice, "Howdy, boys!"

The Indians whirled toward him, grabbing for arrows.

Preacher knew which one of the Arikara warriors was the leader of this bunch: the tall, muscular, ugly one. He brought the Hawken to his shoulder and fired at the chief in one smooth movement, seeming not to aim at all. With a puff of flame and smoke from the muzzle, the rifle roared and kicked against his shoulder. At the last instant one of the other Arikara stepped in front of the chief. The heavy ball caught him in the middle of the forehead, caving his skull in on itself and blowing his brains out the back of his head in a grisly shower that splattered over the chief.

Preacher let go of the Hawken and had hauled out both pistols before the rifle hit the ground. The first man he had shot hadn't hit the ground yet either when Preacher's right-hand pistol blasted. Both balls struck one of the warriors, one of them thudding into his chest while the other just tore shallowly through the side of his neck. That slowed down the second ball and deflected it slightly, but it still had enough force behind it to carry it into the left eye of a third warrior, where it ripped on up the optic nerve and into the brain.

Preacher had killed three members of the war party in a matter of a couple of heartbeats, but he knew that much luck probably wouldn't stay with him. In the next instant, however, two more rifle shots sounded. One of them came from a high rock off to the left, where Preacher had sent Geoffrey. The other originated on the far side of the creek. Preacher had had Jonathan cross the stream half a mile back and then work his way carefully along the creek until he was opposite the spot where the Indians had camped.

Both shots were well aimed and found their targets.

Two more of the Arikara tumbled off their feet as lead smashed through them. That made five down. Preacher fired his left-hand pistol. One of the balls tore through a warrior's lungs and sent him to the ground spewing blood, but the other missed, traveling harmlessly over the shoulder of the chief. The ugly son of a bitch seemed to have a guardian angel. Preacher dropped the pistols and hauled out his knife, ready to go to carvin'.

An arrow whipped past his head as he lunged forward. The warrior who had fired it dropped his bow and grabbed for his tomahawk, but as his fingers closed around it, Preacher's steel drove deep into his body. Preacher twisted the blade and grunted with the effort as he ripped it to the side, opening the Arikara's belly and spilling his guts out on the ground. A hard shove sent the mortally wounded man sprawling into a couple of his companions as Preacher jerked his knife free.

He bent to scoop up the tomahawk that had been dropped by the man he'd just killed, and then in a blur of pantherish motion he was among the rest of them, swinging the 'hawk in brutal strokes and slashing with the knife. Drops of blood flew in the air and fell almost like rain. Dog was in the middle of the fighting too, pulling down one of the warriors and ripping his throat out.

More shots thundered as Geoffrey slid down from the rock and Jonathan splashed across the shallow stream. They fired their pistols at the Indians on the fringes of the melee, being careful not to aim toward Preacher. Some of the Arikara turned to meet this new threat, leaving Preacher with more manageable odds. He caved in a skull, slashed a throat, tripped another man, and then buried the head of the tomahawk in the back of the luckless warrior's head. It was slaughter, pure and simple. Even these hardened Arikara warriors were no match for the frenzy with which Preacher attacked.

Preacher swung toward the kids and saw Hawley trying

to bring a pistol to bear on them. "Stay back, you bastard!" Hawley screamed. "Stay back or I'll kill these little—"

He didn't get any farther, because at that moment, Geoffrey bounded onto the rock beside which the young'uns huddled, and with a spryness that belied his years he launched into a flying tackle that smashed Hawley to the ground. Hawley was bigger and younger and stronger, though, so he was able to throw Geoffrey off.

Preacher was about to go to the older man's aid when he had to dart aside to avoid a slashing blow from the war chief's tomahawk. The Indian swung the weapon again in a backhand that was almost too fast for the eye to follow. Preacher's eyes were not those of a normal man, however, and he was able to drop out of the way of the killing stroke. He rolled to the side and came up lithely onto his feet again.

He was in time to see Hawley drive a knife into Geoffrey's body. The renegade white man pulled the blade free and drew it back to strike again. Preacher threw the tomahawk that was still in his left hand. The throw was accurate. After turning over once in midair, the tomahawk smashed into the back of Hawley's left shoulder and lodged there. Hawley screamed as he fell forward, driven down by the impact of the tomahawk striking him.

That action had occurred in the blink of an eye. Preacher was already turning back to face the chief's challenge. The chief wasn't there anymore, though. Preacher couldn't spot him in the gathering gloom. He saw that all the other members of the war party were down. Jonathan rushed past him, shouting, "Geoffrey!"

Preacher turned and looked and saw that Hawley had staggered to his feet and was running away now, leaving Geoffrey sprawled on the ground behind him. Bending, Preacher snatched up a fallen bow and arrow and let fly after the renegade. The shaft whistled past Hawley as the man ducked into the brush.

Preacher didn't much like it, but he let Hawley go. The renegade vanished into the gloom of fast-approaching night. Preacher hurried toward Jonathan, Geoffrey, and the kids, anxious to see if the young'uns were all right.

TWENTY-ONE

On his way across the clearing where the Indians had planned to make their camp, Preacher picked up his pistols and quickly reloaded them. Dog was nosing around the sprawled bodies of the fallen warriors. Preacher knew if any of the Indians were still alive, Dog would let him know about it.

The kids were already clustered around their great-uncles. Jonathan propped Geoffrey up in a sitting position. "I tell you I'm all right," Geoffrey insisted, but his voice held a thin edge of pain.

Preacher hunkered beside the two older men and said, "Let me have a look." He pulled Geoffrey's coat aside and saw the bloodstain on the man's shirt, just below his right shoulder. It looked like Hawley's knife thrust might have missed anything vital.

A quick further examination of the wound revealed that to be so. Preacher wadded up a piece of cloth and pressed it to the blood-leaking hole. "Hold that there," he told Jonathan, then turned to look at the kids. "Are all you young'uns all right?"

"I'm tired and hungry," Mary said. "And I was scared until you got here, Mr. Preacher."

"None of us are hurt," Nate assured Preacher. "Some of the Indians wanted to kill us when they first caught us, but the chief stopped them."

Preacher grunted. "Prob'ly figured to use you as hostages if'n he needed to. How'd Hawley come to throw in with them?"

Nate shook his head. "I don't know. He was with them when they found us." The youngster looked around. "Where did he go?"

"He got away," Preacher said in disgust. "So did the chief."

"Swift Arrow?"

Preacher nodded. "If that was his name. I wouldn't know."

"That was his name. He spoke a little English and talked to Hawley some." Nate pointed to one of the fallen warriors. "That one there was their medicine man. His name was Badger's Den."

That was the man whose throat had been torn out by Dog. His medicine hadn't been powerful enough to stop the big wolflike creature.

With Swift Arrow and Hawley still on the loose somewhere out there in the darkness, Preacher didn't think they could afford to lollygag around here all night. He said to Geoffrey, "You reckon you can travel?"

"Of course I can, if someone will just tie this bandage in place. . . ."

Preacher did that, and then Jonathan helped his brother onto his feet. Geoffrey was a mite shaky at first, but he steadied himself and nodded to Preacher. "Let's go."

The six of them—seven if you counted Dog—moved out quickly as soon as Preacher had gathered up all their weapons. He took some of the knives and tomahawks that the Arikara had dropped too. You never knew when something like that might come in handy.

Preacher kept up a fast pace, guiding them by the stars and by his own instincts. He wanted to put some distance between them and the scene of the fight with the 'Rees. The fact that Swift Arrow had survived the fracas was worrisome. Preacher didn't think the war chief would try to follow them and attack them by himself, but it was possible, even likely, that he would find the other groups that had split off from the war party earlier in the day and come after them.

Hawley still being alive didn't concern him as much. The renegade was wounded, and Preacher hoped that he would just crawl off in the brush somewhere and bleed to death. That would be just fine.

Preacher knew the kids must be worn out, but they bore up without much complaining. When he finally called a halt a couple of hours later, though, they flopped mighty gratefully on the ground. Jonathan and Geoffrey sat down on a log. Preacher asked Geoffrey, "How you holdin' up?"

"I'm all right," Geoffrey answered, but he spoke between teeth gritted against the pain. "I must admit, though, I'll be quite glad when we get back to the wagons."

"You saved us, Uncle Geoffrey," Nate said. "Hawley was gonna shoot us. I never saw you jump around and fight like that before."

In the moonlight, Preacher saw Geoffrey's rueful smile. "You may never see it again either. I'm, ah, not much of a brawler."

"You did fine," Preacher assured him. "In fact, both o' you fellas handled yourselves well back there. You'll do to ride the river with."

"Thank you, Preacher," Jonathan said, his voice thick with emotion. "Coming from a man like you, that's higher praise than I ever expected to hear."

Preacher said, "You two wait here with the kids while I scout around a mite on our back trail, just to make sure that Arikara chief ain't skulkin' around."

He faded off into the darkness with Dog padding quietly after him. When they came back a few minutes later,

Preacher said, "No sign of Swift Arrow. If you're rested up enough, we'll get movin' again."

"Can't we rest a little while longer?" Mary asked.

"Come on," Nate told her in a tone that brooked no argument. "Don't you want to get back to your folks?"

"I do want to see Mama again," Mary admitted, and her little brother said, "I want Mama too."

"Let's go, then," Nate said as he prodded them to their feet.

Jonathan helped Geoffrey up, and the whole group set out again.

Preacher got them started down a long, narrow valley that they could follow in the moonlight, and then dropped back slightly to bring up the rear. If trouble was going to catch up to them, he wanted it to find him first, so that he could deal with it.

A moment later he saw Nate coming toward him. "Something wrong?" Preacher asked.

"No, I just wanted to come back here and walk with you."

Preacher started to send Nate back ahead with his cousins and uncles, but then he decided it would be all right to let the youngster accompany him for a little while. "All right, but if I tell you to get back with the others, you skedaddle, you hear?"

"Sure, Preacher." Nate hesitated. "Preacher, can I have a pistol?"

The question took him by surprise. "You know how to handle a gun?"

"I've shot one before. They're heavy, but if I hold it with both hands, I can manage."

Preacher chuckled. "You hit what you aim at?"

"Sometimes. And even when I don't, I don't miss by much."

Preacher figured he knew what was going on. Being captured and held prisoner by the Indians must have made Nate feel pretty helpless, and now he wanted a gun so he wouldn't have to feel that way again. Preacher could understand that. He drew one of the pistols from behind his belt and handed it to the boy.

"It ain't primed. You know how to do that?"

"Sure. I'll get some powder from Uncle Jonathan and put it in my pocket."

"Your ma might not like that."

"She won't like me carryin' a gun neither, but I'm goin' to do it," Nate said with a grin.

"Best you remember one thing . . . a gun comes in mighty handy, and it can sure enough save your life out here. But there's problems that it can't solve. You got to use your brain for that. A fella who can think fast and straight is gonna come out on top most of the time."

Nate nodded. "I'll remember." They walked along in silence for a spell, and then Nate said, "Preacher . . . that Indian Swift Arrow kept talkin' about how him and his people had vengeance coming, like we'd done something bad to them."

Preacher had felt all along like the Arikara must have some sort of blood debt they wanted to settle with the Galloway party. Otherwise they wouldn't have tracked the immigrants so far and so stubbornly.

"You got any idea what he was talkin' about?"

"No, not really. But he sure acted like *we* had done something bad to *them,* instead of the other way around."

"Maybe we can figure it out when we get back to the wagons and talk to your folks," Preacher suggested.

"It won't do any good for me to talk to them," Nate said. "I'm just a kid. They won't pay any attention to me."

Maybe not, but they would pay attention to *him,* Preacher thought. He was tired of not knowing what was going on and why the Arikara were so determined to kill them. When they got back to the wagons it would be time for a showdown, time for the Galloways to put their cards on the table.

Preacher intended to make sure of that.

As night fell, Angela sat inside the wagon and studied Dorothy's sleeping face by the light of the single candle that burned.

They had been friends, Angela thought, more like real sisters than sisters-in-law. Why had Dorothy betrayed her by sleeping with her husband?

Angela couldn't answer that question, but she knew what had to be done. She was waiting now for Dorothy to wake up.

John Edward squirmed in his little nest of blankets and pillows next to his mother. His lips made sucking noises. Soon he would be hungry enough to wake up, and when he did, he would demand to nurse and would raise a squalling ruckus if he didn't get the nipple. Angela hoped she would have things settled with Dorothy before then.

A few minutes later, as John Edward stirred even more, Dorothy's eyes flickered open. She was disoriented for a moment, her gaze darting around the room, but then her eyes focused on Angela's gravely solemn face and she whispered, "The baby . . . ?"

"He's right here," Angela assured her, "and he's fine. You'll probably have to nurse him in a few minutes."

Dorothy closed her eyes for a moment and nodded weakly.

"But before then," Angela went on, "we have to talk, Dorothy."

Dorothy looked up at her again and began, "I'm so sorry—"

"Don't. I don't want your apology." Angela saw the pain on Dorothy's face and went on. "I don't know what happened, but I forgive you for your part in it. What's important now is that things don't get any worse. Listen to me, Dorothy. . . . You haven't told Roger about you and Peter yet, have you?"

Dorothy's head moved from side to side, not much but enough to signify her answer. "I . . . I couldn't bring myself to . . . to tell him."

"Then don't." Angela's voice was firm with resolve. "No one needs to know about this but the two of us."

"But the baby . . . looks so much like . . ."

"Roger and Peter are brothers," Angela said. "Yes, the baby looks more like Peter, but that's not unheard of. Peter inherited his dark hair from one of their ancestors. John Edward could have gotten his from the same place."

"I . . . I suppose. But don't you think . . . Roger has a right to know?"

"Roger has a right to be proud of his new son. And since you've been sick, Dorothy, you probably don't know everything else that's been going on. There's been some trouble . . . an Indian attack . . . and now we're headed back east, instead of trying to go on to Oregon."

She hoped that Dorothy was coherent enough to understand what she was being told. Angela didn't say anything about the children being missing. Dorothy was in no condition to do anything about that, and in her weakened, fragile state, the added worry over her son Nate might be enough to send her over the edge. She would have to be nursed along carefully. Anyway, Preacher would be back soon with the children, Angela told herself, and Dorothy wouldn't have to know about any of that until later, when she was stronger.

It was vital, though, for the sake of all of them, that the true identity of the baby's father remain a secret. They had to concentrate on getting safely to Garvey's Fort once Preacher returned with Nate, Mary, and Brad.

"Do you understand, Dorothy?" Angela pressed her. "You mustn't say anything to anyone about you and Peter."

Dorothy closed her eyes and nodded. "I understand," she replied in a hollow whisper. "But I'm so sorry, Angela."

"Don't worry about that," Angela said. She slipped her hands under John Edward just as he began to cry. "You've got something a lot more important to tend to right here."

TWENTY-TWO

Mart Hawley gritted his teeth against the blinding pain as he twisted his body and stretched his right arm in an attempt to reach the handle of the tomahawk. He felt blood trickling out around the edges of the wound. It would probably bleed even worse when he got the tomahawk loose, but that couldn't be helped. He couldn't leave the damn thing stuck in his back.

His fingers touched the branch from which the handle was made. He groaned and stretched a little farther.

He had crawled into this brush-choked gully after running until he collapsed. He expected Preacher to catch up to him at any second, and he knew he couldn't expect any mercy from the mountain man. Preacher was already legendary as a killer. He wouldn't waste any time. He'd just cut Hawley's throat and be done with it.

Hell, Hawley couldn't blame Preacher for that. He'd have done the same thing if the tables had been turned.

Preacher hadn't come after him, though, and the only reason Hawley could think of was that Preacher had probably wanted to get those kids back to safety as fast as he could. He'd been willing to let Hawley go in return for a quicker start.

Bastard was goin' to regret that, Hawley thought with a grimace as he finally got his fingers wrapped around the tomahawk. With a wrench, he pulled it free, crying out at the agony that flooded through him. He felt the warm flow down his back and knew he'd been right about the bleeding. It was worse now. He had to get something on the wound and slow it down, or he might bleed to death right here and now.

Moss was good for that, and he had already felt around in the dark and found some at the base of a tree. He reached out now and got a handful of the stuff. Grunting with the effort, he twisted around and tried to slap it on the wound. He didn't think he was going to make it. . . .

Strong hands plucked the moss from his hand and pressed it to the wound beside his shoulder blade. Hawley let out a yell of fear and surprise. Who the hell—!

"Quiet," Swift Arrow said. Hawley instantly recognized the war chief's harsh tones. "Be still. You not die from this."

"How . . . how did you find me?" Hawley gasped.

"You white man," Swift Arrow said with a grim chuckle. "And you not Preacher. Follow noise."

Hawley slumped in relief and let the Arikara tend his wound. Naturally, Swift Arrow had experience patching up tomahawk wounds. He packed it full of moss and then tied a pad of cloth torn from Hawley's shirt over the wound. The bleeding had already slowed considerably, and although Hawley still felt mighty weak, he didn't think he was going to pass out.

Still lying on his belly, he asked, "What are we gonna do?"

"Kill Preacher," Swift Arrow said. He didn't elaborate, didn't explain how he intended to go about that chore. It was just a simple statement of his intentions.

Hawley sighed. "Take me with you," he said. He was tired and his wounded shoulder hurt like blazes, but the fires of hatred deep inside him burned hotter than ever. Hatred for the mountain man . . .

"You keep up, you be there when I kill Preacher," Swift Arrow said.

"Wouldn't miss it for the world," Hawley said.

Preacher and the others traveled all night, stopping only now and then to rest. Even when he called a halt, Preacher didn't stay still for very long. While his companions caught their breath, he checked their back trail or scouted out ahead, Dog trotting along with him. By the time the moon set and the starlight waned, the terrain had become flatter and Preacher knew they were on the edge of the foothills. They ought to be getting back to the wagons any time now.

He spotted the humped white shapes of the canvas coverings in the gray light of dawn. By that time he was carrying Mary, who was sound asleep. Jonathan had Brad in his arms, with the boy's head resting on his shoulder, and Brad was asleep just like his sister. Nate had taken over the job of helping Geoffrey whenever the wounded man needed any assistance to keep going or to get over some obstacle.

The immigrant camp appeared to be completely asleep. No one moved around the wagons. There was no fire. Preacher had a bad moment during which he wondered if the other members of the Arikara war party had somehow found the wagons and wiped out everybody else. The two old men and the kids might be the only survivors of the group.

But then he saw Angela climb out the back of one of the wagons. She seemed to be all right and didn't act like anything was wrong. She got a bucket and filled it from one of the water barrels.

"Aunt Angela!" Nate cried, unable to restrain himself.

Angela turned sharply and in her surprise dropped the bucket. The water splashed out onto the ground, but no one paid any attention to that. She let out a sound that was half laugh, half sob and ran toward them.

Mary and Brad were stirring. Preacher set Mary on her feet and said, "There's your mama, gal. Go see her."

Mary knuckled the sleep from her eyes and then stiffened as she recognized Angela. "Mama!" she exclaimed as she hurried to meet Angela. A still half-asleep Brad stumbled after her.

Angela went to her knees and swept the children into her arms, gathering them to her like long-lost sheep. She hugged them tightly and shuddered from the depth of the emotions coursing through her. All three of them were crying now.

Preacher, Nate, Jonathan, and Geoffrey stood there smiling as they watched the reunion. Over at the wagons Simon Galloway emerged, and Roger and Peter came hurrying from the trees, carrying the rifles that showed they had been standing guard until the commotion broke out at the camp. They hadn't been doing a very good job of it, Preacher thought briefly, but you couldn't expect much from city folks.

Of course, that wasn't quite fair, he reminded himself. Jonathan and Geoffrey still had a ways to go before they would be seasoned frontiersmen, but they had handled themselves pretty darned well during the rescue mission.

Preacher patted Nate on the shoulder and said, "Go see your pa." Nate looked up at him, and Preacher nodded. With a grin, Nate ran to meet Roger. Roger swung the youngster up into his arms and hugged him.

"Are you all right, Nate?" he asked.

"I'm fine. Not hurt a bit," Nate assured him.

Roger must have felt the gun Nate had tucked behind his belt, because he looked down and said, "What's that?"

"A pistol," Nate said, his tone indicating that that should have been obvious. "I reckon I'm gonna go armed from now on."

Roger looked surprised, but he didn't argue the matter. He was too glad to have his son back alive, safe and sound, when it must have seemed like a strong possibility that he would never see Nate again.

The two old-timers limped forward and were greeted by their brother Simon. Hands were shaken and backs slapped all around, and then Simon said to Geoffrey, "You're hurt!"

"It's nothing," Geoffrey replied. "Just a little knife wound."

"It needs some proper patchin' up," Preacher said as he ambled up. "Any trouble here while we were gone?"

Simon shook his head. "No, but there's a new member of the party. I have a new grandson. John Edward Galloway."

Nate twisted around in Roger's arms to look at his grandpa. "I got a new baby brother?"

"That's right, son," Roger told him.

"Can I see him?"

"Well, I don't know." Roger looked at his sister-in-law. "Angela?"

Angela raised her tear-streaked face. She was still smiling happily at being reunited with her children. "What?"

"Can Nate see his mama and his new baby brother?"

Preacher might have imagined it, but he thought he saw something odd flash in Angela's eyes at that moment. For a second he wondered if Dorothy Galloway had died giving birth. But then Angela said, "They're both asleep right now. Your mama really needs her rest, Nate, so it might be better to wait."

"Aww . . ." Nate said. "I guess it's all right, but I really wanted to see 'em."

"In a little while," Roger promised him.

Nate started to squirm and kick a little. "Put me down, Pa," he said. "I'm too big for you to be pickin' me up."

Roger looked like he might have argued that, but he lowered Nate to the ground.

The sun was almost up now, and the rosy glow in the sky matched the good mood in the camp. Not everything was rosy, though, Preacher reminded himself. There were still at least a couple of dozen vengeance-hungry Arikara out there somewhere, probably no more than a day behind them. Peter was still caught up in hugging and kissing his prodigal children, so Preacher motioned to Roger, Simon, Jonathan, and Geoffrey. They came over to him, with Nate drifting along behind Roger.

Quickly Preacher told Roger and Simon what had happened. He concluded by saying, "Swift Arrow, the war chief o' that bunch, got away, and so did Hawley."

"That bastard," Simon said. "I can't believe he allied himself with savages."

"Well, he did," Preacher said. "I ain't worried all that much about him. He might even be dead by now. But Swift Arrow wasn't hurt, as far as I know, and I reckon he'll be comin' after us as quick as he can. He'll likely try to round up the rest of his war party too. That'll slow him down some, but then he'll come on like a house afire. We got to start puttin' some miles behind us."

Angela heard that comment and came over to join the men. With an assertiveness unusual in women of her era, she said, "We can't go anywhere right now. Dorothy is too weak. I don't think she can stand traveling."

"We don't have much choice," Preacher said. "If we stay here very long, them 'Rees will catch up to us for sure, and then we'll be in for it."

Roger said, "Preacher, if my wife is too ill to go on, then we don't have any choice. We'll just have to hope that once she's a little stronger, we'll still have time to reach the fort—"

Preacher stopped him by swinging an arm toward the

northern sky. "You ain't got that much time, and it ain't just 'cause of the Injuns neither. There's another snow-storm comin', and it'll be a lot worse than the last one."

"Oh, I say!" Simon exclaimed dubiously. "How can you know that?"

"Preacher knows things about this country that none of us do," Jonathan said, and Geoffrey nodded. "Take our word for it, Simon, you don't want to doubt what he says."

"But you're talking about my wife," Roger said miser-ably, his joy at the return of the children momentarily forgotten. "We can't take chances with her life."

"You stay here and you're takin' a chance with every-body's life," Preacher said grimly.

The others started talking all at once, trying to hash things out, and Preacher felt his frustration and impa-tience growing. He had told them how things stood, and while he hated to put Dorothy Galloway in any more danger, what he had said was absolutely right: They would all die if they squatted here for very long, and that included Dorothy.

"I'm goin'," he said curtly, cutting through their bab-ble. "If you folks want to come along, best get ready to move as soon as everybody's eaten breakfast."

They all stared at him. Angela found her voice first. "You'd leave us?" she said. "You'd really abandon us?"

Whether he really would or not was a damned good question, Preacher thought, and he figured the answer was that he wouldn't. But they didn't need to know that, so he kept his bearded features stern and flintlike as he nodded and said, "If you-all are stubborn enough to throw your lives away, damned right I would."

"Then it seems we have no choice," Roger said with a sigh. "We can't get back without your help, so we have to go along. But I'm not going to forget this, Preacher. If my wife dies . . ."

"If you stay here, she will," Preacher said. "You can count on that."

He turned away and went to check on his dun, which he had left with the wagons when he went after the children. He could feel the others' eyes on him as they talked together in low voices, and he figured they were cussin' him up one way and down the other. That was all right, he told himself. He hadn't thrown in with this bunch of immigrants to make friends. His goal was to get them back safely to someplace where they could spend the winter.

He was going to accomplish that goal, and if it had to be in spite of the very people he was trying to help, then so be it.

TWENTY-THREE

Angela gave him the cold shoulder after that, which was probably a good thing, Preacher reflected. He knew that when he had first seen her that morning she had looked mighty damned good to him, and since she was married to somebody else, those weren't feelings he ought to be having.

He checked over all the horses and the mules while Angela was fixing breakfast. The animals were all right. They had probably benefited from having a couple of days to rest. They would need all the strength and stamina they possessed for the long, fast haul to Garvey's Fort.

Nate came over to him when the food was ready. "Preacher, come and eat," the youngster said.

"Much obliged. I'm glad to see you ain't mad at me, Nate."

The boy frowned. "Well, I'm worried about my ma, of course. I wish we could stay here and let her rest after havin' that doggone baby. But Aunt Angela and Uncle Peter and Pa . . . well, they didn't see Swift Arrow close up, nor spend time as his prisoner. Him and Hawley talked about killin' all of us, Preacher. We can't let them catch up to us, or my ma will die for sure."

Since Preacher had said practically the same thing himself earlier, now he just nodded. Nate had a practical streak to him that was a mite unusual in such a young fella.

It would stand him in good stead out here on the frontier, Preacher thought.

He ate a plate of bacon and biscuits and washed it down with good strong coffee. When he was finished, he told the men, "Get those teams hitched up. We'll be pullin' out in a few minutes."

They followed orders without complaint, but he saw the resentful looks Roger and Peter gave him. He didn't give a damn how they felt. They would thank him when they got to Garvey's Fort and still had their hair.

Preacher saddled the dun and then swung up on the back of the rangy horse. He rode to the front of the first wagon and called, "Lead the way, Dog!"

Dog loped out in front of the wagons. Preacher pointed to him and told Jonathan, who had climbed to the seat of the lead wagon and taken the reins, "Follow him."

"We're being led by an animal?" Jonathan asked.

"He'll smell trouble 'bout as fast as I could see it, and he'll take the easiest path too. Fella can do worse in life than to follow a dog. A smart dog anyway." Preacher grinned. "They ain't all overly bright, but then neither are people."

Jonathan shrugged, flapped the reins, and got the wagon rolling.

Preacher reined the dun to the side and waved for the others to follow Jonathan. Roger's wagon came next, followed by Peter's and then the one usually driven by Geoffrey. He couldn't handle a team with his wounded shoulder, though, so Simon had been pressed into service.

When all the wagons were moving, Preacher turned and rode back the way they had come. His eyes roved constantly, searching for any signs of pursuit as he dropped back a couple of miles. He didn't see anything out of the ordinary, and finally he turned and headed east again. Less than an hour later, he caught up to the wagons and got waves of assurance from all the drivers as he passed, letting him know that they hadn't run into any trouble.

That morning, the breeze had still been out of the south. Before noon, the air went dead calm, which Preacher considered a bad sign. Sure enough, a little while later, it began to blow from the north, and it wasn't a breeze this time but rather a hard wind.

A *cold* wind.

Another storm was on the way, just as he had predicted. He had no way of knowing how bad it would be, but his instincts told him it would be worse than the one before. This might be the first of the season's real howlers.

By the time the pilgrims stopped for a late lunch, the temperature was plummeting. Roger looked at Preacher and said, "How in the world did you *know* it was going to do this?"

Preacher shrugged. "I can't explain it. You spend a few winters out here, though, and you get to where you can tell what's comin'. Somethin' about how the air smells maybe."

"Is it going to be worse than last time?"

"Reckon we'll find out," Preacher said. "Just hide an' watch. . . ."

Angela kept tucking extra blankets around Dorothy and John Edward as the temperature dropped during the afternoon. Unlike earlier in the trip when Dorothy had been running a fever, now her body temperature seemed to have gone down, just like the weather. Her lips took on a faint bluish tinge as she muttered incoherently. She was out of her head most of the time, and although Angela didn't want to admit it even to herself, she was losing hope. If Dorothy had been in a comfortable bed, in a nice snug house, being attended to by a physician, she might have stood a chance of pulling through. As it was, rocking along on a pallet in the back of a wagon with nobody to take care of her except a woman with no medical training whatsoever . . . Well, Dorothy's chances weren't nearly as good, Angela thought. She didn't know if Dorothy would make it. She just didn't know.

If Dorothy died, that would leave Roger without a wife and Nate and John Edward without a mother. Angela wouldn't wish that on anyone. Yes, she had been angry when she first discovered that Peter was really the baby's father. If Dorothy had been healthy and had told her that she had slept with Angela's husband, Angela would have cheerfully throttled her. Now, though, she didn't feel anything but sympathy for Dorothy.

The same could not be said about her feelings toward Peter. Speaking of cheerfully throttling someone . . .

But she couldn't do that either, couldn't do anything except keep what she knew to herself, at least until they got back to civilization. When that happened, there would have to be a confrontation. She would have to tell Peter that she knew what he had done. She couldn't keep it all bottled up inside.

"Peter . . ." Dorothy murmured. "Peter, don't, please don't . . ."

Angela leaned closer and frowned. That had sounded like Dorothy was trying to stop Peter from doing something. She was reliving the memory of something, unaware in her ill state of where she was or what was really going on. What could she be remembering except the obvious? Angela asked herself. Was it possible that Dorothy hadn't wanted Peter to do what he had done?

Had Peter raped his own brother's wife?

The thought made a chill go through Angela that had nothing to do with the weather. She had been married to Peter Galloway for almost ten years. She would have thought that she knew him about as well as one human being could know another. My God, she'd had two chil-

dren with the man! To think that he might be capable of
. . . of doing a thing like that . . . was almost beyond Angela's comprehension.

If it was true, she couldn't stay married to Peter. She
didn't know what she would do, but she was certain of
that much. Somehow, their marriage would have to
come to an end.

Of course, between the weather and the Indians, they
might all wind up dead, and then she wouldn't have to
worry about it, Angela thought. She laughed softly, and
even to her own ears, the sound had an edge of hysteria
in it.

The wind blew in more than the cold. Clouds followed
it, racing across the sky. As Preacher glanced at the tumbled gray masses, he thought about how much the
weather had changed since that morning. It had been almost warm then, and now it was like there wasn't even a
vestige of warmth left anywhere in the world.

The clouds overtook the sun and swallowed it whole. As
Preacher rode past the wagons, he called encouragement
to the drivers, who were huddled on their seats in thick
coats and blankets, their hats pulled down tight and tied
with scarves to keep them from blowing away. With the
thick overcast, night would fall early, so Preacher rode on
ahead and started looking for a good place to make camp.
They were on the edge of the plains now, with the foothills
having fallen behind during the day. The terrain rolled
gently, which made for faster traveling but didn't provide
much in the way of shelter. There would be no cliffs or
caves where they could get in out of the wind. The best
they could do would be to draw the wagons in a tight circle and crowd the livestock inside.

The wind was blowing so hard Preacher didn't even
hear the shot. He *felt* the heavy ball go past his ear,

though, only inches from his head. He reined in and twisted in the saddle, looking for whoever had just taken a potshot at him. He saw three riders come boiling over a nearby rise and gallop toward him. Feathered head-dresses streamed out behind them as they rode.

Pawnee! Preacher thought. He never had gotten along well with the Pawnee, and now it looked like he had one more reason not to like them. The three attacking him carried rifles, and another one fired as they came closer. Preacher saw the spurt of flame and smoke from the muzzle.

The ball whined overhead, missing him by a good margin. Some Injuns were good shots, but most of 'em could barely hit anything, especially from the back of a running horse. Preacher lifted the Hawken he carried across the saddle in front of him and spoke quietly to the dun, calming him. Lifting the long-barreled rifle to his shoulder, Preacher drew a bead. The three Pawnee kept coming, riding stubbornly straight at him.

He fired.

One of the Indians went backward like a giant hand had snatched him from the back of his pony. He hit the ground, bounced a couple of times, and then lay still. Preacher knew he would never move again. Anybody who fell like that was dead. But the other two Pawnee were still alive and still after his hair.

Preacher spoke to the dun again as he swapped the empty Hawken for the one in the saddle sheath that was loaded. He cocked and primed the rifle, but by the time he went to lift it and nestle the smooth wood of the stock against his cheek, the Indians had split up and were coming at him from two different directions. So they weren't completely stupid.

He wished he knew which one of them had shot at him before. Whichever one it was hadn't had time to reload, so Preacher would have shot the other one first, figuring the

Pawnee with the empty rifle was less of a threat. But he didn't know, so he just picked one and fired again, the Hawken roaring as it kicked against his shoulder.

As fire geysered from the muzzle of Preacher's rifle, the Indian he was shooting at ducked down, flattening himself along the neck of his mount. Only thing was, Preacher hadn't really aimed at the rider but at the horse instead. He hated like blazes to hurt a horse, but he had figured the Pawnee might do something like that. The heavy lead ball struck the horse in the neck. The animal's front legs folded up, and as the mortally wounded horse fell, the Pawnee on his back sailed through the air over its head. The Indian hit the ground hard, probably knocking the breath out of him and stunning him. A second later the dying horse rolled over him, and Preacher could practically hear the man's bones snapping, even from where he was.

That left only one of the Pawnee, and as he galloped toward Preacher, only twenty yards away now, he thrust out his rifle and fired it one-handed. At the sound of the blast, Preacher knew he had chosen the wrong enemy to bring down first.

It was a lucky shot. The ball struck the barrel of the Hawken in Preacher's hands and tore the rifle loose from his grip. His hands tingled and throbbed from the impact. He kneed the dun and sent the horse lunging forward as the surviving Pawnee reversed his rifle and swung it at Preacher's head like a club.

The blow missed, but the Pawnee recovered with blinding speed and launched himself from the back of his horse just as Preacher was pulling one of his pistols from behind his belt. The collision jolted Preacher out of the saddle. He fell, smashing into the ground with the blood-crazed Pawnee on top of him. The Indian got the fingers of his left hand around Preacher's throat while his right groped for the handle of the knife at his waist. He pulled the blade from its sheath and lifted it high overhead.

Preacher slammed the pistol in his hand against the side of the Pawnee's noggin, sending him sprawling. Preacher rolled the other way, putting a little distance between them. As he came up on his knees, he saw the Pawnee drawing back the knife again, this time getting ready to throw it.

Not wanting to take any chances, Preacher palmed out the other pistol and thumbed back the hammers of both weapons as he lifted them. The pistols were primed and ready to fire, so he let loose with both of them as the Pawnee's arm flashed forward. The next instant he dove to the side so that the knife blade just clipped the top of his left shoulder, slicing his buckskins and nicking the flesh underneath.

The Pawnee wasn't so lucky. All four of the balls from the double-shotted pistols struck him, landing in such a tight pattern at this close range that they blew a fist-sized hole clean through him. He rocked back on his haunches and lived just long enough to gaze down in wonderment at the awful thing that had happened to him. Then he toppled over to the side and was dead when his face hit the ground.

Preacher heard growling and looked around to see Dog standing over the Pawnee who had been thrown from his horse and then crushed by it. Preacher climbed to his feet and walked over to check on the man. He was still alive, but his arms and legs were broken, and from the looks of his body in the bloodstained buckskins, he was all busted up inside too. A swipe across the throat from Preacher's knife finished him off, and Preacher didn't feel bad about doing it either. If he had been hurt that bad, he would have looked on such an act as a kindness.

He straightened and looked around. Evidently the three Pawnee had been alone, because he didn't see any more of them. Probably out on a last hunting trip before the real snows came, and when they had seen a lone white man riding along, they had decided to have some fun with him.

Their sport had backfired on them. Preacher left the bodies where they had fallen, reloaded his pistols, found the Hawken that had been shot out of his hands, and then went back to looking for a place to camp. The storm wouldn't hold up just because he'd been forced to spend a few minutes killing those Injuns.

TWENTY-FOUR

He kept a close eye out for more Indians, just in case those three Pawnee had split off from a larger group. He didn't see any, though. Except for him and the dun and Dog, Preacher thought, the vast plains might as well have been deserted.

A short time later he came upon a buffalo wallow and knew he wouldn't find a better place for the pilgrims to camp. The wide depression in the earth wouldn't offer much protection from the wind, but any was better than none. Preacher marked the spot in his mind and then wheeled the horse to ride back to the wagons.

As Preacher came up to the lead wagon, Jonathan reined the team to a halt and said excitedly, "We heard shots, and then we passed some dead Indians back there a ways. Did you see them, Preacher? Do you know anything about them?"

"Reckon I do," Preacher drawled. "They jumped me a mite earlier this afternoon."

Jonathan goggled at him. "You killed all three of them?"

"Seemed like the thing to do at the time, considerin' that they was shootin' at me and hell-bent on liftin' my hair."

"Yes, of course, I didn't mean to imply that you did anything wrong," Jonathan said quickly. "I was just surprised . . . although I don't know why I should be. I saw how you fought with those Indians when we took the children away from Swift Arrow. Three-to-one odds wouldn't mean anything to you."

"Don't be too sure of that," Preacher told him. "But sometimes a fella's just got to go ahead and do what has to be done, no matter what the odds."

Jonathan nodded. He had come to understand a lot more about life on the frontier than he had when he started this journey.

Following Preacher's orders, the men drove on to the buffalo wallow and bunched the wagons inside the depression, pulling the vehicles close to each other in a circle. The daylight began to fade with a swiftness that surprised even Preacher. The clouds had to be growing very thick overhead for them to shut out the sun that way. For a while, Preacher seemed to be everywhere at once, helping to unhitch the teams and bring them inside the circle of the wagons.

They would have to have a fire, and though there were still clumps of trees here and there, for the most part the landscape since leaving the foothills had become a treeless prairie. That meant firewood was in short supply . . . but not buffalo chips, and they would burn too.

Preacher put the young'uns to work. "See them buffalo chips on the ground?" he said. "I want y'all to pick up some of them and make a big pile of 'em."

"What are they?" Mary asked.

Nate leaned over and whispered in his cousin's ear. Mary made a disgusted face.

"Don't worry, they won't hurt you," Preacher assured her. "And the heat they'll give off when we make a fire out of 'em will feel mighty good tonight when the temperature gets down below freezin'."

"Do you think it's going to snow again?" Nate asked.

"It sure might."

The kids set to work. Preacher motioned for Geoffrey to come over, and when the older man had joined him, he said quietly, "I'd 'preciate it if you'd keep an eye on them young'uns. I know you got a bad arm, but you can handle a pistol a little with your left hand, can't you?"

"Certainly," Geoffrey replied, and from his enthusiasm Preacher could tell that he was glad to have been given something to do. "I'll watch over the children and fire a shot if anything threatens them."

Preacher nodded. "That's the idea. Much obliged." He clapped a hand on Geoffrey's uninjured shoulder for a second, then went on about the task of seeing that the camp was set up properly and safely.

By the time full darkness had fallen, a small, almost smokeless fire was burning next to one of the wagons. The mules and horses were on the other side of the circle, kept there by a rope strung from one wagon to another. That didn't leave the humans much room, but they would make do, Preacher thought. Right now, that livestock was just about as important as the people; that is, if any of them hoped to make it back alive.

Preacher went over to Roger Galloway and asked, "How's that new son of yours?" He hadn't seen Angela since that morning, so he hadn't had a chance to ask her about Dorothy.

Roger had a haunted look in his eyes as he nodded. "The baby seems to be fine. Angela says he has a good appetite and a healthy pair of lungs."

"But your wife ain't doin' so good, is she?"

Slowly, Roger shook his head. "Not at all. She's been either unconscious or out of her head all day." His voice shook from the strain he was under. "I don't know what to do, Preacher. I . . . I want to make things right, but I just don't know how."

"Ain't much you can do right now, stuck out here in the middle of the prairie like we are," Preacher said commiserating with the man. "Time for thinkin' about the right thing to do was before you ever took off for Oregon at the wrong time of year."

"I know that now. I guess we'll just keep trying to make it back to that fort you told us about."

"Pretty much all we can do," Preacher agreed.

Inside the wagon, Angela was thinking about how they would feed John Edward if Dorothy died. She felt terrible about even considering the possibility, but they had to face facts: If Dorothy sank much lower, she wasn't going to make it. If they'd had a milk cow, they might have been able to give that milk to the baby.

But the nearest cow was . . . Angela couldn't even make herself think about how far away. Too far to ever do them any good.

Dorothy broke into her reverie by murmuring, "Peter . . . Peter . . ."

Angela felt herself grow even more tense. She loved Dorothy like a sister, and she had meant it when she forgave her for whatever her part had been in the illicit affair with Peter. But Angela didn't need to be reminded all the time of her husband's adultery.

"Hush now," Angela said quietly as she leaned closer to Dorothy. "The baby's asleep, so you should rest too."

Dorothy's eyes blinked open, and she looked up at Angela with uncommon lucidity. "Angela . . ." she said. "How can you stand . . . to be around me?"

"Shhh. I'm here to take care of you. You have to get well, for the baby's sake."

"The baby . . ." Dorothy repeated weakly. "Your husband's baby, your own husband . . . You're so good, Angela. . . . I don't deserve . . ."

"Hush," Angela said again. Suddenly she felt the wagon shift slightly on its thoroughbraces as someone stepped up at the rear of it. More emphatically she said, "Be quiet now, Dorothy."

Dorothy ignored her plea, though, and her voice chose that moment to grow stronger as she went on. "But Peter is John Edward's father, Angela. You must hate us both."

"No, no, I don't, just . . . just please don't talk anymore—"

"No," Roger said flatly from behind Angela. "Let her speak if she wants to."

Angela jerked her head around to stare at her brother-in-law. Roger's face was bleak and dark with rage in the light from the single candle as he stepped on into the wagon and let the canvas flap fall closed behind him.

"If Dorothy has something to say," he went on, "let her say it."

Dorothy sighed, a long, fluttery sound that made Angela look around sharply. She saw that Dorothy's eyes were closed again. Her breathing was soft and shallow. She had slipped back into unconsciousness, exhausted from those brief moments of awareness.

Without turning to look at Roger, Angela said, "She can't say anything right now. She's resting."

"I heard her," Roger said. "She . . . she was crazy there for a minute, wasn't she? She didn't know what she was saying?"

Angela heard the desperation in his voice, the urgent need to cling to any hope, even the slimmest one. She knew she could lie to him, could agree that Dorothy had been out of her head, but she knew that in the end it wouldn't do any good. Roger had heard for himself the conviction in his wife's voice and knew that Dorothy had spoken the truth.

She turned her head at last to meet Roger's stricken gaze. "It's true," she said. "Dorothy admitted it to me after John Edward was born. Peter is . . . is the baby's father."

Roger stood there without saying anything for a long moment, his breath rasping in his throat as he visibly struggled to control his emotions. He stared past Angela at Dorothy, fixing his gaze on his wife's face. Slowly he moved his eyes down to the tiny, sleeping form nestled next to her. Angela held her breath, thinking that she might see hatred growing in Roger's eyes, but instead, to her great relief, his expression softened and nothing but love shone on his face.

"It's not his fault," he said quietly. "He had no part in this."

Angela shook her head. "No. No, he didn't."

"He's the only truly innocent one among us."

Angela nodded in agreement with that. Since Roger seemed a little calmer now, she ventured, "I think it would be a good idea if we didn't say anything to anyone about this. It won't help anything—"

She stopped as Roger's expression hardened again. "Oh, there'll be something said about it," he told her. "You can count on that."

He turned toward the rear of the wagon.

Angela stood up and hurried to his side, catching hold of his coat sleeve. "Roger, wait! If you confront Peter now, it'll just cause trouble—"

He jerked away. "*He* caused the trouble already! He slept with my wife. The bastard!"

"We don't really know what happened—"

"We know enough." Roger thrust out a hand and pointed at the mother and child bundled up on their makeshift bed. "We know that that baby is no son of mine. I should have realized that! He looks so much like Peter. . . ."

Roger's voice trailed off, and then with a sudden cry he thrust the canvas aside and pushed his way out of the wagon. Angela caught at his coat again, but he pulled away from her with ease and leaped from the tailgate to the ground. As she hurriedly climbed out behind him, he strode toward the fire, where Peter stood along with Simon. Jonathan and Geoffrey were preparing supper, while the children stood nearby. The night seemed huge, with the small fire struggling to hold back the all-encompassing darkness.

"Peter!" Roger barked as he stalked toward his brother.

Peter turned to look at him. "What is it?" he said in alarm as he saw the look on Roger's face. "What's wrong?"

"Wrong?" Roger echoed. "I'll tell you what's wrong!" He jerked a pistol from behind his belt and leveled it at Peter's face, cocking the hammer as he cried, "My brother is a traitorous bastard, that's what's wrong! And I'm going to blow your damned brains out!"

TWENTY-FIVE

Preacher was ranging outside the camp, Dog at his side, when he heard the commotion. Dog heard it too, and laid his ears back and growled.

"Yeah," Preacher agreed, "I reckon we better go see what sort o' trouble them greenhorns are gettin' up to now."

It was even worse than he thought it would be, he saw as he loped into the camp and stepped long-legged over one of the wagon tongues. Roger Galloway had a pistol in his hand and was pointing it right at his brother Peter.

Preacher didn't have any idea what had caused the falling out betwixt them, but he knew that with all the dangers still facing the group, they couldn't afford to go around killin' each other. He called out, "Hold it! Roger, put that damned gun down."

Roger didn't lower the pistol. He stood there with his arm straight out. His face was twisted with anger, and his hand shook a little. Peter stared into the muzzle of the gun. His face was drained of color. Clearly he realized that he was very close to death.

Off to the side, Simon, Jonathan, and Geoffrey watched the confrontation in shocked horror. Mary and Brad sobbed, knowing only that their father was being threatened by his own brother. Nate said urgently, "Pa, no! Don't do it, Pa!"

"Listen to the boy, Roger," Preacher advised. "I don't know what you're so het up about, but it won't make it any better for you to shoot Peter."

"I don't know about that," Roger said tautly. "It might make me feel better to know that I killed the man who slept with my wife."

Carefully, so as not to spook his brother, Peter lifted his hands and held them palm-out toward Roger. "I don't know where you got that crazy idea, but I swear to you—"

"Save your swearing," Roger cut in. "I heard it from Dorothy herself. She was talking to Angela, and she said that you're the father of that baby in there."

Peter swallowed hard. Preacher could tell he didn't know whether to continue denying the charge or if it would be safer for him to admit it. Preacher didn't know either. Roger sure looked ready to pull the trigger on that pistol.

"Roger, please don't," Angela said from the back of the wagon where Dorothy was resting. "Put the gun down and think about what you're doing."

"Think about it?" Roger echoed. "All I've been able to do for the past few minutes is think about it! I can't get that picture out of my head. . . . I can't stop thinking about what he did!"

"Listen to me, Roger," Peter said. "I don't care what she told you, she wanted it as much as I did! I . . . I never forced her—"

"Shut up!" Roger roared.

Preacher wouldn't have thought that Peter could make the situation any worse, but danged if he hadn't just done so.

"You raped her?" Roger went on. "You attacked your own sister-in-law?"

"No, I'm telling you—"

"You've told me enough," Roger broke in coldly.

Simon made an attempt to reason with him. "Son, you can't do this. You can't shoot your own brother."

Roger took a deep breath, and for the first time the barrel of the pistol sagged a little. "You're right," he said in a hollow voice. "You're right, I can't shoot him."

He lowered the pistol the rest of the way and let down the hammer. The gun slipped from his hand and fell with a thud to the ground. Preacher let out his breath when the impact didn't make the weapon go off.

"I can't shoot you, Peter," Roger said. His hands clenched into fists. "But I can beat you to death with my bare hands!"

With that he leaped forward, swinging a vicious punch at Peter's head.

Taken by surprise, Peter didn't have time to avoid the blow. Roger's fist smashed into his cheek and knocked him backward. Though Roger was smaller, he struck again with all the power that rage gave him, and the blow packed enough punch to lift Peter off his feet and drop him to the ground.

Roger went after him, even as those gathered around shouted for him to stop. Except for Preacher, who stood and watched calmly. Sometimes a situation got so bad there was nothing left to do except have it out. Given what he had heard about Peter and Dorothy, he reckoned this was one of those times.

Ignoring the shouts and pleas, Roger drew back his leg and aimed a kick at Peter's head. Peter shook off the effects of the punch just in time to roll out of the way. As he came over onto his back again, he reached up and grabbed his brother's leg. Since Roger was already off balance from the missed kick, it was easy for Peter to heave up on his leg and topple him. Roger fell, landing heavily on his back.

That gave Peter a momentary advantage, and he tried to seize it. He leaped on top of Roger and clawed at his throat, managing after a second to lock his fingers around Roger's neck. Peter planted a knee in Roger's belly to hold him down and began to squeeze.

Peter might have choked the life out of his brother, but Roger cupped his hands and slammed them against Peter's ears. Peter let out an anguished howl and jerked back, and that allowed Roger to break the grip on his throat. Roger bucked up off the ground, arching his back. The move threw Peter off to the side. Roger rolled away, gasping for breath.

"Both of you, stop it!" Angela screamed from the tailgate of the wagon. Behind her the baby wailed, his sleep no doubt disturbed by all the uproar.

Roger and Peter climbed to their feet and faced each other again. A bruise was starting to purple Peter's face where Roger's first punch had landed. Before they could attack each other again, Simon and Jonathan rushed in to grab them and hold them apart.

"Stop it, you two idiots!" Simon commanded as he held on to Roger's arms from behind. "I'm your father! Do what I tell you!"

"You're . . . you're through giving orders to us, Pa!" Roger rasped. His throat was sore from being throttled by Peter. "Let go of me!"

With that he brought his heel down hard on his father's instep. Simon yelped in pain and let go. Roger leaped across the small open space. Peter tore away from Jonathan and lunged to meet him.

Nobody could have more of a knock-down-drag-out fight than a couple of brothers, Preacher thought, unless it was a father and son. For the next few minutes, Roger and Peter fought with all they had, standing toe-to-toe and slugging it out. The thick coats both men wore made it difficult for them to strike with much effect at each other's bodies, so they aimed their punches at their opponent's heads instead. Blood began to fly as knuckles opened cuts, smashed lips, and pulped noses. It began to look like they might actually beat each other to death if the fight continued long enough. Preacher started to think about stepping in and ending it.

He didn't get the chance to. A gun roared, the loud noise echoing over the prairie. Startled by the shot, Roger and Peter both stopped swinging their fists. Everyone looked around to see Angela standing at the rear of the wagon, smoke curling from the barrel of the pistol in her left hand. In her right she held another pistol, and this one was pointed at the two combatants instead of into the air.

"I'll shoot the next man who strikes a blow," she declared. "That's a promise."

"Angela!" Peter cried. "Shoot him! Stop him!" When Angela didn't respond, he said raggedly, "For God's sake, I'm your husband!"

"You should have thought of that about nine months ago," Angela said, her voice flinty with anger.

"I don't care if you shoot me," Roger mumbled through swollen lips. "I'm still gonna kill him." He started to shuffle toward Peter.

Preacher got in his way. "You ain't gonna kill nobody, old son," he said in a flat voice that allowed for no arguments. He put a hand on Roger's chest. "Back off. Fight's over."

Roger's fists were still balled. For a second he looked like he was going to take a swing at Preacher, but the thin smile on the mountain man's bearded face must have warned him that that wouldn't be a good idea. Glaring, he stepped back, then turned and walked unsteadily toward the wagon where Angela stood. He went past her to lean against the vehicle, where he lifted a hand and dabbed the back of it against bleeding lips.

"Pa," Nate said as he came up to Roger. "Pa, can I help you?"

Roger summoned up a pained smile as he looked down at his son. "Thanks, Nate," he said thickly. "But I reckon it's too late for that."

Angela still had the pistol lined on Peter. He glowered at her and snapped, "For God's sake, put that gun down. It's liable to go off accidentally."

Preacher never had held a very high opinion of Peter Galloway's intelligence, and it went down another notch now. If Peter couldn't see that if that pistol went off it wouldn't be an accident, then he was damn near too stupid to live.

Still, they might need every warm body they could muster before this journey was over, so Preacher said, "Might be a good idea for you to lower that pistol, ma'am. We don't need any more shootin'."

His calm words got through to her. Slowly she lowered her arm until the pistol was pointed at the ground. Preacher took it from her and eased down the hammer. He set the weapon on the tailgate.

Angela turned away. Instead of going to her husband, she stepped over to Roger's side and put a hand on his arm. "Come inside the wagon," she said. "We'll put some salve and plaster on those cuts on your face, and your hand should probably be wrapped up too. You may have some broken knuckles."

Peter stared at her in disbelief. She ignored him as she helped Roger into the wagon. Nate climbed in after them.

Preacher tightened his jaw to hold in a chuckle as he looked at the expression on Peter's face. "You prob'ly made some big mistakes in your life, mister, but none bigger'n this'un."

"I don't need any advice from you," Peter said.

"Wasn't offerin' any, just commentin' on what a damned fool you are. A fella don't go messin' with his brother's wife." Preacher found himself growing a little angry. "And out here, a man who forces hisself on a woman usually winds up dead in a hurry—shot if he's lucky, kickin' his life out at the end of a hang-rope if he ain't."

"Are you threatening me?"

"Just tellin' it to you straight, so you'll know not to cross me."

Peter muttered a curse under his breath and turned away, clearly not wanting any further confrontations tonight. He pulled a rag from his pocket and started wiping at the blood on his face. His two young'uns just stared at him, unsure of what they were supposed to do. It had to be mighty unsettling for them, seeing their mama point a gun at their papa that way.

"Simon, grab a rifle and go stand guard," Preacher said. "Everybody else, go back to what you were doin'. Fight's over, and if we're lucky, there won't be any more trouble tonight."

Grudgingly the others went back to their chores, even Mary and Brad, who resumed piling up buffalo chips near the fire. Nate hadn't returned from the wagon where Angela was patching up Roger's injuries.

Preacher wasn't sure what to do with Peter. If the man really had raped his sister-in-law, he ought to be punished, but there was no law out here on the frontier to do it. The nearest law was back in St. Louis. Everywhere west of there, folks took care of their own problems.

And to complicate matters even more, there was still the threat of the Arikara war party lurking behind them. Peter might not be much of a man, but as long as he could point a gun and pull a trigger, he was valuable to the rest of them.

For the time being Roger was going to have to call a truce with his brother. They couldn't be tussling or threatening to shoot each other all the time. They had to find a way to get along. The safety of the whole bunch might depend on their cooperation.

Preacher hoped it never came down to that, though, because if things were that bad, then they were sure enough in trouble.

Roger climbed down out of the wagon, followed by Angela and Nate. He had bits of plaster stuck here and there on his bruised, battered face, covering up the worst of the cuts and scratches. He still looked very angry, but he was in control of himself again. Angela must have been talking to him as she worked on his injuries, Preacher thought. She must have argued some sense into his head.

"Peter," Roger said.

Peter had his back to his brother. He turned slowly and said, "What are you going to do now, take another punch at me?"

Roger shook his head. "No, I'm through fighting. You're not worth it. I can see that now. But you're no longer my brother."

"Oh, come on. Brothers fight. You know the old saying about blood being thicker—"

"No," Roger cut in. "I'll never forgive you, Peter. I see you now for what you are. You're nothing but a selfish coward, and you don't care about anyone except yourself. You've been causing trouble ever since this trip started." An even more bitter edge crept into Roger's voice as he added, "If it weren't for you, those damned Indians wouldn't even be after us."

Preacher's ears perked up. He had thought from the start that there was more to the story than he had been told.

Maybe he was about to find out what it was.

TWENTY-SIX

Preacher stepped forward even as Peter waved a hand and said disgustedly, "I don't know what you're talking about."

Preacher didn't believe him for a second, and judging by the stricken looks on the faces of Jonathan, Geoffrey, and Simon, they knew that Peter wasn't telling the truth either. Just as Preacher had suspected, something had happened back along the trail that had sent the Arikara war party after the immigrants. The men had hidden the secret among themselves, but it could stay hidden no longer. Preacher was about to drag it out into the light.

"All right," he said heavily. "Time you fellas put your cards on the table. Roger, what are you talkin' about?"

Roger hesitated now, as if he might regret what he had said. But then his resolve stiffened, and he ignored the warning looks from the others as he met Preacher's intent gaze and said, "Peter killed one of the Indians. A young man. It happened not long after we passed their village."

"That's a lie—" Peter began, but Preacher silenced him with a hard glance.

"Go on," Preacher told Roger. "I thought you said you hadn't never seen any 'Rees before."

"Well, we didn't stop at their village. We saw it before we got there, and we were afraid of them—they're savages, after all—so we went around. They didn't see us, didn't know we were there."

Preacher would have been willing to bet that the Arikara had known good and well the little wagon train was passing close by. They just hadn't bothered to do anything about it. The tribe had a habit of letting other people alone unless something happened to rile them, as it had in this instance.

"We moved on," Roger said, "and then the next day, while we were stopped at noon, Peter went out to do some hunting. We wanted some fresh meat."

Preacher looked at Peter and guessed. "Instead you ran into an Injun."

Peter looked like he wanted to deny it, but then he shrugged and shook his head as if to ask what was the use of that. "I didn't set out to hurt anybody," he said, a note of whining defensiveness in his voice.

"Just tell me what happened," Preacher said. "Don't leave anything out."

Sullenly Peter said, "I was walking through some trees along a creek, and then suddenly there he was. He looked, well, savage, like he wanted to kill me. He had bones in his hair, like those others, and he was carrying a bow. When he saw me, he said something—I didn't understand him, of course—and then he reached behind his back, like he was reaching for an arrow. You have to understand, I thought my life was in danger. I thought he was going to get an arrow and shoot me."

"So you shot him first," Preacher said, knowing where this story of misunderstanding and violence was going. It had been repeated many times across the frontier, ever since the white man had started pushing westward into the domain of the red man.

"I was defending myself," Peter insisted. "My rifle was ready, so I just lifted it and pointed it at him and pulled the trigger." He swallowed hard. "The ball hit him in the chest and knocked him back into the creek. I pulled him out, but it was too late. He was dead."

"What did he have behind his back?" Preacher asked, guessing that he still hadn't heard everything.

Peter looked down at the ground. "A couple of rabbit carcasses on a string. I . . . I think he was going to offer one of them to me."

Preacher's hands clenched tight in anger on the Hawken. "I expect you're right," he said. "As a rule, the Arikara are generous folks. The fella you shot was prob'ly out huntin' too, and he asked you if you wanted to share in the game he'd bagged." Preacher thought of something else. "Roger said the Injun was young. How young?"

"I don't know." Peter waved his hands helplessly. "Fifteen or sixteen years old, more than likely. But I thought he was a full-grown man when I first saw him. I . . . I never really took a good look at him until after I'd pulled him out of the creek."

"So you just blazed away and killed a fella who didn't mean you no harm." Preacher struggled to keep his temper reined in. "What did you do then?"

"There . . . There was a little gully close by. I put him in it and . . . put some brush and rocks on top of him."

"Hidin' what you'd done," Preacher snapped accusingly.

"I didn't want to take the time to bury him," Peter said. "I knew someone might have heard the shot."

"The other Injuns, you mean."

Peter shrugged again. "I just thought it would be best to put him where he couldn't be found easily. And it wasn't totally selfish on my part, you know. I . . . I was trying to lay him to rest the best I could."

Preacher knew such thoughts had never entered Peter's head; the man hadn't even considered anything except saving his own hide. But he didn't waste any breath arguing. He just said, "Then you went back to the wagons."

"That's right."

"And you told your brother and your pa and your uncles what had happened."

"Not right away, he didn't," Roger said. "I suppose he was too afraid of what he had done. But a day or two later, he told us. We all agreed that the best thing to do would be to go on and keep what had happened to ourselves. We didn't think it would matter once we got to Oregon."

"You didn't figure the rest of the Injuns would come after you?"

"We hoped they wouldn't find the body," Roger said.

And for a while they must not have found it, Preacher thought. Otherwise the wagons wouldn't have gotten such a big lead on the war party that had set out to avenge the young man's murder. It had taken time to find the body and then to locate the trail of the one responsible for the killing. The Arikara, in their quest for vengeance, wouldn't really care which of the immigrant party had pulled the trigger. They would wipe out all the whites in order to even the score.

Preacher wondered if the slain young man had been the son of the chief or the leader of one of the warrior societies. That would help explain a little more the determination of the Arikara to find and kill this bunch of pilgrims. It wasn't necessarily the case, though. They would have valued the life of any of their young men and considered his murder a debt that had to be paid in blood.

"Why didn't you tell me all this when I threw in with you?" Preacher demanded of the circle of men.

"We had agreed to keep it our secret," Simon said.

"And we didn't see how telling you would really change anything," Jonathan put in. "The Indians were already after us, and you seemed to be convinced those first ones who attacked us weren't just a small band of renegades, Preacher. How could you have done anything differently?"

Preacher dragged a thumbnail through the close-cropped beard on his jaw and frowned. "Maybe I would have staked out Peter and left him for the 'Rees. I reckon they would've figured out he was the one to blame for the killin' and might've been satisfied with tor-turin' and scalpin' him."

Peter stared at him, eyes wide with horror, and the others looked just about as appalled. "You can't mean that!" Simon exclaimed.

"Don't be so sure," Preacher grated. "Out here when a fella makes a mistake, he usually pays the price for it hisself, without draggin' a bunch of other folks down with him."

Geoffrey stepped over beside Peter and squared his shoulders, even the wounded one. "We never would have allowed such a thing," he said. "Peter made a mis-take, all right, a bad one, but he's still family."

"That's right," Jonathan said, moving up alongside Geoffrey. Simon closed ranks on Peter's other side.

Preacher looked at Roger. "How about you? You was ready to kill him yourself a while ago."

Roger appeared to think it over for a moment, lead-ing the others to glare at him for his hesitation, but then he said, "They're right. As much as I hate Peter right now, I wouldn't turn him over to the savages. I just couldn't do that."

"Suit yourself," Preacher said. "I don't reckon they'd take him now anyway. There's been too much fightin'. Too many of them have been killed. For them, it's all or nothin' now."

"You mean . . ."

"Either we die," Preacher said, "or all of them do."

* * *

Inside the wagon, Angela Galloway had listened to the men talking, and though she wouldn't have thought it possible, her loathing for the man she had called her husband grew even stronger. Peter had slept with his brother's wife, possibly even raped her, and now Angela discovered that he was a killer as well, the murderer of an innocent young man.

Of course, Peter had acted out of panic when he shot that Indian, Angela told herself. He probably really had feared for his life. But his impulsiveness was liable to cost them all dearly. The other Indians wouldn't turn back, wouldn't give up. She had heard Preacher say that the Arikara intended to kill all of them. She didn't doubt it for a moment.

The baby began to kick and fret. Angela turned and picked him up, holding him against her as she snuggled him tighter in the blankets around him. The wind was still blowing hard, and it was very cold inside the wagon. Drafts found their way in no matter how snugly she closed the canvas flaps over both entrances. Poor John Edward, she thought. He was cold and hungry, and his mother was dying and his father was a coward and a liar and an adulterer. How could any child stand a chance in the world with odds like those against him?

"I'll take care of you," she murmured, knowing that the baby couldn't understand her but feeling compelled to say the words anyway. "I know I'm not your mother, but I won't abandon you. Neither will Roger. He may not be your real father, but he loves you. That . . . That's more important. He loves you, and so do I."

John Edward settled down as she spoke quietly to him, and a moment later he was sound asleep again. He must not have been too hungry, Angela thought. She laid him down carefully and then brushed a hand over Dorothy's forehead. The poor woman was colder than ever, and when Angela checked her pulse, she found it weak and rapid. Despair gripped her, despair for Dorothy, for John Edward, for Nate and for her own children as well, because all of them were threatened by the weather and the Indians. If any of them survived, it would be a miracle.

But Preacher was still with them, Angela reminded herself, and if anyone on this wild frontier was equipped to work a miracle, it was the man called Preacher.

Simon Galloway had drifted back into camp when the argument of Peter's killing of the Injun youngster had started. Now Preacher sent him out again to stand guard, and he took Dog and the Hawken and went out himself, circling the buffalo wallow in the howling wind.

The night's revelations had been stunning ones, and yet Preacher wasn't all that surprised. He had known from the start that Peter was rash and reckless and inclined to get into trouble. He just hadn't known how bad that trouble was. It took a special breed of bastard to cuckold his own brother. As for shooting the Injun when it wasn't necessary, well, that was something that had happened before, all the way back to when Cap'n Lewis and Cap'n Clark had gone up the Missouri and set out for the Pacific. Lewis and Clark had been a good ways north of here, and it had been a Blackfoot Lewis had shot in a dispute over a gun, Preacher recalled, but still it was a hasty act that had had plenty of repercussions over the years. The Blackfeet never had been friendly toward the whites after that, and more than one scalped trapper could lay part of the blame for his grisly fate at the feet of ol' Meriwether Lewis.

Dog suddenly growled and bumped his muscular body against Preacher's leg. Preacher looked down at him and asked, "What is it, Dog? Somethin' wrong?"

A second later, he got the answer to that question as the blizzard hit him like a brick wall.

TWENTY-SEVEN

He had just *thought* the wind was blowing hard before. Now he staggered as it smashed at him with incredible force. Not only that, but he was blind, instantly surrounded by an ocean of white flakes driven with stinging force by that terrible wind. Preacher had been battered by heavy rainstorms before, but he had never known that *snow* could hurt.

He held his hat on and lowered his head so that the wide brim protected his face, at least to a certain extent. He went to a knee before he could be bowled over by the gale. "Dog!" he shouted, not knowing if the animal could hear him or not.

A moment later, the great furry body pressed against him and he felt Dog's warm breath against his ear. Preacher looped his right arm around Dog's neck and buried his hand in the thick fur.

"We got to get back to camp!" he shouted. "Come on!"

Relying on his inner sense of direction, he came up in a crouch and started moving toward the buffalo wallow. At least, he hoped that he was going the right way. If he wasn't, if he became completely disoriented by the storm, he might wander around out here for hours until he finally collapsed and froze to death. He kept his hand knotted in Dog's thick coat, knowing how keen the wolflike creature's senses were and knowing as well that Dog would head for the camp.

Preacher felt the ground under his feet change its pitch. He was moving down a fairly gentle slope now, and relief washed through him as he realized it was probably the buffalo wallow. He still couldn't see anything except the sea of white that had swallowed him, but a few moments later he ran into something big and unyielding. It took him only a second to feel of it and realize it was a wagon wheel.

He groped his way along the wagon until he came to the back of it. Stepping up on the tailgate, he pulled the canvas flap aside and tumbled inside. It wasn't much warmer, but at least he was out of the wind. For the most part anyway, since the canvas cover popped and billowed and let in some of the howling monster.

"Who's that?" someone exclaimed loudly as Preacher entered the wagon. "Who's there?"

Preacher recognized Jonathan Galloway's voice. "Take it easy, Jonathan," he assured the older man. "It's just me, Preacher."

"Thank God! We were afraid you were lost out there in the blizzard."

"I came damn close to it," Preacher told him. "But Dog helped me get back."

And speaking of Dog, Preacher thought, where was he?

As if in answer to the question, he heard claws scratching at the tailgate and turned to put his head and shoulders outside the flap. He reached down and caught hold of Dog under the animal's front legs. As big and heavy as Dog was, even Preacher had to grunt with effort as he helped him climb into the wagon.

"Hope you don't mind some more company," Preacher said as he settled back with Dog beside him. He pulled the flap closed and tied the thongs on it to keep it shut.

Geoffrey answered this time. "Not at all. Every bit of body heat we can get is more than welcome."

"Injuns sleep with dogs during the winter for warmth. The colder it is, the more dogs you need."

"Well, then, we could use a whole pack of them tonight," Jonathan said.

Preacher found himself warming up a mite now that he was out of the worst of the wind. His teeth stopped chattering after a few minutes, and he said, "Is everybody else in the wagons? Everybody accounted for?"

"I think so," Jonathan replied. "The only one I'm not sure about is Simon. He was out standing guard, you know. But he wasn't very far away, and he must have come back when the storm hit."

Preacher frowned in the darkness. "You saw ever'body else? You know they're in the wagons?"

Geoffrey said, "That's right. Roger, Dorothy, and Angela are in Roger's wagon, and the children are with Peter in his wagon."

"But you don't know for sure about Simon?"

"Well . . . no. We just assumed. . . ."

"You don't think he's still out there, do you?" Jonathan asked.

"Only one way to find out, I reckon," Preacher said grimly.

"My God!" Geoffrey said. "You can't mean you're going back out there?"

"To the other wagons at least. Until I find Simon."

"Do you want us to come with you?" Jonathan asked. Preacher heard the reluctance in his voice, mixed with worry about Simon.

"No, we don't need any more lost sheep," Preacher said. "Stay here with Dog. I'll be back."

He ordered Dog to stay, then loosened the flap and

climbed out of the wagon. The icy wind pounded at him and the snow stung him fiercely as he fastened the canvas behind him. He moved to the front of the wagon, keeping at least one hand on it all the time. When he came to the wagon tongue, he worked his way along it until he could reach out and touch the next wagon in the circle. He stuck his head in the back and asked who was there, but no one answered. That came as no surprise. According to what Jonathan and Geoffrey had told him, one of the wagons should have been empty, unless Simon had crawled into it, and obviously he hadn't.

With his head bowed against the wind, Preacher moved along the second wagon to the third one. This time when he climbed onto the tailgate and put his head through the flap, someone inside screamed. A childish voice yelled, "Indians!"

"No, it ain't Injuns," Preacher said. "Peter, you in here?"

In this catastrophic weather, the earlier conflicts had been forgotten. Preacher thought he heard relief in Peter Galloway's voice as the man answered, "I'm here. And all three children are with me. We're all right, Preacher."

"What about your pa?"

"What about him? He's in one of the other wagons, isn't he?"

"You ain't seen him since this blizzard started?"

Peter hesitated. "No. I don't think I have."

"You don't think so, or you're sure you ain't?"

"I'm sure," Peter said. "I got the children together and brought them in here when the storm hit, and we've been in here ever since."

The uneasy feeling inside Preacher began to grow stronger. He said, "All right. Stay here, and don't come out until the storm lets up. It'll last all night, and it might even last all day tomorrow."

"We have food," Peter told him. "We'll be all right."

Preacher nodded, even though they couldn't see him in the snow-choked darkness, and closed the flap. There was just one wagon to go, and if Simon Galloway wasn't in it, then the unavoidable conclusion was that he was out there somewhere in the storm, definitely lost and maybe already dead.

One more time, he felt his way along the wagon and came to the last one. As he paused at the tailgate, he saw a narrow strip of light coming from inside, through a gap in the canvas cover. The occupants of this wagon had managed to keep a candle going, even with the drafts that had to be blowing through there. He pulled the canvas aside, and the light flickered as the wind made the candle flame waver.

"Who—" Roger Galloway began excitedly.

"Preacher. Take it easy, folks. It's just me."

He climbed in and closed the flap behind him, and as the candle flame grew steady and bright again, he saw Roger and Angela sitting on either side of the thick pallet where Dorothy lay. Both of them were wrapped in blankets, and Angela had a bundle in her lap that had to be the baby. Preacher looked at the pale, haggard face of the woman lying on the pallet and realized he was seeing Dorothy Galloway for the first time. He had heard plenty about her during the time he had been with the wagons, of course, but until now he hadn't laid eyes on her.

There was no sign of Simon Galloway inside the wagon.

Preacher's spirits sank for a moment as he realized that. He hadn't particularly liked Simon—the man struck him as weak and lazy—but Preacher wouldn't wish freezing to death on him either. And he knew as well that he was going to have to go out in that blizzard and look for Simon. He had to at least make the attempt.

"It's good to see you, Preacher," Roger said. "We were

worried about you. I thought, though, that if anyone could make it back here once that storm hit, it would be you."

"What about your pa?"

"What about him?" Roger asked with a frown. "He's with Peter, isn't he? Or Jonathan and Geoffrey?"

Preacher shook his head. "He ain't in any of the wagons."

Angela lifted a hand to her mouth. "Oh, Dear Lord. You mean . . ." She couldn't go on.

"He's out in . . . in that?" Roger finished for her, horror in his voice and on his face.

"I reckon he must be. There ain't no other place he could be."

Roger hurriedly started to get up. "We have to find him! It may not be too late!"

That was true. Simon was probably still alive, since he wouldn't have frozen in the time that had passed since the storm hit. But he wouldn't be able to last much longer.

Preacher put a hand on Roger's shoulder and held him down. "Stay here," he grated. "I'll find him."

"But how? We . . . We can't afford to lose you, Preacher."

"You got any rope? I need as much as you can muster."

Roger nodded. "We have several coils. If we tie them all together, they'll probably stretch six or seven hundred feet."

That ought to be long enough, Preacher thought. The buffalo wallow was about a hundred yards across. Likely Simon wouldn't have gone any farther than that to stand guard. Unless, of course, he had tried to get back to the wagons when the storm hit, gotten turned around, and moved farther and farther away instead of coming closer. If that was the case, there was no telling where he could be by now.

"Stay put and tell me where the rope is." Preacher was ready to go. Waiting wouldn't make things any better.

Roger told him where to find the rope in one of the storage packs slung underneath the wagon. Preacher gave Roger and Angela a reassuring nod and then crawled out into the snow and wind once more. He found the ropes and began knotting them together. His fingers were stiff from the cold, and that, along with the gloves he wore, made the task difficult and awkward. Preacher took the necessary time, though, to make sure the ends of the ropes were knotted together securely. If they came apart while he was searching, he might be in big trouble.

Once he was satisfied, he moved around to the outside of the wagon, dragging the heavy coils of rope with him. He found an end and tied it around a wagon wheel, making sure that knot was secure too. Then he gathered the rope in his arms and started walking straight out from the wagon, paying out the makeshift lifeline as he went.

Of course, there were risks. As long as he had hold of the rope, he was confident that he could follow it back to the wagons. But if he lost it for any reason, he might not ever be able to find it again. Then too, there was no guarantee that he would find Simon Galloway by doing this. He might pass within five feet of the man and never see him. All he could do was work his way out to the end of the line, move over a little, and start back in. When he got to the wagons, he could move again and go back out. It would be a slow, tedious process . . . maybe too slow to do Simon any good.

But as far as Preacher could see, it was the only chance Simon had. He trudged ahead, buffeted by the wind, stung by the snow, hoping that once again luck would be with him.

TWENTY-EIGHT

It took Preacher a good ten minutes to walk to the end of the rope, leaning over into the wind the whole way. Keeping a firm grip on the lifeline, he faced back the way he had come, moved some ten feet to his right, and started back in, gathering up the rope as he went. The return trip went a little faster since the wind was now at his back. When he reached the wagon the rope was tied to, he turned around and started out at a different angle this time.

He was pretty sure he was checking the general vicinity where Simon had gone to stand guard. There was no way of knowing, though, how much Simon had moved around once he was out here. And Preacher's mind kept coming back to the possibility that Simon could have easily wandered off even farther after he was blinded by the blizzard.

The minutes seemed to race past, because Preacher knew that with each one that went by, the chances of him finding Simon alive were less. Out to the end of the rope, back to the wagons . . . Again and again, Preacher moved along the lifeline, back and forth, out of the buffalo wallow and then back in. He lost track of how many times he had made the trip and how long he had been here. His fingers and toes were getting numb. He knew he couldn't stay out in the blizzard for much longer, or he would risk losing them.

A fella ought to be in somewhere snug and warm on a night like this, he thought. In his own cabin maybe, with a fire roaring in the fireplace and a pretty gal to share a buffalo robe in front of that fire. A girl like Jennie . . .

He saw it plain as day in his mind's eye, the two of them snuggled together while the storm raged outside, secure in the knowledge that they were together and would never be parted. With the kids asleep up in the loft and Dog at their feet . . . Jennie had loved Dog and he had loved her, had in fact nearly lost his life trying to protect her. It sure made a pretty picture, Preacher thought. Never would happen, of course, couldn't happen because Jennie was dead, but for a moment, as Preacher trudged through the snow, he felt almost warm as he thought of it. What might have been, Lord, what might have been if only things had worked out different. . . .

Maybe he was warm because he was freezing to death, a part of his brain warned him. He had heard that was what happened just before a fella drifted off to his final sleep, the one from which he never woke up.

A moment later, he tripped over something and went to his knees in the deepening snow.

The fall made the rope slip out of his left hand. It slid in his right too, so that only two fingers were around it. He clutched desperately at it, knowing that if he let go the wind might whip the rope around so that he could never find it again. Should have tied it on to his belt, he thought wildly, but the idea hadn't occurred to him. Now that oversight might be the death of him.

His flailing left arm tangled in the rope. He grabbed on firmly with both hands and knelt there for a few seconds, letting his racing pulse slow down a little. When it had, he wrapped the rope completely around his waist and knotted it there. Then he reached out to feel around and locate whatever it was he had tripped over.

He knew what it was, of course, before he found it, or at least he was afraid he knew. And as his fingers touched something and explored it until he was sure it was a face, his guess was confirmed. He ran his hand over the man's head and felt the lack of hair on top. Simon Galloway had been mostly bald.

Preacher checked for a pulse, a heartbeat, a breath. Nothing. He even leaned down and pressed his cheek against Simon's. The flesh was cold and hard.

Preacher bit back a curse. He hadn't liked Simon Galloway, had considered the man pretty much useless most of the time. But his death still bothered Preacher, even though the mountain man knew it wasn't his fault. He had sensed that a storm was coming, but he'd had no way of knowing it would be as bad as it was. The frontier could be a harsh, unforgiving place, and Simon had been unlucky enough to bear the brunt of its fury on this night.

Simon was a good-sized man. Preacher couldn't pick him up and carry him. He had to settle for dragging the body back to the wagons. When he got there, he took it to the empty wagon, lowered the tailgate, lifted Simon enough to prop him against it, and slid the body inside. Then he untied the rope from his waist and went to tell the others.

He stopped first at the wagon where Jonathan and Geoffrey were. As he climbed in, Jonathan asked, "Preacher? Is that you?"

"It's me," Preacher said heavily. He recalled that these two didn't know he had been out searching for Simon. The last they had seen of him, he had been headed for the other wagons to check on everyone else.

He went on, "I've got bad news, fellas. Your brother n't in any of the other wagons."

"My God!" Geoffrey exclaimed. "You mean he's out in this storm somewhere?"

"We have to go look for him!" Jonathan said.

"I already did," Preacher said, "and . . . I found him."

The ominous tone in his voice told the two older men what they didn't want to know. Still, they had to ask. Geoffrey said, "Is . . . is he . . . ?"

"He's dead," Preacher confirmed. "I figure he tried to make it back to the wagons when the storm hit, got turned around, and finally couldn't go any farther."

Jonathan muttered something, and after a second Preacher figured out it was a prayer for Simon's soul.

"I brought him back in," Preacher went on. "He's in that empty wagon."

"What can we do?" Geoffrey asked, his voice thick with grief.

"Nothin', at least not tonight. Come mornin', we'll see about diggin' a grave, if the ground's not frozen too hard already."

He left them talking quietly with each other, no doubt reliving some of the good memories of their brother's life. Bypassing the wagon where Peter was staying with the young'uns, Preacher went to Roger's wagon.

He pushed the flap back a little and called softly, "Roger, come out here."

A moment later, Roger climbed out of the wagon. He was followed, to Preacher's surprise, by Angela, who clutched a blanket tightly around her.

"Ain't no need for you to be out here, ma'am," Preacher told her. "You ought to be in there watchin' over the other lady and the little one."

"They're both asleep," Angela said. "They don't need me right now. And if you have news about Simon, I want to hear it. He's my father-in-law, you know."

"Yes, ma'am, I know. And I'm mighty sorry to have to tell you—both of you—that I found him out yonder a good ways. Looks like he froze to death, so I reckon he went pretty peaceful-like and prob'ly didn't really know what was goin' on."

Angela let out a sob, and Roger flinched almost like he had been struck. "Dear Lord, is there no end to the tragedy?" he said. He put his hands over his face for a moment, then found the strength to straighten slightly and ask, "Where is he now? Were . . . were you able to bring him back?"

Preacher nodded. "Yeah, I put him in that wagon with nobody in it. I already told your uncles, but I ain't said anything to Peter. Didn't want the young'uns over-hearin' and gettin' upset any sooner than they have to."

"Thank you. I'll tell Peter." Roger took hold of Preacher's arm for a second, squeezing hard in his grief. "And thank you for . . . for finding him. I feel a little better knowing that he . . . he wasn't left out there in the storm all night."

Preacher didn't say anything. It didn't matter to Simon where he spent the rest of the night, but then, after a fella was dead, nothing mattered. All the gestures and rituals that went with death were for those who remained behind, not the one who had already crossed over the divide.

Angela said, "Come inside where it's at least a little warmer."

"I'm obliged, ma'am, but I reckon I'll go back and spend the rest of the night with Jonathan and Geoffrey. Quarters are already a mite cramped in there, and I don't want to disturb the baby."

"You're sure?"

"Yes, ma'am."

Preacher left them and felt his way back along the line of wagons. The storm hadn't eased any. The wind was blowing just as hard and the snow was just as thick as it had been earlier.

He climbed into the other wagon to find that Geoffrey and Jonathan had lit a candle too. They sat huddled over it, as if the tiny, flickering flame would ward off not only the darkness but the cold. It wasn't doing a very good job of either of those tasks.

Jonathan held out a jug as Preacher settled down beside them. "We're drinking to Simon's memory," he said. "We'd be honored if you'd join us, Preacher."

"Well, I ain't one to take a drink except ever' now and then . . . but I reckon this is a righteous time." Preacher took the jug and said, "To Simon Galloway," before lifting it to his mouth and taking a swallow of the fiery whiskey.

"To Simon," both of the older men said quietly.

It had already been a long night, Preacher thought, and it would be longer still until morning.

Jonathan and Geoffrey got roaring drunk. Preacher took a few more swigs from the jug, but for the most part he just passed it back and forth between the other two. When they weren't drinking, they were telling stories about the times when they and Simon had been kids and then young men. Preacher heard more yarns about the Galloway family than he ever wanted to hear.

They had been a pretty normal bunch, growing up in Philadelphia, the sons of a printer who had been friends with Ben Franklin, Tom Jefferson, and the other fellas who had led the colonies in their revolt against the English. Those must have been exciting times, Preacher thought. He had been born too late for the revolution, but he had taken part in the war that had finally finished it up, back in '14. Despite the fact that he had fought against them, he didn't bear any particular hatred or even dislike for the English. Like every other nationality, there were some good ones and some bad'uns.

"What did you fellas do when you grew up?" Preacher asked.

"Geoffrey and I took over the printing business," Jonathan replied. "Simon became a banker. He was the most successful one in the family. In fact, he paid for most of the wagons and supplies for this journey."

"Damn shame he didn't make it to see the end of it."

"Yes, it is," Geoffrey agreed.

"Any other brothers or sisters?" Preacher asked.

"Yes, but they're all back in Philadelphia." Jonathan laughed. "They all believe that we're insane for leaving the city and coming west. I'm afraid they don't have any adventure in their souls."

Preacher nodded. How well he understood that. He had left home at the age of twelve, determined to go out and see the world, to take care of himself and make his own way. He had been on his own ever since, his solitude broken only by occasional sojourns with friends, or with Jennie when she was still alive.

At times he suspected he would spend the rest of his life alone. That frightened him near as much as that grizz he had tangled with, back in the days when he hadn't been long in the mountains, but fate was called that for a reason. A fella chose his own path, his own way of getting there, but in the end he had a destiny to live out, and there wasn't much that could change it.

"What are you plannin' on doin' when you finally get to Oregon?"

"Well, we'll want to see Roger and Peter settled first, of course," Geoffrey replied. "They plan to have a farm . . . although, given the hard feelings between them now, they may have to have *two* farms. After that . . ."

"After that we're going to be mountain men and go exploring," Jonathan finished, eagerness in his voice.

Preacher grinned. "Mountain men, is it?"

"That's right." Jonathan frowned. "You think we can

do it, don't you? I know we're rather old to be starting out on such a career, but . . ."

"If that's what you really want to do, you'll find a way to do it," Preacher assured them. "Don't forget, I've seen you fellas in action. You handle yourselves pretty good. Just keep your eyes and ears open, and learn as much as you can."

"Just being around you seems to be an education in itself, Preacher," Geoffrey said with a smile.

Preacher chuckled, glad that they had gotten their minds on something other than grieving for their lost brother. Sorrow was a good thing in many ways, but it had to be tempered with hope.

And he was a good one to be thinking that, he told himself, considering how he had felt since Jennie's death. Had he had any hope, truly, or was he just going through the motions? The Galloways still had time to mourn Simon. Maybe it was time for him to move on, though, Preacher thought.

"You know, if y'all are gonna be mountain men, you'll need some good nicknames," he pointed out.

"What's wrong with our real names?"

"Not a thing, but out here folks tend to be a mite less formal. You don't reckon I was born with the name Preacher, do you?"

"What is your real name?" Jonathan asked.

Preacher grinned at them. "Arthur." He didn't give them his last name; he had kept that to himself ever since the night he had sneaked out of his parents' house and gone out to see the world.

"Well, that's a fine name," Geoffrey said. "Like King Arthur and his knights."

"I ain't got no fellas in armor followin' me around, though, and I'd just as soon not. The Injuns had trouble sayin' the name when I first come out here, so they called me Artoor. That is, until they started callin' me

Preacher like most ever'body else. Ever' now and then, though, I run across one of the old trappers who calls me Art."

"I think we'll stick with Preacher," Jonathan said. "What should our nicknames be?"

"Well, I'll have to think on that. It'll come to me, though, and when it does, we'll have a drink on it."

The older men nodded, and Geoffrey said, "That's a promise."

TWENTY-NINE

During his time in the Rockies and on the Great Plains, Mart Hawley had seen quite a few snowstorms and even raging blizzards. None like this one. This bastard was one for the ages.

He was glad that he and Swift Arrow had found the other two bunches of the Arikara war party and merged them back together into one group that would continue to pursue Preacher and the Galloways until vengeance was done. He was even more glad that they had come upon a small cave at the edge of the foothills before that blizzard hit. If they had been out in the open, with no shelter at all, they wouldn't have stood a chance.

Hawley's back still hurt like blazes where the tomahawk had lodged in it. Swift Arrow had given one of the members of the war party, a young brave called Corn Man, the job of caring for Hawley's wound. Corn Man didn't speak any English, or if he did he was keeping it to himself. He was surly too, and Hawley could tell that he hated whites. Still, Corn Man's respect for—and fear of—Swift Arrow was enough to insure that he followed orders. He had cleaned the wound and bound it up again when the blizzard forced them to halt, and now Hawley leaned against the wall of the cave with his right shoulder and felt drowsiness stealing over him. The Injuns had built a fire out of buffalo chips and a little wood, and enough of the heat it gave off was trapped in the cave to make the temperature bearable. It was still cold enough so that Hawley was grateful for the buffalo robe, though.

Swift Arrow came over to him and hunkered down to talk to him. "Where whites go?" he asked.

"Well, it's obvious that kid lied to us, or at least made us think he was lyin' on purpose," Hawley replied. "Tricky little bastard. The wagons didn't head south. They're still hittin' east, I reckon, makin' for Garvey's Fort. They won't be goin' anywhere in this blizzard, though."

Swift Arrow grunted. "Sahnish not travel in blizzard either. Whites freeze to death?"

"Hard to say," Hawley answered with a shrug. "They're bound to be a good ways out on the plains by now, and if they don't have any shelter 'cept those wagons, they might be in a bad fix. You got to be ready, Chief, for the possibility they might be dead already when we catch up to 'em."

"What good you be then?" Swift Arrow asked, and Hawley thought he saw cruel amusement glinting in the war chief's eyes.

"I been a friend to your people, ain't I? I done ever'thing I could to help you get your vengeance on that bunch. It ain't my fault things ain't worked out so far."

Swift Arrow didn't say anything, just regarded Hawley intently, as if trying to figure out what to do with him.

Hawley swallowed and went on. "Anyway, I didn't have nothin' to do with whatever it is that's got you folks so het up. You don't have any score to settle with me. 'Twouldn't be honorable to do me any harm."

Swift Arrow's hand shot out and gripped Hawley's injured shoulder. The war chief's lip curled in a snarl as he twisted Hawley's shoulder and brought a cry of pain from the trapper. The other Indians ignored the cry.

"Speak not of honor," Swift Arrow growled. "Your skin is white. You know nothing of honor."

"I . . . I didn't mean nothin' by it," Hawley gasped, blinking as tears began to roll down his cheeks into his beard. "I just meant that I'm your friend, and I want to stay your friend!"

Swift Arrow brought his face close to Hawley's. "You know why Sahnish kill whites?"

Hawley managed to shake his head mutely.

"Whites kill young Sahnish brave. Go hunting, never come back. Days go by. We look, find young warrior, killed by white man's rifle. Follow tracks that lead to wagons. Wagons that went by Sahnish village days before."

"I'm sorry," Hawley said, still struggling to control his pain. "Did they shoot him for no reason?"

"No reason to kill," Swift Arrow agreed. "Not painted for war."

"Reckon whoever killed him must not have known anything about that. Those greenhorns are pretty dumb, Chief. They really thought they could get across the mountains to Oregon at this time of year."

Swift Arrow shook his head at the sheer stupidity of that idea. Finally, he let go of Hawley's shoulder and allowed him to slump back against the rock wall of the cave. Hawley sighed in relief as the pain subsided a little.

"Who was the young fella who got shot?" he asked as an afterthought.

"Name Cloud Seeker." The war chief's face was as stony as the wall of the cave. "Was son of Swift Arrow."

When Preacher climbed out of the back of the wagon the next morning, he stepped down into more than two feet of snow. The stuff immediately worked its way into his high-topped moccasins and made his feet even colder.

The wind had died down some, but it was still blowing and snow still fell thickly from the leaden sky. It was impossible to tell for sure what the time was, but the sun was up; enough light made it through the snowstorm for Preacher to know that. He felt like the hour was pretty early.

Behind him in the wagon, both Jonathan and Geoffrey snored loudly. They had dozed off into a drunken slumber far into the night. Preacher had slept too, rolled in a couple of blankets. Eventually the cold and the racket had roused him.

He wasn't that worried about the Arikara war party right now, he thought as he took a look around the camp. Chances were, the Indians were holed up somewhere, probably back in the foothills. They didn't have even the meager shelter of covered wagons; if they had been out on the plains when the storm hit, they might be done for. That would certainly simplify matters, although Preacher wasn't sure he would wish such a fate even on his enemies.

The mules and the horses were all still alive, having huddled together for warmth during the long, cold night. They were pressed up against the wagon where Simon Galloway's body lay. Preacher moved outside the circle and headed on around to check on the people in the other wagons.

Peter Galloway climbed out in response to Preacher's soft-voiced call. The man's teeth chattered as he rubbed his hands wearily over his reddened face. "The children are all right," he said in reply to Preacher's question. "Cold, of course. Can we build a fire?"

Preacher nodded. "We'll clear off a space and build a shelter, and then we'll get a fire goin'. That'll make everybody feel a mite better." He paused for a moment, then said, "I reckon your brother told you . . . ?"

"About our father?" Peter nodded. "He did. Thank you for going out and finding him. Knowing that he's not lost out there is scant comfort, but it's better than nothing."

"You and Roger ain't gonna go to whalin' on each other again, are you?"

"I'm sure I deserve it," Peter said stonily, "but I think we've called a truce, at least for the moment. In a situation like this, we can't be trying to kill each other."

"That's the damned truth. Let me check on everybody else, and then I'll get started on that fire."

"Let me know if you need any help," Peter offered.

Preacher went on to the remaining wagon, pulled the canvas flap aside a little, and said quietly, "Roger? You awake?"

A moment later, Angela's face appeared at the opening as she answered the summons. "Roger's asleep," she whispered. "Do you need me to wake him?"

Preacher shook his head. "Nope. Just checkin' to see how everybody's doin' this mornin'."

Angela didn't say anything, but she pulled the flap back farther and slid out of the wagon. She stepped over the tailgate and held out a hand to Preacher. He instinctively took it and helped her leap lightly down into the snow. She wore a hooded coat and had a blanket wrapped around her in addition to that. A scarf muffled her throat and the lower part of her face.

"It snowed every winter in Philadelphia, of course," she said, "but it's been a long time since I've seen this much on the ground. And it's still coming down."

"May be four or five feet 'fore it's over," Preacher said.

"How can we travel in that?"

He shook his head. "We can't. We'd be stuck here until some of it melted or blew off. The wagons can manage about three feet, but that's all."

"Then if it snows the rest of the day and on into the night . . ."

"We likely won't be goin' anywhere for a week or more."

Angela frowned. "We have enough food. I suppose we could wait it out if we had to. But what about those Indians?"

"They'll be pinned down too, but they'll probably be able to move again quicker'n we will. So we better hope that we ain't stuck."

"There's no chance that they might just . . . give up? Go home because of the weather?"

Again Preacher shook his head. "It's hard to tell what a Injun will take a notion to do, but as stubborn as this bunch has been so far, I don't reckon they'll give up. They want blood too bad."

"Killing all of us won't bring back that young man, or any of the men they lost when they attacked us the first time."

"No, ma'am, it sure won't, and they know it. But that won't stop 'em from liftin' all our scalps if they get a chance to do it."

Angela shuddered. "I . . . I just don't understand how anyone can be so savage, so heartless." She glanced at the wagon where her husband was. "But then, there are a lot of things in life that I just don't understand," she added meaningfully.

"Yes'm, you and me both." To change the subject, Preacher asked, "How's the mama and the baby this mornin'?"

"John Edward is all right, though I don't think he's getting enough to eat. Dorothy is very low. I . . . I don't think she's going to last much longer."

"That's a terrible shame," Preacher said. "Things betwixt her and Roger, did they ever get worked out?"

With sadness on her face, Angela said, "Dorothy was lucid for a time during the night. She and Roger were able to talk for a while. I . . . I tried not to eavesdrop, but

I couldn't help overhearing some of what they said. She begged for his forgiveness, and he gave it. He wanted to know if Peter attacked her, and while she wouldn't admit that, wouldn't blame him for what happened, I'm sure that none of it was Dorothy's idea, even if she did cooperate and he didn't have to rape her."

That was her husband she was talking about, Preacher reminded himself, and it was remarkable that she could stand there and say such things in such a calm, strong voice. The whole messy business had to be tearing her up inside too, but as long as the others needed her, she wasn't going to give in to what she was feeling, wasn't even going to show her pain.

In some ways, he supposed it had simplified things that the one woman he had ever loved was a prostitute. He had been young and inexperienced enough when he first met Jennie that he didn't fully understand what was going on in the back of that wagon owned by the man who had taken her in, but he had caught on quickly enough. It might have bothered some fellas to be in love with a whore, even a reluctant one, but for Preacher, that was just the way things had always been. Jealousy never really entered his mind.

"Well, it's good that they settled things," Preacher said now, referring to Roger and Dorothy. "Might make things easier . . . later on."

Angela nodded in solemn agreement.

"I'm gonna clear some ground, get a shelter up, and build a fire," he went on. "We can have some hot coffee and food in a while."

"That will be wonderful." Angela hesitated. "What about Simon?"

"It's cold enough the body'll keep," Preacher said. "I ain't tryin' to be callous about it, just practical. When the weather gets a mite better, we'll get a grave dug and say some words over him 'fore we move on. That's the best we can do."

"Yes, I suppose you're right. I just wish—"

Preacher never found out what she wished, because at that moment, a ragged cry came from inside the wagon. "Dorothy!" Roger Galloway wailed. "Oh, my God, no! Dorothy!"

And Preacher knew that before they left this place, they would have two graves to dig.

THIRTY

Dorothy's eyes were open but lifeless. Her face was so pale it seemed to have been completely drained of blood. Her lips were blue.

"She was still bleedin' inside somewhere most likely," Preacher told Jonathan. The older man had climbed into the wagon to help him with the body. Roger and Angela were back in the other wagon with Geoffrey. They had taken the baby with them, of course. Preacher wasn't sure how they were going to continue feeding the infant with Dorothy gone. Preacher was not optimistic about the poor baby's chances of survival.

"It never should have come to this," Jonathan said bitterly. "She was a good woman, and she shouldn't have died this way."

"Can't argue with that."

"If only Roger and Peter and Simon hadn't pushed so hard to leave Philadelphia. We could have waited until next spring, but no, they had to start. There couldn't be any delays. They were just too . . . too anxious to get to the Promised Land. But like Moses, Simon will never enter it. He won't even see it."

Preacher wouldn't have compared Simon Galloway to Moses, but he knew what Jonathan meant. "Best get on with the job at hand," he said. "Let's wrap this blanket around her nice and snug."

With Dorothy no longer needing all the blankets and quilts that had been around her for warmth, the two men used only one blanket as her shroud. They wrapped the body securely, and Preacher tied the blanket in place with several lengths of cord. Then they picked up the body, Preacher at the head and Jonathan at the feet, and carried it out of the wagon.

It took them only a few minutes to place Dorothy in the other wagon with the body of her father-in-law. With that unpleasant task accomplished, Preacher got to work on the chore that he had hoped to have done by now, getting a shelter built and a fire burning.

Using a shovel from the farm tools stored in one of the wagons, Preacher cleared the snow as best he could from an eight-foot-wide circle and then angled some stakes in the ground, tying them together at the top. He used a couple of pieces of canvas to rig a makeshift tepee on the framework. It was crude but it would work. The canvas would protect the fire from the wind and snow, and the opening at the top would let the smoke out. If everyone crowded inside, it might even be halfway warm. Since it looked like they might be here for several days, they needed something like this in order to survive.

He dug buffalo chips out of the pile the young'uns had made, shook the snow off them, and carried them into the tepee. A few minutes of diligent work with flint, steel, and tinder got a tiny fire started. Preacher leaned over and blew on the flames until he was confident they wouldn't go out. He held his hands above the fire for a moment, enjoying even the little bit of warmth that the flames gave off.

Jonathan stuck his head in through the opening where the pieces of canvas came together. He said, "I've got the coffeepot and the frying pan and our supplies. If you'll move over, Preacher, I'll get to work on breakfast."

"Sounds mighty fine to me," Preacher said with a nod.

"I'll go take a look around, just to make sure there ain't nobody tryin' to sneak up on us."

With Dog at his side, Preacher trudged up the slope and out of the buffalo wallow. Although visibility was much better than it had been the night before, the snow was still swirling and blowing enough so that Preacher couldn't see very far. He made a complete circle around the camp, knowing he had gotten back to the place where he had started because he could still see the path he had broken through the deep snow. The tracks might fill up if the snow continued coming down, but it would take quite a while. Not having seen anything threatening other than the weather itself, he went back down to the wagons and inside the circle. He caught a brief whiff of coffee brewing, and the aroma made his mouth water. He went to the tepee and bent over to step inside quickly, so as not to let out warm air and let in cold.

He found Jonathan, Geoffrey, and the two younger children sitting by the fire. Mary looked up at him and said, "Good morning, Mr. Preacher. This is just like an Indian's house, isn't it?"

Preacher hunkered on his heels next to her. "It sure is, little missy. They build 'em a mite better than I do, but I reckon we can get by with this'un."

The youngsters wore solemn expressions, and Preacher figured they had heard about their Aunt Dorothy's passing. He said quietly to Geoffrey, "Where's everybody else?"

"Roger and Angela and Nate and the baby are in our wagon," Geoffrey replied. "I'm not sure where Peter is."

Preacher felt a faint stirring of alarm. "He wouldn't wander off in this storm, would he?"

"I'm pretty sure he's in his wagon brooding. Don't worry about Peter; he's prone to doing foolish things, but not anything that will hurt him directly." Geoffrey spoke quietly, and the children didn't seem to be paying any attention to him. Preacher was glad of that, since Geoffrey was talking about their father. As sorry a human being as Peter Galloway was, Preacher didn't believe in talkin' down a man in front of his kids.

Jonathan had bacon frying and some left-over biscuits warming, and the coffee was ready. When the food was done, Preacher ate sparingly. These pilgrims might believe they had plenty of food, but Preacher knew first-hand how quickly supplies could disappear, especially when a trip took longer than anyone thought it would. He didn't want them to run out of rations before they got back to Garvey's Fort. He poured himself a full cup of coffee, though, and savored it.

The others had eaten by the time he swallowed the last of the strong, black brew. "Stay here," he told them. "I'll go let the others know breakfast is ready."

"Is there room in here for everyone?" Geoffrey asked.

"It'll be a mite cramped, but I reckon ever'body can squeeze in. Be warmer that way too." Preacher just hoped there wouldn't be any more ruckuses between Roger and Peter. Peter had promised that they would get along, but Preacher wasn't convinced of it yet.

He walked across the camp to the wagon where Roger, Angela, Nate, and the baby were and stepped up at the back of it to put his head through the flap. "Mornin', folks," he said, keeping his voice pleasant but not cheery. These people were bereaved, after all. Roger had lost a wife, Nate and John Edward a mother, and Angela a sister-in-law. "There's food and coffee, if anybody wants any. And I'd recommend that you eat. We all got to keep our strength up."

Angela sat on one of the bunks built into the side of the wagon, cradling the blanket-wrapped infant in her lap. Roger and Nate were on the other bunk. Roger had an arm around his son's shoulders. Preacher almost thought of Nate as Roger's older son, then reminded himself that Roger wasn't really John Edward's father.

It might be best all around if Roger *did* regard himself as the baby's pa. John Edward could be raised that way and might not ever have to know the difference. Preacher didn't pretend to be an expert on such things, though. He knew about huntin' and trappin' and trackin' and fightin', and everything else that went with staying alive on the frontier. He had explored places where no white man had ever set foot. But like most folks, the human heart was still largely uncharted territory to him.

"I don't think anyone is very hungry right now," Angela said. She smiled sadly. "Except for this little fellow here." The baby squirmed a little in her lap and made tiny crying noises.

"Better eat anyway. Won't do nobody any good to starve, and it might even make y'all feel a mite better."

"My mama is dead, Preacher," Nate said dully. "How can I feel better?"

"Well, now . . . did you ever fall down when you was runnin' and scrape your knee or bust your shin against somethin'?"

"Yeah. I guess I did."

"Whenever that happened, I'll just bet you your ma tried to make it not hurt quite as much, didn't she?"

Nate hesitated but finally said, "Yeah."

"Then I reckon she'd prob'ly like it if you didn't hurt quite so much now, wouldn't she? It'd make her happy if you weren't so sad?"

"Maybe," Nate said. "I never really thought about it like that."

"Well, you ponder it, and if you want some bacon and biscuits whilst you're ponderin', just come on over."

"Thank you, Preacher," Roger said in a voice choked with emotion. "I think we'll do that. Won't we, Nate?"

"Sure, Pa. If you say so."

Preacher looked at Angela. "Be warmer on you and the babe in the shelter I made too."

She nodded, and there was gratitude in her eyes for more than the offer of food and coffee. "Let's all go," she said to Roger. "Just let me wrap up the baby a little better. . . ."

A short time later, they had joined the group already inside the tepee. Dog was in there too, lying between Mary and Brad, enjoying the petting they were doing. There was a time when he'd been too touchy to let himself be loved on like that, Preacher thought. The big, wolflike creature was getting more tolerant as he got older.

That left Peter as the only one who wasn't in the tepee. Preacher figured he ought to go get him. That might make things a bit tenser, but they didn't need anybody else freezing to death right now.

Preacher tromped through the snow to Peter's wagon and thumped a fist on the tailgate. "Come get some breakfast!" he called. "Coffee and bacon—good for what ails ye!"

There was no response from inside the wagon.

"Galloway!" Preacher called. "You hear me?"

When there was still nothing but silence, Preacher frowned. Earlier, Jonathan and Geoffrey had said that Peter wouldn't wander off in the storm or do anything else to hurt himself, but Preacher wasn't so sure of that. If the man had even an ounce of humanity left in him, he had to be feeling pretty damned bad right now about everything that had happened. He hadn't put a pistol to his head—Preacher would have heard the shot—but there were other ways for a fella to end his own life if he was determined enough to do so.

Muttering under his breath, Preacher pulled himself up, stepped over the tailgate, and pushed into the wagon. It was very dim inside, and he couldn't see well.

He could smell, though, and the reek of raw whiskey hit his nostrils. His foot bumped something lying on the floor of the wagon bed, and when he knelt and reached out, he put a hand on Peter's shoulder. The man groaned when Preacher shook him.

Dead drunk, Preacher thought. And if he stayed here like this, maybe just plain dead. The temperature was still below freezing, and Preacher had heard that cold weather was even harder on a fella when he was full of rotgut.

"Come on, damn it," Preacher said as he slipped an arm around Peter's shoulders and rolled him onto his back. "We better get you by the fire so's you can thaw out."

Peter was a big, muscular man. It took some effort for Preacher to get him onto his feet and wrestle him out of the wagon. Peter was only half-conscious, and he fell when Preacher tried to guide him over the tailgate. He plunged down into the thick snow, which cushioned his fall. He came up sputtering and pawing at the snow that covered his face. The cold had shocked at least some of the drunkenness out of his system.

"What . . . what the hell—"

Preacher grabbed his arm and swung him toward the tepee. "We're gonna get some black coffee in you."

"Let go of me, damn you!" With that, Peter swung a wild, shaky punch at Preacher. The mountain man easily avoided the blow and gave Peter a shove that sent him stumbling several feet away. Preacher expected him to fall, but somehow Peter managed to remain on his feet.

"Listen to me," Preacher grated, and his voice was low and dangerous. "I know you been in there guzzlin' Who-hit-John all night 'cause you feel sorry for yourself. But I reckon you're the only one who feels sorry for you. I sure as hell don't. And if you swing at me again, I'll bust you, sure as shootin'."

"I'm not . . . not afraid . . . of you," Peter said thickly.

"You damn well better be."

After a moment, Peter shook his head gingerly, mumbled a curse or two, and wiped the back of a gloved hand across his mouth. "You said something about . . . coffee?"

"Come on. And you best behave when you get in there. The mood ever'body's in, if you cause any trouble they're liable to line up to thump you." Preacher added grimly, "And I ain't gonna stop 'em neither."

THIRTY-ONE

It stopped snowing about the middle of the afternoon, but the sky remained thick with clouds. When Preacher stepped out of the tepee and regarded the heavens through squinted eyes, he couldn't tell if the snow was really finished or just holding up for a while. He hoped the storm was over. There were some three feet of snow on the ground. He thought the mule teams and the wagons could negotiate that much, if they avoided the deeper drifts. With any luck, they might be able to pull out early the next morning.

He took up the shovel he had used to clear the ground where the tepee now stood and said, "Come on, Dog." Together they walked up the slope to the edge of the buffalo wallow. Before he stepped out onto the prairie, he took a good look around. The thick white carpet of snow would make it easy to see anyone who was coming toward the camp. Preacher didn't spot any movement anywhere in the vast sweep of the plains.

He found a spot where the wind had scoured some of the snow off the ground, leaving only a thin covering. The shovel had a difficult time biting into the dirt when he began to dig, but the ground wasn't frozen so hard yet that it was impossible. He had been working at it a while, enough so that he was starting to feel a mite warm in his buckskins and heavy coat, when footsteps came crunching through the snow behind him.

"Let me help," Peter said. When Preacher turned to face him, he was holding out his hand for the shovel.

Preacher grunted and handed over the tool. Peter took it and began to dig. He went at it hard and fast, his breath fogging thickly in front of his face. After standing by and watching for a few minutes, Preacher said, "That ain't gonna change anything."

Peter paused and looked up at him, breathing heavily. "What?"

"No matter how hard you dig, it won't change what you did. And it won't bring back your sister-in-law or your pa."

Peter gave him a surly glare. "I'm just trying to help."

"And I appreciate the help. I'm just tellin' you not to think it means more than it really does . . . 'cause it don't."

Peter stared at him for a long moment, then finally said, "You're a hard man, aren't you, Preacher? Your heart's as cold as all this snow."

"I've stayed alive this long and aim to stay alive a while longer. And I don't really give a damn what you think of me."

Peter drove the shovel into the ground with a grating sound. "The feeling is mutual."

He went back to his digging. A few minutes later, Preacher saw another figure trudging up from the center of the buffalo wallow. As the man came closer, Preacher recognized him as Jonathan Galloway.

"I thought I'd come lend a hand," Jonathan said as he walked up to the other two men.

Peter stepped out of the shallow hole and handed the shovel to his uncle. "Don't work too hard at it," he advised, "or Preacher will insult you."

Jonathan frowned in confusion but didn't press the

matter. He turned to Preacher and said, "Roger told me he thinks it would be all right to dig one grave for both Simon and Dorothy. They got along well enough in life, he said, that they can stand to be buried together."

Preacher nodded. That was the practical thing to do, of course. He was glad Roger had suggested it, though, so he hadn't been forced to.

Jonathan worked on the grave for a while, but being older, he tired more easily. Preacher took the shovel back from him and went to town with it. The ground was softer the lower he dug, and the work went fairly quickly. By the time the light was beginning to dim, he had a big enough hole to do the job.

Peter had already gone back to the wagons, but Jonathan was still there, keeping Preacher company while the mountain man completed the grim task. As Preacher stepped up out of the grave, Jonathan said, "I'll go tell the others we're ready."

Preacher nodded. There was no point in putting it off. Now that the grave was dug, it would be better to go ahead and get it over with.

He followed Jonathan down to the camp and found Peter sitting alone in his wagon, rather than in the tepee with the others. "Come on," Preacher told him. "You and me'll take the bodies up there."

"Why me?" Peter asked, still surly from the earlier confrontation.

"Because you're the strongest of the bunch next to me. Besides, I'll be damned if I'm gonna make your brother carry his own wife's body."

"Don't you have any feelings?" Peter choked out. "I . . . I loved her too, you know."

"You keep your trap shut about that," Preacher warned. "Take your hat off when the words are bein' said over 'em and look sad all you want, but don't you say a damned word."

Peter glowered at him for a moment, then shrugged. "I'm not going to waste my breath arguing with you."

"Good."

They went to the wagon where the bodies lay and one at a time carried the blanket-shrouded figures up the slope to the grave. They took Simon Galloway first and then returned for Dorothy, and as they brought her to her final resting place, the others left the tepee and walked slowly and solemnly behind them. Angela held the hands of her children, while Roger carried the baby and Nate walked alongside him. Jonathan and Geoffrey brought up the rear of the gloomy procession, at least as far as the humans were concerned. Dog padded along through the snow behind them.

The grave was wide enough so that Simon and Dorothy could lie side by side. Simon was on the left, Dorothy on the right. The mourners gathered around the grave. Despite the cold, the men removed their hats.

"I'm now the oldest one in the family," Geoffrey began, "so I'll begin. We've come here to lay to rest these two fine people. Simon Bartholomew Galloway was brother, father, and grandfather to us, and we loved him very much. He was a kind man, a hard-working man."

Preacher thought Geoffrey was being a mite generous, based on what he had seen of Simon Galloway, but hell, the man was talking about his brother after all. It was understandable.

"And Dorothy Elizabeth Corrigan Galloway was a fine, loving woman, a dear wife to Roger, a devoted mother to Nathan and John Edward. So devoted to her children that she gave her own life to bring the newest member of the Galloway family into the world. She will be deeply missed." Geoffrey looked around. "If anyone else would care to say a few words . . ."

Preacher meant no disrespect, but his mind wandered some as Jonathan, Roger, and Angela all spoke glowing,

emotional tributes to the two people who had passed on.
He had buried quite a few friends over the years, and beyond a simple prayer, not much had been said at those
services. The frontier taught those who dared to live
there how to be practical and efficient in all things, including their ceremonies. Also, he was standing so that
he could keep an eye on the country to the west, because
that was where the pursuing Arikara war party would
come from. He watched for any sign of movement now
that the storm was over. It wouldn't surprise him a bit if
the Injuns were already on the move again, coming after
the wagon train they had tracked halfway across the
plains, into the mountains, and back out again. He
didn't see anything moving against the snow, however,
except a distant animal that his keen eyes identified as
an antelope. He found himself wishing the creature
would come within rifle range. Some antelope steaks
fried over the fire would be mighty good tonight.

He lowered his head and closed his eyes as he realized
that Geoffrey was praying, commending the souls of the
departed to the Lord, asking that He welcome them into
heaven. If they were going to get there, Preacher
thought, they were already there, having ascended the
Starry Path to Man Above, as the Indians put it. Preacher
knew he would take that Starry Path himself one of these
days, even though he was still relatively young, and the
prospect didn't worry him overmuch. He had already
crossed the earthly divide several times; when he finally
crossed the heavenly one, it would be just one more new
country to explore.

"Amen," Geoffrey said, and everyone murmured,
"Amen." Peter had done as Preacher told him and remained silent throughout the service. Now he remained
behind with Preacher as the others turned and walked
back down the slope to the camp. Out of consideration
for them, Preacher waited until they had gone into the

tepee before he picked up the shovel and went to work filling in the grave. Those folks didn't need to hear the thud of earth falling onto the blanket-wrapped forms.

"I'll help," Peter said after a few minutes. Just as he had earlier, he reached out for the shovel.

Preacher gave it to him and stepped back. As Peter tossed shovels of dirt into the hole, he went on. "You think I'm one sorry son of a bitch, don't you?"

Preacher's silence spoke volumes.

"Well, you don't understand," Peter grated as he pushed the shovel into the mound of earth beside the grave. "You can't understand what it's been like. You don't know everything that's happened."

"The Injuns have a sayin' about walkin' a while in the other fella's moccasins," Preacher said. "I reckon that's pretty hard to do, though. Why do you care whether or not I understand you, Galloway?"

"I don't," Peter snapped. "I'm just telling you not to be so damned high-and-mighty. If you were in the same position I was in, you'd probably do the same thing I did."

"I don't reckon."

"But you don't *know*. Nobody knows what they'll do until they're faced with a situation. You may believe you'd handle it a certain way, but you could be wrong."

"This conversation ain't gettin' us nowhere." Preacher stepped forward. "Gimme that shovel."

He took it and resumed filling in the grave. Peter moved back. A humorless laugh came from him.

"You know I'm right," he said. "You know it, Preacher. You just don't want to admit that you're fallible too. You try to act like you're not human, but you are. You make mistakes just like everyone else."

Preacher stopped his work and faced the other man. "Sure, I make mistakes," he admitted. "Make 'em all the time more'n likely. The difference 'tween you and me is that I don't try to excuse mine away or blame 'em on other folks. I own up to what I've done."

"Always?" Peter asked mockingly. "You didn't come to me and apologize after you looked at my wife with lust in your eyes."

Preacher's hands tightened on the shovel. "Miss Angela's a fine woman," he said. "I wouldn't never dishonor the friendship she's showed me."

"That didn't stop you from wanting her. Would you like to know what she's like in bed, Preacher? How it feels to have her under you—"

Preacher took a step toward him and drew back the shovel. "Shut your filthy mouth," he warned, "or by God I'll bash that head o' yours in!"

Peter laughed again. "Go ahead. Put me out of my misery. You'll just have to dig another grave."

Slowly, Preacher lowered the shovel. He glanced toward the camp, hoping that none of the others had seen him threaten Peter. No one was in sight. He supposed they were all still inside the tepee. Even if someone had been out and about, it was getting dark, and they might not be able to see very well up here where the grave was.

"I'll finish this," he said. "You go on down."

"Suit yourself." Peter turned and stalked toward the wagons.

Preacher stood there for a moment, leaning on the shovel as he tried to get control of the anger roiling around inside him. When his pulse wasn't thudding quite so hard in his head, he went back to work and finished filling in the grave. He patted down the rest of the dirt and then stepped back.

Pausing before leaving, he took off his hat and said, "I didn't say nothin' before, I reckon because I never knew you hardly at all, ma'am . . . and Galloway, I knew you but didn't much like you. Still and all, none o' that really matters now. We walk our paths in life, and we walk our paths in death. Here's hopin' that y'all's have led you home."

He put his hat back on and started down the hill carrying the shovel, not looking back.

He was only about halfway to the camp when he heard the loud, angry voices and knew that the trouble wasn't over yet.

Somehow, that didn't surprise him at all.

THIRTY-TWO

When Preacher stepped over one of the wagon tongues into the circle, he saw that the argument had spilled out of the tepee into the open. Roger and Peter stood facing each other, fists clenched, faces red with anger.

"I won't allow it!" Roger declared. "I'll be damned first!"

"You don't have any say in the matter!" Peter shot back.

"The hell I don't! He's my son!"

Peter shook his head and said, "No, he's not, and you know it."

Angela came running from the tepee and got between the two men. "Stop it!" she cried. "Have you two no decency? Simon and poor Dorothy are barely in the grave, and you're ready to kill each other again!"

"No one is taking my son away from me," Roger said, his voice shaking with emotion. "Least of all *him*." Undisguised loathing dripped from the words.

"John Edward is my son, and you know it," Peter said. "You heard Dorothy admit it. Since I'm his father, I have a right to raise him as I see fit."

Angela swung toward him, her previous role as would-be peacemaker forgotten for the moment. "What about me?" she asked. "Don't I have any say in this?"

"No," Peter said flatly. "You don't."

"That baby will be raised believing that I am his father," Roger insisted. "It's only right and proper."

"It's neither of those things. You know you can't keep such a secret from him forever. Too many people know about this, Roger." Peter adopted a more reasonable tone. "Wouldn't it be better and easier for John Edward if he knew the truth all along?"

"Never!" Roger practically spat at him. "He'll never be your son!"

"Then go to hell!" Peter shouted as he shoved Angela aside and launched a punch at his brother's head.

Angela cried out as she stumbled, tripped, and fell into the snow. Roger ducked the blow and grappled with Peter. They swayed back and forth for a second, clawing at each other's throat, before Preacher reached them. He grabbed each of them by the coat collar and flung them in opposite directions, his great strength sending them flying through the air. They crashed to the ground and skidded in the deep snow.

Preacher reached to his waist and grasped both pistols. He brought them out and leveled them at Roger and Peter, earing back the hammers as he did so.

"No!" Angela screamed from the ground.

"Preacher, wait!" Jonathan called from the tepee, where he and Geoffrey had just pushed out through the gap in the canvas cover.

"Don't shoot them!" Geoffrey added.

Preacher stood there for a moment, then growled a curse and lowered the hammers on the pistols. "I wasn't goin' to shoot 'em," he said, "though I was sore tempted there for a spell." One at a time, he tucked the weapons back behind his belt. "You two get up," he snapped at the men on the ground. "What's all this about?"

Roger and Peter climbed to their feet and started brushing snow off their clothes. "He says he's going to take John Edward away from me," Roger said, nodding to Peter.

"Yeah, I reckon I got that." Preacher turned to Peter. "What ever gave you that idea?"

"He's my son," Peter insisted. "I have a right to raise him."

"His mama should have had a say in that."

"His mother is dead," Peter said flatly. "The decision is mine to make. Legally—"

"Now there's an idea you got to get out o' your head," Preacher cut in. "The nearest court is one hell of a long way from here, and the only judges who got any jurisdiction west o' the Mississippi are cold steel and hot lead. The only law is what's right, and you got to enforce it yourself."

"That's what I was trying to do."

Preacher turned back to Roger. "You want that boy, don't you?"

Roger wiped his mouth and said, "I . . . Yes, I do. He's part of Dorothy, and God help me, I love him, just like I loved her. I never stopped loving her."

Preacher looked at Jonathan and Geoffrey. Behind them, the three older children were peeking out of the tepee, curious about what was going on but at the same time scared to see all the grown-ups so upset. "What do you fellas think about this?" Preacher asked the two older men.

They looked uncomfortable at being caught in the middle of the dispute. Jonathan said reluctantly, "It seems to me that a child ought to have both a mother and a father. I know Roger means well by saying he'll raise the boy, but . . ."

"But if Peter and Angela raise him," Geoffrey said, "he'll have two parents—"

"Wait a minute," Angela interrupted. "You're assuming that Peter and I are going to stay married."

"What?" Peter exclaimed, thunderstruck by the implications of her statement.

She looked coolly at him. "I'm not sure I intend to remain married to you, Peter."

He gave a harsh laugh and said, "You can forget about that. You heard what Preacher said. There are no courts out here, which means there are no divorces. Such a thing is practically unheard of anyway. Why, it . . . it's unholy! A marriage is sacred and forever."

Angela crossed her arms over her chest and took a deep breath. "Yes," she said. "I can go in there and look at that poor baby, and see for myself just how sacred marriage is to you, Peter."

He didn't have anything to say to that.

Night had fallen while the argument was going on. Preacher said, "We ain't goin' to settle anything tonight, I don't reckon. And if it don't snow no more tonight, then first thing in the mornin' we'll be pullin' out, so there won't be time to fuss about it then. Seems to me that right now, we're all sort o' responsible for takin' care o' that baby, so let's just leave it at that."

"That's the best idea I've heard," Jonathan declared.

"I agree," Geoffrey put in. "We'll sort it all out later."

Preacher looked back and forth between Roger and Peter. "What do you say?"

"All right," Roger said grudgingly. "I'll never give up my son, though."

"We'll see," Peter said. "This isn't over yet."

Preacher was beginning to wonder if it ever would be.

Far into the night, the clouds began to thin, with stars peeking through the gaps. As the overcast broke even more, the moon appeared and showered silvery light that was reflected and made brighter by the snowfield.

In fact, it was almost as light as the past couple of days had been.

That's what Mart Hawley thought as he trudged along in the wake of the Indians. Swift Arrow was in the lead, tirelessly breaking a trail through the snow for the others. The war chief drew strength from his hatred and his thirst for vengeance on the whites.

Swift Arrow had gotten them moving again when the clouds began to break. Hawley hadn't wanted to leave the warm, dry cave, but Swift Arrow had made it plain that his choices were either going along with the war party or staying there with his throat cut. Hawley hadn't taken very long to make up his mind. He knew he was lucky that Swift Arrow had left him alive to start with. The Arikara didn't really need him, although it was possible they might be able to make use of him in a trap for the immigrants, if it came down to that.

The deep snow made it impossible to find any tracks left behind by the wagons, so Swift Arrow was steering his course by the stars and heading as much due east as possible. He thought they would be able to see the wagons against the snow if they passed anywhere within a couple of miles of them. Hawley figured that was pretty likely. And by starting out while it was still dark, they had a chance to cut down considerably on the lead that the pilgrims had. The snow hadn't stopped until mid-afternoon, and Hawley thought it was likely that wherever the Galloway party had waited out the storm, they wouldn't get moving again until morning. They might not leave even then; the snow could be too deep for the wagons.

The two dozen Arikara warriors strung out behind Swift Arrow, with Hawley bringing up the rear. His wounded shoulder ached, and he was cold, clean through. Walking in deep snow wore a man out about as quick as anything. It would have been better if they'd had snowshoes, but the war party hadn't expected to be away from their village this long and that was one thing they hadn't brought with them. They were running a little low on rations too. They wouldn't starve—they were Injuns after all, and able to live off the land where a normal man couldn't—but they were liable to be pretty thin and hungry by the time they got back home.

Hawley slowed down more and more and fell farther and farther behind the others. He began to wonder what would happen if he lagged far enough behind that the Indians forgot about him. Could he just stop and let them go on without him? Surely, sooner or later Swift Arrow would notice that he was gone. The question was whether or not the war chief would take the time to turn around and come back after him. The more Hawley thought about it, the more he doubted whether that would happen. Chances were, Swift Arrow would just keep going.

Hawley's mouth stretched in a thin smile under the muffler that was wrapped around his neck and the lower half of his face. He slowed down some more. The nearest Arikara warrior was now a good thirty yards in front of him. Hawley dawdled until that gap had increased to fifty yards.

The war party came to a gully where the snow had drifted even deeper. Swift Arrow paused on the lip of it for a moment, studying it. The gully ran north and south as far as the eye could see in both directions, and Swift Arrow didn't want to take the time to try to get around it. Besides, it might run for miles and miles, both ways. He slid down the bank, floundered through the drifts, and then climbed up the other side. The rest of the war party came after him. No words had been spoken; no words needed to be.

Hawley had hung back as much as he dared during that little delay. When he came to the gully, he climbed down into it as well. But instead of clambering up the far bank, he turned and began making his way along the bottom of the gully, heading south. The snow was above his waist, but he forced his way through it for several hundred yards until he came to an overhang. He rested there with his back against the bank and listened. The night was deathly quiet. He knew that angry voices would have carried well in the thin, cold air. Either the Injuns hadn't discovered that he was no longer with them, or they just flat didn't care.

Every minute that passed meant that he was safer, because it would take longer for Swift Arrow to come back and kill him. Swift Arrow knew that Hawley hadn't had anything to do with the death of his son. The war chief wouldn't waste the time to murder one white man just on general principles. Hawley clung to that hope.

Finally, when an hour or more had passed, he was convinced that the Injuns weren't coming back. He came out of his hidey-hole and climbed up the bank to the plains. Turning slowly, he looked all around and saw nothing in the silvery moonlight except the snow-covered prairie. He was alone, he thought exultantly. He had escaped.

And he was *alone,* he thought again, as the realization hit him that he was indeed by himself, wounded and without food, in the middle of a vast, snowy wilderness.

A sob of fear came from his throat as he asked himself what the hell he was going to do now.

THIRTY-THREE

The weather had improved by the next morning. Even before sunup, Preacher could tell that the sky was clear. Once again, a storm had come and gone.

Unfortunately, the atmosphere in the camp hadn't gotten better since the night before. That storm was still raging.

At least Roger and Peter didn't come to blows as everyone began to stir and get ready for the day. They made a point of avoiding each other as much as possible, although that was difficult given the close confines of the circled wagons.

Preacher had spent most of the night on guard, sleeping only for a short time early that morning. Peter had retreated alone to his wagon, while Roger, Angela, and all the children remained in the tepee. Jonathan had taken a short turn on watch while Preacher slept, and Geoffrey had gotten up before the rest of them to start on breakfast. His wounded arm was still sore, but it was healing and he was able to use it more now.

Preacher and Dog walked out onto the prairie to check the snow. It was deep, but not quite as deep as in the buffalo wallow. Preacher thought the wagons would be able to handle it, although the going would be slow. When he walked back down to the camp to report as much, he found Roger and Peter glaring at each other.

"Now what?" Preacher asked, not bothering to suppress the weariness and impatience in his voice.

"Now he's not only trying to steal my son, but my wife as well," Peter said accusingly.

"You're insane," Roger shot back. "If you make any more evil insinuations about Angela, I'll—"

Peter broke in by saying, "See? See the way he defends her? He's in love with her! And she spent the night with him in that tepee, like she was some sort of . . . Indian squaw! It's not proper, I tell you—"

He fell abruptly silent as Preacher stepped up to him and grated, "Shut your damned mouth. You ain't the one to be talkin' about what's proper and what ain't. Miss Angela spent plenty of nights in Roger's wagon whilst she was tryin' to save Miss Dorothy's life. Now she's lookin' after the kids. I reckon that's all."

Peter sneered at him. "You're just saying that because of the way you feel about—"

"Shut . . . up," Preacher whispered, "or I swear I'll take my knife and open you up from gizzard to gullet, you son of a bitch."

He ached with the desire to smash a fist into Peter's face and carve him up with the heavy hunting knife, just as he had threatened. Peter swallowed, paled slightly, and backed off a step. "I didn't mean to get everyone upset," he muttered.

"That's a damned lie," Roger snapped. "All you want to do anymore is upset everyone."

Peter turned his back, saying, "Go to hell." He headed for his wagon.

Preacher let him go. He wanted to get the wagons moving again as soon as possible, and wasting time on Peter Galloway just wasn't in his plans.

"Soon's we eat, we'll get the tepee taken down and them teams hitched up," he said, and Roger and Jonathan nodded in agreement.

The next half hour was a busy one. Everyone ate quickly, and then Preacher assigned each of them a job, even the young'uns, who helped Geoffrey take down the tepee. They rolled up the sections of canvas and stowed them away in one of the wagons, along with the stakes that had formed the structure's framework. If they needed to set up the tepee again, it would be faster and easier next time.

Roger and Jonathan hitched up some of the mules while Preacher and Peter tended to the others. Preacher didn't like working with the man, but he knew better than to tell Peter and Roger to work side by side. When the teams were all hitched and the supplies had been loaded, Preacher walked over to Geoffrey and asked, "Can you handle a team with that wounded arm?"

"I reckon I'll have to," Geoffrey replied, sounding more like a frontiersman than ever. "Angela can drive, but she'll have to take care of the baby and the other children."

"I can take a team if I need to."

Geoffrey shook his head. "We need you on horseback, Preacher, scouting ahead of us and watching our back trail."

"That's true, I reckon. We'll try to rest as much as we can along the way—"

"Not on my account," Geoffrey insisted. "Let's get moving, and put as much distance between us and those Injuns as we can."

Preacher grinned and said, "Sounds like a fine idea to me."

There was a solemn moment as the wagons rolled out of the buffalo wallow and then halted while everyone looked back at the lonely grave where Simon Galloway and his daughter-in-law Dorothy lay in eternal rest. Preacher sat his dun beside the lead wagon, where Jonathan was at the reins. The older man said, "It doesn't seem right to just leave them there like that, without even a marker." He looked at Preacher. "Could you find this place again come spring?"

"I reckon I could," Preacher said with a firm nod.

"Would you come back and put up a marker of some kind, so that if anyone else comes along and sees it, they'll know who's buried there? I . . . I hate to think about them being completely forgotten."

"Sure," Preacher said quietly. "I can do that."

"I'd be glad to pay you for your trouble—"

"No need. We've fought side by side. We're pards now, you and me, and Geoffrey too."

"You're sure?"

"You say anything else about payin' me, and I'm liable to get a mite insulted," Preacher told him.

"Well, all right then. I really appreciate it, Preacher."

Preacher shrugged to say that it was nothing. He didn't bother explaining to Jonathan that any marker he put up on the grave probably wouldn't last more than a year before the elements claimed it. After a few years had gone by, all signs of the grave would be gone for sure. It would be just another small stretch of prairie, just like the other hundreds of miles of prairie.

That didn't really matter, Preacher thought. The memories that folks kept in their hearts were the best and most lasting markers of all.

The wagons rolled steadily eastward all day, with only occasional stops to rest the teams or to clean out hard-packed snow that had piled up underneath the wagon beds and slowed them down. The snow had one other disadvantage besides making travel more difficult, Preacher thought: They were leaving a clear path behind them now, a trail that a blind man could follow. If those Arikara warriors stumbled on it, they wouldn't have any trouble knowing where their quarry had gone. And Preacher knew that once they had the trail, they would come on fast.

He rode back a mile or more, Dog bounding through the snow beside him. Stopping and scanning the plains for as far as he could see, Preacher didn't notice anything out of the ordinary. Then, suddenly, he did, his keen eyes picking out some small dark dots against the white sweep of snow.

"Damn it," he said under his breath. The Injuns were back there, and they were moving quickly. He wheeled the dun and put it into a trot, knowing it didn't matter if the Arikara had seen him or not. Chances were they had, since he had spotted them and they probably had pretty good eyes too.

He rode hurriedly after the wagons. Peter was last in line, with the wagon Geoffrey was handling in front of him, then Roger, and finally Jonathan in the lead. Preacher didn't stop to talk to Peter, but he rode alongside the vehicle where Geoffrey was perched on the seat and said quietly, "I think I done spotted the Injuns back there a ways."

Geoffrey's breath hissed between his teeth. He looked at Preacher with a frown and asked, "Are they catching up? They can't catch up, can they? I mean, they're on foot and we have wagons and mule teams."

"Even with the snow, those warriors can run faster than them mules can pull the wagons," Preacher said. "If they keep on a-comin', they'll catch up. It's just a question of how long it'll take 'em."

"How long will it take us to reach Garvey's Fort from here?"

"With luck we might get there tomorrow, or more likely the next day."

"We're that close?" Geoffrey asked with despair in his voice. "We could make it in less than forty-eight hours?"

"I reckon."

"My God . . . What do we do now, Preacher?"

"Keep movin'," Preacher said. "When the Injuns get closer, maybe we can find someplace to fort up. If not, we'll just have to stop, circle the wagons, and fight 'em as best we can."

"We're only five men. There are still at least a couple of dozen of them."

"Nate can handle a rifle, I reckon, and maybe Angela too, unless we decide we want her to load for us. One way or another, we'll have some cover. The Injuns'll have to come at us over open ground. Don't give up, Catamount."

"I won't . . . What did you call me?"

"Catamount," Preacher said with a grin. "That's another name for a mountain lion. I figure you were fightin' about like one when we had that tussle with the Injuns back yonder in the foothills."

"Catamount," Geoffrey repeated. "I think I like it."

"It suits you," Preacher assured him. With a wave, he rode on ahead to break the news that they were being followed to Roger and Jonathan.

After Preacher had told him about the Arikara, Roger asked quietly, "Should I tell Angela and the children?"

Preacher thought about it, then shook his head. "No need to worry 'em just yet. They'll find out what's goin' on soon enough."

Roger nodded in agreement. "What should I do?"

"Just keep drivin'," Preacher told him. "Just keep drivin'."

Like his brother and his nephew, Jonathan took the news calmly. "I suppose this means a fight," he said.

"I reckon it does. Sooner or later. The Injuns won't turn back."

"Well, we have plenty of ammunition, and they don't outnumber us as much as they once did."

Preacher couldn't help but chuckle at the optimism in

Jonathan's voice. "That's a good way to look at it, Silver-tip."

Jonathan's face lit up in a grin. "Silvertip? Is that my mountain man name?"

"That's right. You got some silver in your hair, just like a silvertip grizzly bear. Built a mite like a bear too."

Jonathan threw his head back and laughed. "That's the greatest thing I've ever heard!" he exclaimed. "I'll carry the name with pride, Preacher. What about Geoffrey?"

"You mean Catamount?"

That brought another laugh from Jonathan. Then he grew more sober and said, "You've given us those names because we're running out of time. You think we may not survive the day."

"That's true of ever'body, every day they open their eyes and go on livin'. I sure as hell ain't givin' up, if that's what you mean."

"No," Jonathan said, "I suppose you're not. And I don't intend to either. How do we proceed?"

Preacher leveled an arm and pointed east. "Keep goin'," he said. "I'll let you know when to stop."

Jonathan nodded, flapped the reins, and called out to the mules, urging them on. The wagon wheels continued turning, crunching their way through the snow.

The snow wasn't as deep here as it had been farther west, telling Preacher that the storm hadn't been quite as intense. A little less than a foot of the stuff was on the ground. The sky was a bright blue overhead, but the temperature was still below freezing. That was all right with Preacher. The wagons could move faster on snow-covered, frozen ground than they could through mud, and that was what they would have out here once all the snow melted.

By the time that happened, either the wagon train would have reached Garvey's Fort . . . or it would never get there.

THIRTY-FOUR

A short time later, Preacher rode back to check on the pursuit. The Arikara were still back there, coming on at a steady pace that ate up the ground. He figured they were about two miles behind the wagons. When they had cut that lead to, say, half a mile, it would be time to stop and get ready for the inevitable attack.

Preacher glanced at the sky. The hour was well past noon, and that wasn't good. Darkness would be the ally of the Indians. It would be much easier to sneak up on the wagons after night fell. The immigrants would lose the slight advantage they had because of their rifles. Preacher had hoped to pick off some of the Arikara before the war party came within arrow range. The defenders couldn't hit what they couldn't see to aim at, though.

Preacher galloped back to the wagons, snow flying high as it was kicked up by the dun's hooves. Peter had found out somehow that the Indians were closing in on them, because he raised a hand and hailed Preacher. When the mountain man stopped, Peter said, "Is it true? Are they right back there?"

"A couple of miles," Preacher replied with a nod.

"Can we outrun them?"

"Nope. I don't think so."

"What if we keep moving all night?"

Preacher shook his head. "Then they'll sneak up on us and take the wagons one at a time. We'll have a better chance fortin' up and makin' a stand."

"Forting up where?" Peter waved a hand at the trackless expanse around them. "There's nothing out here!"

"It ain't quite as flat as it looks. If we can find a little rise, or somethin' like that . . ."

Preacher wasn't confident of finding such a place, but he wasn't going to give up hope either. He heeled his horse into a trot again and rode to the front of the wagon train, waving at Jonathan as he moved past.

About half a mile farther on, he felt his spirits begin to lift a little. The ground sloped down slightly into a broad, shallow valley that was at least a quarter of a mile wide. On the far side, the terrain sloped up to a small rise dotted with brush. The rise wouldn't provide much shelter, but Preacher knew it was the best he was likely to find in this mostly flat country.

Some people had started referring to the vast plains between the Mississippi River and the Rocky Mountains as the Great American Desert. Well, it wasn't a desert by any stretch of the imagination—Preacher knew the prairie teemed with life, both animal and plant—but it was a mite sparse when it came to geographical features. That little rise was the closest thing to a hill that this vicinity boasted, and Preacher was glad to have found it.

He reined in at the crest and waited. Before long, the wagons lumbered into view. He waved them on, and when Jonathan's wagon finally rolled up the slope and over the top of the rise, Preacher called to him, "This is where we'll make our stand!"

For the next few minutes, he was busy supervising the preparations for defending this high ground, such as it was. He had the drivers pull the wagons into a loose box shape, one on each side, with enough room left in the center for the livestock. By now Angela had figured out what was going on, and she came to Preacher to say, "I can fight. Just give me a rifle."

"Figured you'd say as much," he said with a smile. "Hold on a minute."

He called Nate over, and when the boy came running up, Preacher said, "Nate, you know how to load a rifle, don't you?"

"Sure, Preacher," the youngster replied.

"That'll be your job then."

Nate's face fell. "Aw, Preacher, I was figurin' that I'd get in on the fight too."

"You'll be in on it, never you worry about that," Preacher told him. "What you'll be doin' is just as important as anything we'll be doin'. Ever'body'll have two rifles, and it'll be your job to keep that second one loaded. Liable to be so much shootin' you can't keep up, but do your best."

Nate nodded. "I will, Preacher. I promise."

Preacher turned back to Angela. "I reckon that leaves you free to handle a gun, ma'am. The only thing is, can you shoot?"

"Well enough. We all practiced some with the rifles on the way out here."

"Shootin' at targets, you mean?"

"Well . . . yes. Does that make a difference?"

"A target don't shoot back at you," Preacher said. "It don't have a family neither. When you got one o' them Arikara in your sights, you got to be able to forget that he's just a fella who's probably got a squaw and a passel o' kids back in whatever village he comes from. You can't be thinkin' about how his old ma's gonna carry on when she hears he's dead." He made his voice deliberately harsh, so that he could be certain he was getting through to her. "All you can think about is how, if that warrior gets his way, him and his friends are gonna rape you until you're half-dead, and then he's gonna cut your throat and lift your hair."

Angela was pale and wide-eyed, but she kept herself under control and nodded. "I can shoot a man, if that's what you're getting at," she assured him.

"Good . . . because it ain't just what he'll do to you that you got to remember. He'll kill your kids too if he gets the chance."

"Just give me a couple of rifles," Angela grated.

Preacher nodded. "You'll do."

He hated putting a woman on the front line of defense, but Angela was probably in better shape than Geoffrey, who, while stronger than before, would have trouble handling a rifle with that wounded arm. Preacher walked along the rise, glancing from time to time toward the west, where the war party was now visible. They were approaching the far side of the valley, moving out in the open and not bothering to hide. Everyone on both sides of this conflict knew exactly what was going on and what was going to happen. There was no need for secrecy.

The defenders would use the wagon parked just beyond the crest of the rise for cover. Preacher put Roger at the rear of the wagon and Peter at the front. Angela and Jonathan were stationed underneath the vehicle, where they could lie down side by side and fire over the crest. The kids, except for Nate, were all in the wagon that formed the back end of the box. Geoffrey would stand guard over them and was well armed with several pistols.

The Indians stopped on the far side of the valley. When they didn't come any closer, Preacher frowned. That war chief, Swift Arrow, was a cunning fella. He knew that the rifles wielded by the white men had a longer range than the Arikara bows. If he led his men in an attack on the wagons now, while the sun was still up, the defenders would have a chance to pick off quite a few of them before they ever got close enough to inflict any damage of their own.

"Damn," Preacher muttered as he stared across the quarter mile or so of open ground.

"What is it?" Roger asked. "What are they doing?"

"What I was afraid they'd do. They're waitin' for night. If they came at us now, it'd be a turkey shoot for us. But if it's dark, we won't be able to see 'em comin', especially if they hit us before the moon comes up, and I reckon they will."

"What do we do?"

"Nothin' we can do but wait. At least they still have to come up a slope at us, and we ought to be able to see them a little against the snow, so that's somethin' else on our side too. But it'll still be mighty tricky shootin', and chances are they'll be amongst us before we can kill all of them."

"My God," Roger said softly. "They're going to overrun us, aren't they?"

"We'll give a good account of ourselves," Preacher said, his voice gruff.

"But we'll still die, no matter how many of them we kill. There are just too many. . . ."

"A fight ain't over until it's over," Preacher insisted. "And I ain't in the habit o' givin' up."

Roger looked toward the other end of the wagon and said bitterly, "None of this would be happening if it weren't for Peter. He doomed us all when he killed that Indian."

Preacher didn't say anything. What had doomed them was their decision to start west at the wrong time of year. Even if Peter hadn't shot that Arikara brave, the whole bunch would have died up in the mountains, probably when the first blizzard roared through. They were just too green to live.

But they still had a chance to fight their way out of this. They couldn't give up hope.

Suddenly, Peter stalked up behind Roger and grabbed his shoulder. As he jerked his brother around, Peter snapped, "I heard what you said! You're blaming me for everything, just like you always do!"

Roger knocked Peter's hand off his shoulder. "Get away from me. It's bad enough we have to fight on the same side. If I'm going to die, I don't want you anywhere near me."

"Damn it, we're brothers!"

"You should have thought of that before you . . . you . . ." Roger couldn't bring himself to say it, but they all knew he was talking about Dorothy.

"This isn't my fault," Peter insisted stubbornly. "I only killed one Indian. Preacher killed a dozen of them! Jonathan and Geoffrey attacked them too."

Angela crawled out from under the wagon. "Peter, just stop it," she said with an infinite weariness in her voice. "It doesn't matter now. Go back where Preacher told you and do the best you can. That's all any of us can do now."

Peter turned to her and reached out. "Angela, at least you can say you forgive me," he pleaded. "We've meant so much to each other. You . . . You can't just turn away now. . . ."

"You turned away from me, Peter," she whispered. Her hands tightened on the rifle she held. "No matter what happens, it's over between us. I can't ever love you again."

"Angela . . ." Peter looked and sounded utterly wretched.

"I'm sorry, Peter. But we can't change what's happened."

He looked around. Confusion, anger, sorrow, resentment . . . All those emotions and more played across his face. Finally he said in a surly tone, "All right, if that's the way you want it, that's the way it'll be, I guess." He went

back to the other end of the wagon and took up his position there, staring dully out across the open valley
toward the Indians, who still waited there.

"Are they out of rifle range where they are now?"
Jonathan asked from under the wagon when Angela had
rejoined him there.

"No, but it'd be a heck of a shot if any of us hit one of
'em from here," Preacher said. "I could maybe do it, especially if I had a shot or two to sight in, but if we start
shootin', they'll just pull back and then we'll have wasted
some powder and lead."

"This waiting is hard," Jonathan mumbled.

"That it is, Silvertip, that it is."

The sun was low in the western sky by now, and its red
glare reflecting off the snow made the defenders squint.
Preacher wondered for a moment if Swift Arrow might
try an attack just as the sun went down, in hopes that the
white men on the rise would be blinded. He didn't think
the war chief would risk that, preferring to wait until
dark when sneaking up on the wagons would be even
easier, but where Injuns were concerned, nothing could
be ruled out. They usually did whatever they took a notion to, whether it made sense to a white man's way of
thinkin' or not.

"Anybody wants anything to eat or drink, now's the
time," Preacher said a short while later. "Or if you just
want to stretch your legs."

Angela and Jonathan came out from under the
wagon. Angela went to check on Geoffrey and the children while Jonathan got a dipper of water from one of
the barrels. The water had ice crystals in it but hadn't
frozen solid yet. He and Roger stood talking quietly
while Preacher said to Nate, "How you doin', partner?"

Nate's head bobbed in a nod. "I'm all right. I'm
scared, though, Preacher."

"So am I."

"Really?" Nate looked up at him as if he couldn't believe that. "I didn't think you ever got scared, Preacher."

"Sure. I been scared plumb half to death plenty o' times in my life. Like when I had to fight that grizzly bear. Only a fool wouldn't be scared goin' up against an ol' grizz like that. Or when we was at war with the British, and the outfit I was part of had to fight 'em at New Orleans. That was mighty scary too. I couldn't even begin to count the times I been scared."

"But you never quit. You never ran."

"Well . . ." Preacher rubbed his bearded jaw. "When the Good Lord was handin' out the things that fill up a man and make him what he is, He didn't see fit to put a whole lot of back up in me. It ain't somethin' I did a-purpose, you understand. It's just the way I am."

"I wish I could be as brave."

"You plan to keep them rifles loaded, like I asked you?"

"Yeah, sure," Nate said.

"If a fella does what's got to be did, no matter how scared he is, then he's just as brave as anybody else."

"As brave as you, you mean?"

Preacher squeezed the youngster's shoulder for a second. "I sure do."

Nate grinned. "Thanks, Preacher. I—"

Whatever he was going to add remained unsaid, because at that moment Angela let out a startled cry and said, "Oh, my God! Peter! What's he doing?"

Preacher wheeled around, feeling a flash of anger toward himself because he had let the conversation with Nate distract him. He hadn't been keeping an eye on the situation as well as he should have. He hadn't noticed when Peter Galloway left the wagons.

By now, Peter was a hundred yards away, striding out into the valley, heading straight toward that Arikara war party.

THIRTY-FIVE

Preacher stared at Peter's retreating back, for a second unable to comprehend what the man thought he was doing. Then Preacher stepped out away from the wagons and bellowed, "Galloway! Damn it, get back here, Galloway!"

Peter ignored him and kept walking toward the Indians.

Angela clutched Preacher's arm. "Stop him!" she said. "For God's sake, he's going to get himself killed!"

Maybe that's just what he wants, Preacher thought. It sure as hell looked like that was what Peter was trying to do.

Preacher shook off Angela's hand and trotted forward, snapping a command over his shoulder. "Ever'body stay here. Take your positions and be ready to fire."

Then he hurried after Peter, who still didn't look back, even when Preacher shouted at him to stop.

Preacher kept an eye on the distances involved. Peter wasn't in range of the war party's bows, but if he kept up that fast walk for much longer, he would be. Preacher started to yell at him again, but before he could, Peter began to shout. The words were directed at the Arikara war chief.

"Swift Arrow! Swift Arrow, can you hear me?"

There was no response from the Indians, but Preacher knew they could hear Peter just fine.

"Swift Arrow, I'm the one you want! I killed your brave back there near your village! Take me, and let the others go!"

Preacher kept trotting after Peter, and finally Peter glanced back. He broke into a run, but he didn't stop yelling at the Indians.

"I surrender!" Peter shouted. "The others had nothing to do with it! Let them go, and you can have me!"

The damn fool didn't realize that the Injuns already had him. His surrendering now wouldn't change a blessed thing. The war party wanted vengeance, not only for the young man Peter had murdered, but also for the warriors they had lost when they set out to even the score. Peter thought he was making a noble gesture—maybe in an attempt to redeem himself at least partially in his wife's eyes, Preacher thought—but in reality all he was doing was throwing away his life and making the odds for everyone else even worse.

Preacher would have to catch the dumb son of a bitch, though, before he could explain all that. And there might not be time for that, because Peter was almost close enough for the Indians to risk a shot . . .

In fact, it was just a second later when an arrow came whistling through the air. It fell short, but Peter still didn't stop. "Kill me!" he shrieked. "Kill me and let the others go!"

"Galloway, stop now!" Preacher roared. His long legs had cut the gap between them until he was only about twenty yards behind Peter. "They're gonna—"

They did. The next arrow flew true and slammed into Peter's chest. He cried out in pain as the flint arrowhead tore into his body, burying itself deeply. He stumbled but stayed on his feet and kept running toward the Indians. "Take me!" he croaked. "Don't kill the oth—"

Two more arrows thudded into him, one in the chest, one in the belly. Preacher heard screams coming from the wagons far behind him as Angela saw her husband being pincushioned with arrows. Peter staggered and twisted around so that Preacher saw the shafts protruding from his body. Peter turned his head and looked back at Preacher, his eyes wide with pain and the realization that he was doomed. Preacher began to back away, knowing that he was dangerously close to being in range himself.

"I'm . . . sorry," Peter choked out, and then another arrow ripped into his side. He twisted the rest of the way around under the impact, so that he was facing toward Preacher and the wagons. He fell to his knees.

A final arrow hit him in the back of the neck and penetrated all the way through so that the bloody arrowhead emerged from his throat. Peter opened his mouth but couldn't scream or say anything else because of the flood of crimson that came from his mouth. He flopped forward, landing awkwardly because of all the arrows sticking out of his body.

Preacher wheeled around and lit a shuck for the wagons.

He heard the Arikara a-whoopin' and a-hollerin' behind him. An arrow zipped past him, and fluttering sounds behind him told him that more arrows were falling short. He risked a glance over his shoulder and saw that the war party was giving chase. One of their most hated enemies had come close to them, almost in their grasp, and they hadn't been able to resist the temptation to come after him.

A grim smile tugged at Preacher's mouth. This might work out after all. It would all depend on how fast he could run. . . .

It was a fantastic race with stakes of life and death there in the fading light. Preacher was a hundred yards ahead of the Indians, but he had to cover almost three hundred yards to reach the relative safety of the wagons. He was a fast runner, though. The snow slowed him down a little, but his pursuers had to contend with the same obstacle.

He remembered hearing about John Colter's epic race with hostile Blackfeet back in the fall of '08. This was nothing like that, of course; Colter had been stripped naked by his Indian captors and then had to run five miles to escape from them. Preacher had all his clothes and had to cover less than a quarter of a mile. But he still thought about Colter as he thudded across the open ground with the Arikara howling in pursuit.

Preacher slowed down. He could have run faster, but he didn't want to. If he drew away from them, they would realize they couldn't catch him and would turn back. He didn't want that. He wanted to pull them on, so he let them come closer and closer to him. Some of the Indians stopped, nocked arrows, and let fly at him again. The feathered missiles rained around him. Preacher kept going.

He was about a hundred yards away from the wagons when the defenders opened up. He heard the roar of exploding powder and saw puffs of smoke from around the wagon that was parked just beyond the rise. Behind him, one of the 'Rees yelled in pain, and when Preacher glanced back, he saw that two of them were down. The others came on, but they were slowing now that they realized Preacher had become the bait in a trap.

Jonathan, Roger, and Angela had had all the rifles loaded before they fired their first volley. That allowed them to fire again quickly, and they did so, the heavy lead balls whistling over the prairie to thud into the bodies of some of the onrushing Indians. Preacher stopped and whirled, throwing the Hawken to his shoulder. He cocked the rifle and drew a bead in the blink of an eye, then pressed the trigger. Flame spurted from the muzzle as the Hawken blasted. Another Arikara warrior spun off his feet as Preacher's lead tore through him.

Preacher pulled his right-hand pistol and fired, was rewarded by the sight of blood spraying in the air from a warrior's shattered shoulder. He didn't delay any longer. Turning toward the wagons, he broke into a run again, and this time he didn't hold back.

More shots came from the wagon, irregularly spaced now instead of together in a volley. With Nate's help, the defenders were reloading and firing as fast as they could. Preacher threw a look over his shoulder and saw that the Indians were retreating, leaving their dead and wounded behind for the moment, although he was sure they would come back for them later. He counted six bodies on the ground, and he thought one or two more of the fleeing warriors were limping and staggering from their wounds. Peter's crazy notion had allowed the others to strike a heavy blow at the enemy.

But they were still outnumbered by more than two to one, Preacher thought, and it would be dark soon. Swift Arrow wouldn't give up either. He would still rush the wagons as soon as night had fallen.

Preacher slowed to a trot as he went up the rise to the wagons. His heart slugged heavily in his chest. He was all whipcord, whang leather, and muscle, but that had been a hard run in cold, thin air. He would be glad for a chance to catch his breath.

Jonathan met him. "We got some of them!" the old-timer exulted. "I saw some of them go down!"

"You sure did," Preacher told him. "I figure we done for five or six of 'em, and there's a couple more wounded, maybe 'bad enough so they're out of the fight."

Jonathan's grin vanished, to be replaced by a solemn look. "Peter . . . ?"

Preacher shook his head. "He never had no chance."

Angela crawled out from underneath the wagon in time to hear that. A sob caught in her throat. Roger went to her and put an arm around her shoulder to comfort her. Both of them had lost a spouse in the past couple of days. Even though Angela had come to despise Peter and had declared their marriage over, there had still been enough of a bond remaining between them so that she felt his loss. It had to hurt, Preacher thought. Best to let her cry it out.

But only for a short time, because the sun was gone and its light was beginning to fade from the sky. In less than an hour, Preacher thought, Swift Arrow and the rest of the Arikara war party would be coming, and one way or another, this would be the end of the long chase.

While he had the chance, Preacher went to check on Geoffrey and the younger children. Mary and Brad were sniffling, still frightened by all the shooting that had gone on earlier. If they knew that their father was dead, Preacher couldn't tell it. He didn't say anything about what had happened to Peter, but he could tell from the bleak look in Geoffrey's eyes that the older man knew about it. "What now?" he asked.

"Same as before," Preacher said. "When the time comes, we fight as best we can."

Geoffrey nodded grimly. He sat on one of the bunks with four loaded pistols at his side. If it came down to it, Preacher was sure that Geoffrey would defend the young'uns to his last breath.

Preacher dropped down from the tailgate and saw Nate coming toward him in the dusk. "Preacher," the boy said, "did I do all right?"

"As far as I could tell, you done just fine. You ready to do some loadin'?"

"Yes, sir."

Preacher patted his shoulder. "Well, it shouldn't be too long now."

He went back to the first wagon and nodded to Roger, who stood there leaning on a rifle, the butt resting on the snowy ground. "That was terrible," Roger said quietly, keeping his voice low so that Angela, who was at the other end of the wagon with Jonathan, wouldn't overhear. "I didn't know Peter had that much courage. It was a grand gesture."

It was a stupid gesture, Preacher thought, and hadn't accomplished a damned thing except to cost them a defender. Still, Peter had been Roger's brother, and just as with Angela, there were still bonds there despite all the trouble. Roger had lost a father, a wife, and a brother in mighty short order.

Those deaths gnawed at Preacher's innards too. He had thrown in with these immigrants with the goal of getting them back to safety. *All* of them. He had known from the start how unlikely that was, of course, but still, losing any of them bothered him. He hadn't had anything to do with Dorothy Galloway's death, of course, and he had tried to get Peter to come back and not throw his life away. But there was a way of looking at Simon's death that made Preacher to blame for it. After all, Preacher had sent him out to stand guard before that storm hit and froze him to death.

Of course, somebody had to stand guard, and if it hadn't been Simon, it would have been somebody else. Jonathan or Geoffrey or Roger might be dead now instead of Simon. Preacher wasn't going to lose much sleep over what had happened—assuming he lived through the perilous night to come—but he wouldn't forget about it either. Tragedy had dogged this expedition even before he joined it, and he hadn't been able to prevent it completely since then.

"Got all the guns loaded?" he asked.

Roger nodded. "Loaded and primed. All we have to do is cock and fire. But once it's dark, how will we know the Indians are attacking?"

"We'll have to let them make the first move," Preacher said. "It's risky, but we don't have much choice."

"So they take the first shot and we hope they miss?"

"Yeah, pretty much," Preacher said with a grin.

"How many of them are left?"

"Twelve, fourteen, somewhere along in there."

"And there are five of us," Roger mused. "More than three to one odds."

"I've faced worse and come through all right."

Roger turned to look at him, but Preacher couldn't read his expression in the fading light. "Angela is quite fond of you. You'll take care of her, if you both live through this."

"This ain't the time to think about that."

"And the children," Roger said, ignoring Preacher's comment. "Someone will have to look after them."

"That'd be a good job for the two of you," Preacher pointed out.

"The two of . . . You mean Angela and me?"

"Y'all been through a lot together, and you both love them kids. I ain't sayin' or meanin' any more than that. I reckon right now you're thinkin' that you ain't got a lot to live for, Roger. I'm just sayin' that maybe you do."

For a moment, Roger didn't say anything. Then he said quietly, "You're an odd man, Preacher."

"So I been told," Preacher replied with a chuckle.

"You see hope where there shouldn't be any. You don't back down and you don't give up. Talking to you, I almost find myself thinking that maybe we will make it."

"Remember that," Preacher told him, "and keep on

a-fightin' even it looks like there ain't no use. We'll pull through, one way or t'other."

Roger nodded and looked out across the open ground in front of the rise. "I'm ready," he declared.

That was good, Preacher thought, because the sky was black and the stars were out and in a matter of minutes the Arikara would be coming to wreak their vengeance on the hated whites.

That meant it was time for him to go.

THIRTY-SIX

He made sure everyone was back in position and ready for what was to come. Every gun in the darkened, makeshift stronghold was loaded. All the defenders were alert, their eyes turned in the direction the Indians would come from. When Preacher was sure he had done everything he could to prepare them for the battle, he drifted back into the shadows and said softly, "Dog." The big animal followed him soundlessly as he slipped away from the wagons.

It would be a few minutes before they noticed he was gone, he thought. They might not even tumble to that fact until after the Indians launched their attack. By that time it would be too late for the defenders to waste any time wondering about his disappearance. They would be too busy fighting for their lives.

He catfooted along in a low crouch just behind the rise, moving about seventy-five yards before he dropped to hands and knees and began crawling. Within minutes his hands and knees were soaked and cold from the snow, but he ignored the discomfort as best he could. Beside him, Dog bellied along, following Preacher's example. Neither of them could afford to be spotted, not until they were good and ready.

He stretched out flat as his senses warned him that someone was moving nearby. Several shapes ghosted past him about twenty yards away. The war party had spread out, and now the Indians were closing in. Preacher glanced toward the wagon at the top of the rise, barely able to make out its bulk in the thick darkness. The stars were bright, but what light they gave off seemed to be swallowed up by the heavens before it ever reached the earth. It was as dark as the bottom of a well, and as Preacher came up in a crouch again and began to move, he was guided by instinct as much as he was by sight.

Smell helped too. He caught a whiff of bear grease and knew he wasn't far now from the Injuns.

As he came up soundlessly behind them, he began to be able to pick them out better, indistinct shapes here and there, dark against the snow. He heard one of them take a deep breath and knew that was his signal to go into action. They were getting ready to charge.

Preacher stood up straight, about ten feet behind one of the skulking Indians, and leveled his Hawken. He snapped, "Dog!" and then pulled the trigger.

Dog leaped forward, choosing one of the other warriors as his prey. The rifle roared and bucked against Preacher's shoulder and the heavy ball that it launched exploded through the body of the Arikara brave, smashing him face-first to the ground. Dog hit his target an instant later, his ferocious charge landing him on the startled Indian's back. The man cried out as he went down, but the yell ended in a grotesque gurgle as Dog's teeth sank into his throat and ripped it out.

Preacher dropped the Hawken and yanked out the brace of pistols. They were double-shotted and loaded with heavy charges, and they boomed like pocket cannons as Preacher fired. Three more of the Arikara went down, knocked off their feet by the scything lead.

"Open fire!" Preacher yelled. "Open fire!" He knew the shout would reach the defenders at the top of the rise. He hoped they wouldn't hesitate for fear of hitting him once they realized he was right in there among the Indians. He had known what he was doing when he decided to hit the war party from behind, and he was willing to take his chances.

Welcome spurts of flame came from the rifles around and underneath the wagon as Preacher bounded forward. As a dark shape loomed in front of him, he struck with one of the pistols and felt the satisfying crunch of a skull being crushed by the blow. Preacher shoved the dying man out of the way and dropped the empty pistols. He reached behind his back and brought up two more, loaded and primed. His thumbs found the hammers and pulled them back as feet rushed at him from the side.

He pivoted smoothly, bringing up the right-hand gun. The flame that licked out from the muzzle as he fired briefly lit up the face of the warrior who took both balls almost point blank. Then most of his head disappeared in a bloody spray of brains and bone, blown right off his shoulders by the double charge.

Preacher heard fierce growling and screaming and knew that Dog was still in the middle of the fracas, pulling down his prey just as his wolf ancestors had done for untold centuries. A grunt of effort warned Preacher in time to prompt him to duck under the sweeping blow of a tomahawk. As the warrior who wielded the 'hawk stumbled against him, thrown off balance by the miss, Preacher slammed the barrel of the empty pistol across the bridge of his nose, shattering bone and sending deadly splinters up into the man's brain. Jerking as he died, the Indian toppled off his feet.

Preacher still had a loaded pistol in his left hand. The next instant, he needed it as two of the warriors rushed him. He fired, hoping to take both of them down with the double shot, but only one man was hit. That one died on his feet, his heart pulped by the ball, as he continued to stumble forward for a few steps before diving face-first into the snow. The other one crashed into Preacher and bore him over backward. The Indian landed on top of him and knocked all the air out of his lungs, and for a moment all Preacher could do was lie there stunned as the Arikara warrior drove the blade of a knife at his throat.

The defenders had been taken completely by surprise when Preacher started yelling and shooting from *behind* the Indians. None of them had realized he was gone. But the uproar about fifty yards in front of the wagons gave them something to aim at. Everyone who pressed the trigger of a rifle worried about hitting Preacher, but they fired anyway, knowing that the survival of the entire group depended on winning this fight.

The rifle in Roger's hands was empty when he saw one of the Indians closing in on him. The Arikara howled a war cry and fired an arrow that clipped the sleeve of Roger's coat as it went past. The warrior dropped his bow and grabbed his tomahawk instead, lunging at Roger with his arm upraised to strike a killing blow.

Roger reversed the rifle and leaned in, swinging it like a club. The stock shattered on the Indian's jaw and broke bone as well. The warrior went down. Roger struck again and again with the broken rifle, using the breech to batter in the enemy's skull. He knew he was fighting and cursing like a madman, but he didn't care. All the fear and grief and anger of the past few days came flooding out of him in an incoherent cry as he beat the Indian to death.

Under the wagon, Jonathan and Angela fired as fast as they could, taking the reloaded rifles that Nate slid up to them. But then several of the Indians were right there in front of them, and Jonathan shoved Angela back as he crawled forward to get in front of her and shield her with his own body. He rammed the barrel of an empty rifle into the belly of an onrushing warrior, and as the Indian doubled over in pain, Jonathan reached up and got him by the neck. He came to his feet and slammed the man's head against the sideboard of the wagon.

Pain lanced into his side like fire. He gasped and reached down to grasp the shaft of an arrow. It hadn't lodged deeply, so he was able to rip it loose. As another Indian grappled with him, Jonathan jammed the arrowhead at the man's left eye. It went in cleanly. Jonathan heard the eyeball pop and felt the spray of liquid from it on his face. The Indian staggered back, shrieking and pawing at his destroyed eye.

Jonathan saw a couple of them run past him and tried to get in their way, but he was too late. They were heading straight toward the wagon where Geoffrey stood guard over the children, Jonathan saw. "Geoffrey!" he shouted in warning.

As one of the Indians leaped to the tailgate, a pistol roared inside the wagon and knocked him backward. The children began to scream. Inside the wagon, Geoffrey dropped the empty pistol and snatched up another one as he crouched beside the rear opening. He was too late. A buckskin-clad figure lunged through the opening and crashed into him. Geoffrey went down. He cried out as cold steel bit deep into his belly. The stench of bear grease filled his nostrils, mixed with a coppery smell that a detached part of his brain knew came from his own blood. Feeling himself about to pass out, he summoned up the last of his strength, jammed the barrel of the pistol under the Indian's chin, and pulled the trigger. The Arikara warrior had been grunting with effort as he ripped his knife back and forth in Geoffrey's midsection, but those sounds ended abruptly with the roar of the pistol.

Mary and Brad kept crying in terror, along with the

thin wailing of the baby. The children's shrieks redou-
bled as another dark figure clambered into the wagon.

A fierce, furry shape barreled into the Indian just before the blade found Preacher's throat. Dog bowled over
the warrior and went to work on him with slashing teeth.
The Arikara tried to fight back and managed to land a
long gash on Dog's shoulder before the powerful jaws
crunched down on his throat, ending his life.

Preacher rolled over, came up on his knees, and dove
to the side as he saw a tall, powerful figure lunging at
him. Swift Arrow, he thought. Had to be. The war chief
was the biggest of the Arikara.

Swift Arrow came at him, starlight glittering on the
knife in one hand and the tomahawk in the others.
Preacher leaped to the side to avoid a flurry of slashing
blows. He still had an empty pistol in his left hand. He
used his right to pull his own hunting knife from its
fringed sheath.

It was almost like a dance then, across the shadowed,
blood-spattered snow, as Preacher and Swift Arrow
darted and lunged and circled, each man attacking and
parrying in turn, moving with blinding, deadly speed.
Swift Arrow's knife slashed across Preacher's upper arm,
leaving a bloody wound behind, fortunately not cutting
deep enough to sever any nerves or muscles. An instant
later, the barrel of Preacher's pistol thudded with numb-
ing force on the top of Swift Arrow's left shoulder. The
war chief stumbled but caught himself before Preacher
could press the advantage.

Back and forth they struggled. Breath rasped in
Preacher's throat. His foot suddenly caught on something concealed underneath the snow, and he staggered
and went to one knee. Swift Arrow rushed in at him.
Preacher went on down, letting the Indian's attack go

over his head. He bowled forward, knocking Swift Arrow's legs out from under him. Both men rolled away to put some distance between them, then came up to face each other again.

Preacher had dropped his pistol, but the tomahawk had slipped out of Swift Arrow's fingers. They came together, knives flashing, and suddenly they were locked motionless, less than a foot apart, each man with the fingers of his free hand wrapped desperately around the wrist of his opponent's knife hand. They strained against each other's grip, putting all their incredible strength into the effort, but for long moments neither man could budge the other.

Then Swift Arrow's left arm buckled slightly, and the tip of Preacher's blade came nearer the war chief's chest. Though Preacher didn't know it, Swift Arrow's left shoulder was broken where Preacher had hit him with the pistol. Swift Arrow struggled on anyway, gritting his teeth against the terrible pain as shattered bones ground together.

Preacher had his own problems. The gash on his left arm had bled quite a bit, and he felt himself weakening and growing light-headed. If he passed out, even for a second, the fight would be over. Swift Arrow's knife would be in his heart in the blink of an eye. Preacher reached inside himself, drawing on all the reserves he had left. He sensed that Swift Arrow was growing weaker too. If he could just hold out, hold out a little longer . . .

Swift Arrow's left arm buckled again, and this time there was no holding back the thrust that Preacher made. The knife penetrated the war chief's buckskins, slipped through skin and flesh and muscle. Preacher shoved hard and felt the steel grate on bone as the blade passed between ribs. Swift Arrow said softly, "Ahhh . . ." Preacher pushed harder, driving the knife through the tough fibers of the Arikara's heart. He twisted the blade.

Swift Arrow's knees buckled. His hand opened and he dropped his knife as he sagged. Preacher ripped his knife free and stepped back. Swift Arrow fell to his knees, looked up at Preacher, and died. He toppled to the side like a falling tree.

Then and only then did Preacher realize there was no more shooting going on. The battle was over, he told himself as Dog came up to him and nuzzled his hand. He looked around and saw dark shapes sprawled everywhere on the ground. Then he lifted his gaze toward the wagons and saw someone hurrying toward him. His fingers tightened on the handle of the knife. He didn't know if he could fight anymore, but damned if he was going to surrender.

"Preacher!" Jonathan Galloway shouted. "Preacher, is that you?"

"Damn . . . Silvertip . . ." Preacher husked as Jonathan came up to him and reached out toward him. "I'm mighty glad . . . that's you . . ."

Jonathan grabbed his arm and held him up long enough to get an arm around his waist. Then he began helping Preacher back toward the wagons.

"Anybody . . . hurt?" Preacher managed to ask.

"I've got a cut in my side from an arrow," Jonathan said, "but it's not too bad. Roger and Angela and the children are all right. None of them were hurt. It's a miracle."

"Not . . . a miracle. Just . . . hard fightin'." Preacher forced himself to concentrate on what Jonathan had just said. "Your brother . . . Geoffrey . . . ol' Catamount . . ."

"He . . . died . . . protecting the children. I found his body when I climbed into the wagon. The Indian who killed him was lying on top of him with his head blown off."

"Aw, hell," Preacher said, and meant it.

Tears sparkled on Jonathan's cheeks, sparkled in the

light of the rising moon. "He died fighting, like a mountain man. That's another marker you'll have to put up, Preacher."

"I'll do it," Preacher promised.

"At least it's over now," Jonathan said. "All the Indians are dead. We're safe. All we have to do is make it to Garvey's Fort."

"That's right. Safe," Preacher repeated. They had suffered losses, heavy losses, but now the rest of them would make it. He was sure of it.

That same night, about twenty miles to the east, four men rode through the gate in a high wall made of sod and bricks. The wall ran around the compound of several buildings that made up Garvey's Fort, the trading post and lone bastion of civilization in this part of the country. The riders were lean, hard-faced men, and when they dismounted, they went into the trading post's barroom and asked if anyone knew the whereabouts of a family called Galloway. . . .

THIRTY-SEVEN

Again they dug a single grave in the morning, and laid Geoffrey and Peter to rest side by side in it. Preacher was getting mighty tired of lowering blanket-shrouded shapes into the ground. He figured Garvey's Fort was only about twenty miles away, though, and with the threat of the Arikara war party taken care of, he hoped they could make it the rest of the way without running into any more trouble.

One thing he noticed as he checked the bodies of the warriors was that Mart Hawley was no longer with them. He wondered what had happened to the renegade trapper. It could be that Swift Arrow had gotten tired of him and killed him, or maybe Hawley had sickened and died from the wound he'd suffered during the fight back in the foothills. Or maybe he had just frozen to death. Preacher hoped that whatever had happened, he had crossed paths with Hawley for the last time.

He didn't like leaving the bodies of the Arikara for the scavengers, but there was no handy gully or ravine where they could be placed, and he didn't want to take the time necessary to dig a grave big enough for a dozen corpses. Still, it bothered him, and when he said as much, Jonathan frowned at him and said, "Why? They were trying to kill us. I don't see why you'd worry about not burying them."

"You've learned a lot about frontier ways, Silvertip," Preacher told him, "but you still got some things to learn. Them old boys were our enemies, sure enough, but they weren't without honor. They were tryin' to avenge a wrong that was done to their people."

"The murder of that young man," Jonathan said solemnly.

Preacher nodded. "That's right. The way they looked at it, they was just after justice. I can't say as I disagree with 'em."

"And yet you helped us. You probably killed more of the Arikara than the rest of us put together."

"And if they'd just gone after Peter, I might've stayed out of it. But it wasn't right for them to try to kill the rest of you either." Preacher shrugged. "Most of the time in life, there ain't no right or wrong answers, just shades of good and bad on both sides. You got to go with which side looks the best."

"Most of the time?"

"Yep. But there's such a thing as pure evil too, and now and then you run across it. When you do, you fight it. Simple as that."

Jonathan shook his head. "I don't think there's anything all that simple about you, Preacher."

"You just ain't known me long enough," the mountain man said with a grin.

There had been a heap of crying over Geoffrey and Peter, but everybody was dry-eyed again as the wagons rolled eastward later that morning. White clouds floated in the sky, pushed around by a breeze from the south that was still cold, but not as cold as it had been. Just as before, they would have a few days of better weather before another storm came roaring down out of Canada, Preacher thought as he rode out ahead of the wagons with Dog at his side. By the time that happened, they would be safe and sound at Garvey's Fort.

Angela and Nate had to each drive a wagon now. The young'un was nervous about handling a team, but his pa and his uncle had given him some pointers and Preacher was confident that Nate would do just fine. The boy had the right stuff in him.

Roger had come through the fight without a scratch, as had Angela. Jonathan had a shallow arrow wound in his side, but Angela had cleaned it and bound it up, and with any luck it would heal just fine. The injury was stiff and sore but not enough so to prevent Jonathan from driving one of the wagons.

The temperature remained cold enough to keep the snow from melting very fast, although the sun took care of some of it. The wagons made good time because Preacher kept them moving all day with only short, occasional stops. He wanted to cover enough ground today so that they could reach the fort the next day. By nightfall, he was fairly certain that they had. He thought he could have ridden ahead and reached Garvey's place that night, but that would have meant leaving the wagons and he didn't want to do that. He could wait until the next day and ride in with them.

That night they had a good fire and a hot supper, and although the mood was still solemn because of the losses the group had suffered, there was also talk about what would happen the next day when they reached the fort, and even a mention or two of going on to Oregon in the spring. Preacher sipped from a cup of coffee as he looked across the fire at Roger and Angela sitting together on a wagon tongue. They had been through a hell of a lot, and while the friendship they shared might or might not blossom into anything else, at least they would always have that friendship. Preacher hoped it stayed strong.

Far behind the wagons, Mart Hawley walked along, his feet scuffing in the thin coat of snow on the ground. He saw the faint, distant eye of the fire and knew the pilgrims were there. He wasn't trying to catch up. The shape he was in, he didn't want another showdown with Preacher. He had food now, and weapons, all scavenged from the bodies of the Arikara war party when he came on them earlier in the day. He would survive and grow stronger and recover from his wound, and maybe one of these days, when the time was right, his trail would cross Preacher's once again.

An ugly grin tugged at Hawley's mouth as he thought about that. He wouldn't forget, and he sure as hell wouldn't forgive, all that Preacher had done. Sooner or later he would have his revenge.

One of these days . . .

The flat terrain meant that the walls of the fort were visible long before the wagons reached them. Preacher, ranging out ahead on the dun, saw them before anyone else and galloped back to tell the others. "Hallelujah!" Jonathan exclaimed. A short time later, when the wagons came in sight of the fort, the children began chattering excitedly. Preacher couldn't even begin to imagine what a grueling, terrifying journey this had been for them.

People inside the fort must have seen them coming, because the gates opened and several riders emerged. As they came closer, Preacher recognized one of them as a trapper he knew, Cephus Rattan. He lifted a hand in greeting and called, "Howdy, Cephus!"

Rattan reined his horse to a stop and stared at the wagons trailing behind Preacher. "Whoo-eee!" the lean, bearded trapper exclaimed. "What you got there, Preacher? Been pickin' up strays?"

"I reckon you could say that," Preacher replied with a

grin. "I ran into a whole family of pilgrims who thought they could make it over the Rockies with winter comin' on."

Rattan shook his head at the sheer damned foolishness of that idea.

"I got 'em turned around and brought 'em back here," Preacher continued. "Figured they could try again next spring."

"That was smart of you," one of the other men said. He was tall, powerfully built, and sported a thick black mustache. "Fred Garvey," he said introducing himself as he thrust out a hand. "This is my place."

Preacher shook hands with the trader, whom he had never crossed trails with before. "Pleased to meet you." He jerked a thumb at the wagons. "Those folks behind me are the Galloways."

"Galloway?" Rattan repeated, sounding surprised.

"From Philadelphia?" Garvey asked.

Preacher tensed. Something was wrong here. "Yeah, that's where they're from," he said. "How in blazes did you boys know that?"

Rattan, Garvey, and the other men, who looked like trappers but were unknown to Preacher, glanced at each other, and then Garvey said, "There are some men inside the fort looking for a family name of Galloway that came out here from Philadelphia. They rode in a couple of days ago."

"Hard-lookin' bunch too," Rattan said, leaning over in the saddle to spit on the ground.

"We told them we didn't know any Galloways," Garvey said, "and it was true at the time. They said they'd stock up on supplies and rest their horses for a day or two before they left."

"And they're still there?" Preacher asked sharply.

Garvey nodded. "Still there. They keep to themselves

and don't say much, but like Cephus said, they look like hard cases."

"I'm obliged for the information," Preacher said with a nod of gratitude. "I'll try to find out what it's all about." He wheeled the dun and rode back to the wagons, about seventy-five yards behind him. Rattan, Garvey, and the other men trailed behind him.

Preacher held up a hand, signaling for Roger to stop. Roger was at the reins of the lead wagon now, with Jonathan bringing up the rear and Angela and Nate second and third in line, respectively.

"Why are we stopping?" Roger asked. "We're almost at the fort. I can see it right up there."

"There's somethin' we better talk about first," Preacher said, leaning forward to ease himself in the saddle. "Some men at the fort are lookin' for a family named Galloway. A family from Philadelphia. I don't reckon that's a coincidence, do you?"

Roger's face tightened. "What sort of men?"

"A bad sort, accordin' to what I been told. What's this all about, Roger? Who are those fellas?"

Roger sighed and said, "I was hoping . . . we all hoped . . . that no one would follow us."

The other wagons had stopped behind Roger's, and now Jonathan came forward, carrying a rifle. "What's the holdup?" he asked. "Why aren't we going on into the fort?"

Roger turned to look at his uncle. "There's trouble, Jonathan," he said. "Some men are there looking for us."

"For us? What in the world for?"

"Money, I suspect," Roger said heavily. "They've been paid to track us down."

"Spit it out," Preacher said, his voice like flint now. He had suspected all along that there was more to the story than he had been told, and he was tired of having the truth hidden from him.

Angela hopped down from the wagon she was driving and came forward too, in time to hear Roger say, "My father paid to outfit us for this trip, but what none of the rest of us knew except for Peter and myself was that most of the money was . . . well . . . stolen."

"Stolen!" Jonathan exclaimed. "Simon was a thief?"

"He took the money from his partner, but only because the man was a thief to start with! He had been cheating Pa for years." Roger's voice lost some of its certainty. "At least, that's what Pa said. . . ."

"So now this old partner of your pa's has a grudge against him and hired men to come out here and look for him," Preacher said, having no trouble connecting up the rest of the story. He added contemptuously, "Bounty hunters."

"That's what I suspect, yes," Roger said.

"Why didn't you tell the rest of us, or at least Geoffrey and me?" Jonathan wanted to know.

Roger shook his head. "I suppose Pa was ashamed. I . . . I guess he really *was* a thief. But he asked Peter and me to keep it to ourselves, and we decided to honor his wishes."

"So that's why we had to leave so quickly," Angela said, "why there was such a hurry about getting out of Philadelphia. Simon wanted to get far away before his crime was discovered."

Roger nodded miserably. "That's right."

Well, things made a heap more sense now, Preacher thought, but there was still one very important question left unanswered: What were they going to do now?

"Those men who are looking for us . . ." Roger said. "When we tell them that Pa is dead, I suppose they'll go back where they came from and report that to the man who hired them?"

"Maybe," Preacher said. "It just depends on how much

vengeance the fella wants. He may have given them orders to go after the whole bunch of you."

"But that's not right! Pa was the one who took the money. The rest of us had nothing to do with it."

"Yeah, and your brother was the one who shot that Arikara brave too, but that didn't stop the 'Rees from wantin' to lift the hair from all of you."

Roger paled. "My God! You mean they may try to . . . to murder the rest of us?"

"I wouldn't put it past 'em. I could be wrong, though. Only one way to find out."

"Yes, we'll go in and talk to them—" Roger began.

"Nope. *I'll* go in and talk to 'em, try to find out just how bad they want you folks."

"No, Preacher, that's not fair," Jonathan said. "You've done so much for us already, we can't ask you to risk your life for us again."

Preacher ignored him. "Keep the wagons right here," he told Roger. "Don't you come on in unless me or Cephus here rides out to tell you it's all right." He glanced at Rattan. "That all right with you, Cephus?"

The trapper nodded. "Sure, Preacher."

Fred Garvey spoke up, saying, "I can't take sides in this. I've got to do business here—"

"Sure," Preacher said. "I understand, Garvey. We'll settle this amongst ourselves, without gettin' anybody else mixed up in it."

"I'm obliged for that."

Preacher lifted the dun's reins, but Angela stepped forward and stopped him by laying a hand on the horse's shoulder. She looked up at him and said, "Why are you doing this for us? I'm not sure we deserve it."

Preacher wasn't sure they did either, and yet he had been around them enough to know that there was good in all of them, especially Angela and Nate and Jonathan.

But he didn't know how to explain that, so he just said again, "Stay here. I'll be back."

Then he turned and rode toward the fort.

THIRTY-EIGHT

Rattan, Garvey, and the other men who had come out from the fort followed Preacher. The gates were still open. Preacher rode through them and turned to ask Garvey, "Where are those fellas now?"

"In the bar inside the trading post. That's where they've spent most of their time since they got here."

Preacher reined to a stop in front of the long, low building that housed the trading post. The building was constructed of blocks of sod carved out of the prairie, but instead of the usual thatched roof it had a wooden one, made of thick planks that must have been carted out here by wagon from St. Louis. That had probably been expensive.

He swung down from the saddle and looped the reins around a hitchin' post next to the building's low porch. When he swung open the heavy door and stepped inside, it took his eyes a few seconds to adjust to the dimness. The trading post had no windows and was lit by candles and a few lanterns hung on pegs, so the air inside was close and stuffy, hazed by smoke, and smelled of the buffalo chips being burned in a potbellied stove in the corner. Even inside, Preacher's breath fogged a little from the cold. The stove didn't do much to ward off the chill.

Preacher's instincts helped him recognize the men he

was looking for. There were four of them. They sat bunched around a rough-hewn table, a jug of whiskey and four cups in front of them. All of them wore thick coats and high boots. One sported a fur cap while the others all had floppy-brimmed felt hats much like the one Preacher wore. Their coats were open, and Preacher saw the butts of pistols sticking up behind their belts.

He walked toward them. They watched him warily as he approached. Coming to a stop a few feet from the table, he nodded to them and said, "I hear you fellas are lookin' for a family called Galloway."

"That's right." The words came from the man in the fur cap, who seemed to be the spokesman. "You know where we can find them?"

"How come you're lookin' for 'em?"

"That's our business," Fur Cap said. "Might could make it worth your while, though, if you can put us on their trail."

Preacher shook his head. "You don't want to go messin' with the Galloways. They're pretty good folks. They've had a passel o' bad luck, and they need to be left alone."

That sharpened the interest of all four men. They leaned forward eagerly, and Fur Cap said, "It sure sounds like you know where they are, mister. You'd be well advised to tell us and then keep your nose outta our business."

"Never was too good at that," Preacher said, his voice deceptively mild. His tone hardened as he went on. "Simon Galloway is dead. He froze to death a few nights ago and is buried about thirty-five or forty miles west o' here. Go back to the man who hired you and tell him it's all over."

For a long moment, none of the men said anything as they studied Preacher. Then Fur Cap sneered and said, "You know the whole story, do you?"

"Enough of it."

Fur Cap shook his head. "No, you don't know enough. You don't know me, mister. Once I take on a job, I do it. I been paid to settle up with the Galloways, and that's what I intend to do. That's what we all intend to do."

The other hard cases nodded their agreement.

"What about the money?" Preacher asked harshly. "If you get some of it back, is that enough to satisfy you—and the man who hired you?" He didn't know how much of the stolen money, if any, the Galloways still had, but he thought it was worth a try.

Fur Cap shot down that hope by slowly shaking his head. "It ain't about the money anymore. Like I said, it's about settlin' the score."

"Well, then, you'll have to start with me," Preacher said quietly.

Fur Cap's eyes narrowed. "Who the hell are you anyway?"

Preacher would have answered, *A friend of the Galloways,* but he didn't get a chance to. Rattan and the others had followed him into the trading post, and now the lean trapper laughed and said, "Why, mister, that there is Preacher."

Fur Cap's breath hissed between his teeth. "Preacher!" His hand darted toward the gun at his waist as he kicked backward and came up out of the chair. "Get him!" The other three went into action an eyeblink later.

But that was an eyeblink too late, because Preacher's hands had already swept underneath his coat and closed around the butts of his pistols. He brought them out and up and flame spurted from the muzzles, throwing a garish red glare on the corner where the four hired killers had been sitting. One of the balls from the left-hand pistol thudded into the center of Fur Cap's forehead and blew a sizable chunk of his brains out the back of his head. The other ball missed, but it wasn't needed. Both lead missiles from the right-hand pistol struck one of the other men at the point where his arm met his shoulder and nearly tore the limb off. Blood fountained as the arm flopped loosely, held in place only by a couple of strands of gristle. The man fell back in the corner, screaming and gurgling as he bled to death.

Preacher threw himself forward as the other two men fired. The shots went over his head. The roar of exploding powder was deafening at such close range. Preacher slid across the table and barreled into both men, spreading his arms so he could take them down. They all crashed to the floor.

Swinging one of the pistols in a short, backhanded arc, Preacher broke one man's jaw. The man rolled away moaning, out of the fight for the moment. The other man grappled desperately with Preacher, forcing him to drop both pistols. The bounty hunter fumbled at the handle of a heavy-bladed knife sheathed at his waist. Preacher got a hand on the man's wrist just as the knife came free. He pinned the man's arm down and locked the fingers of his other hand around his opponent's throat. Preacher hung on tight as the man kicked and spasmed underneath him, face turning dark and tongue bulging. Finally the man went limp. Preacher didn't know if he was dead or had just passed out, and didn't particularly care which it was either.

The other man, the one with the broken jaw, hit him from the side then, mouthing incoherent curses as he knocked Preacher sprawling. He went for Preacher's throat, but Preacher was too fast for him. Preacher's arm looped around the man's neck and pressed down like a bar of iron, and as they rolled over and over on the hard-packed dirt floor, a sudden loud cracking sound signaled a broken neck. The last of the hired killers jerked violently and died.

Slowly, Preacher climbed to his feet. He wiped the

back of his hand across his mouth, then bent to pick up his hat, which had fallen off when he tackled the two men. As he settled the hat on his head, he looked around at Garvey, Rattan, and the other men in the trading post and said, "I'm obliged to you for not mixin' in that, boys. It was my fight."

"Didn't figure you really needed the help," Rattan said with a grin. "Hell, there was only four of 'em. 'Tweren't really your fight, though, Preacher. You was just takin' up for them Galloways."

"Somebody's got to take up for folks what can't take up for theirselves." Preacher shook his head. "I hate to think what it'll be like in this world if people ever forget how to do that."

Then he walked out of the trading post, swung up onto the dun, called Dog, and rode out to tell the Galloways it was safe to come in.

All four of the hired killers were dead. "The fella who hired 'em won't know for a long time, if ever, what happened to them," Preacher told Roger and Jonathan that night as they sat at a table in the trading post. "By the time he finds out, you folks ought to be in Oregon next year, makin' a new life for yourselves."

"You're sure you won't guide us there?" Roger asked.

Preacher shook his head. "No need. Cephus says he's got a hankerin' to see the Pacific Ocean, and he's a good man, damn near as good as me. He'll get you there just fine."

"And what will you do?" Jonathan wanted to know.

"Thought I might head south," Preacher said with a grin. "Find someplace warmer to spend the winter. There's a place called Texas I ain't never been to yet. It's part o' Mexico, but things like that don't mean much to me. Lines on a map only matter as long as a fella lets them."

"We'll miss you," Jonathan said. "We owe you more than we can ever repay. We've learned so much from you."

"Well, you're what they call the patriarch o' this family now, Silvertip. You'll do just fine. Take care o' each other, that's the main thing." Preacher looked at Roger. "You and Angela got kids to raise. Raise 'em up right."

"We will," Roger promised solemnly.

Preacher drained the last of the whiskey in the cup in front of him, then stood up. "Come next spring, I'll put those markers up," he promised.

"You're not leaving now?" Jonathan exclaimed, startled.

"No reason to stay. It's a clear night with a big moon. Dog an' me can put some miles behind us 'fore we settle down for the night."

"But . . . but you just got back to civilization!"

Preacher grinned. "For some of us, that's all the more reason to light a shuck."

He shook hands with both of them and left the trading post, walking out into the cold, clear night. He regretted a little bit not saying good-bye to Nate, but he figured the youngster would understand. Nate had some of the same restless nature in him that had always been a part of Preacher. He had already seen that in the boy.

"Preacher."

The soft word was spoken as he reached to untie the dun's reins. The horse had been fed and watered and rested and was up to traveling a ways yet tonight. First, though, Preacher turned and saw Angela come out of the shadows on the trading post's porch.

"You're leaving?"

He nodded. "I reckon it's time."

"I . . . I hoped you'd spend the winter here too."

"Oh, I don't reckon I could do that," he said. "Bein' around people all the time, sleepin' with a roof over my head . . . some of us just ain't made for that kind o' life. We need to be out in the wild, lonesome places."

"You . . . you never wanted to stay somewhere . . . to stay with someone?"

Preacher remembered Jennie, for a change seeing her face clear as day, seeing the smile of wistful farewell on her lips, and for the last time, he allowed himself to think about what might have been.

"Once maybe," he whispered in reply to Angela's question, "but that was a long time ago." Then he bent down, brushed a kiss across her forehead, and said, "Roger's got the makin's of a good man, but he needs a good woman, and all those kids need a mama."

Clearly embarrassed, she said, "Preacher, I . . . I don't know what to say. . . ."

"Don't say nothin," he told her. "Just think on it." Then he swung up into the saddle, said, "Come on, Dog," and galloped out through the open gate into the night.

Texas was waiting. Someplace he'd never been before.